GOOD WIVES AND
SECRET LIVES

GOOD WIVES AND SECRET LIVES

Stories of Exceptional Women

Janey Kaya

Matador
9 Priory Business Park,
Wistow Road, Kibworth Beauchamp,
Leicestershire. LE8 0RX
Tel: 0116 279 2299
Email: books@troubador.co.uk
Web: www.troubador.co.uk/matador
Twitter: @matadorbooks

ISBN 978 1789010 084

British Library Cataloguing in Publication Data.
A catalogue record for this book is available from the British Library.

Printed and bound in the UK by 4edge Limited.
Typeset in 11pt Minion Pro by Troubador Publishing Ltd, Leicester, UK

Matador is an imprint of Troubador Publishing Ltd

To Yasmin, a very special young lady,
I wish you all the luck and love this world
can bring!

Little girls dream of fairy-tale weddings,
handsome princes,
And happy ever afters!
But that is just for princesses in children's
books.
Our women have to deal with a whole lot
more
Lies, Affairs, Drugs, and Money.
They do what it takes to get through the
worst of times,
To get to the best of times.
A dedication to
Love, faith and friendships,
And to exceptional women all over the world.

CHAPTER ONE

Sherrie & Angie

Sherrie

My full name is Sherrie Lynne Tammy Rae Boutine, my ma was the one for naming us all like Nashville stars.

There is nothing more likely to give away your country poor roots than having a name like mine. My two younger sisters, Gabby-June Loretta and Patsy Rose-Anne, adored their names, this was just one of the differences between us.

My pa, Edward, or Teddy Rae as he was known amongst friends, was a transient ranch hand, he came to the farm to work for my granddaddy one harvest time, and stayed a while, long enough for Ma to turn sixteen and find herself with child; he shot off pretty fast and no one ever saw or heard from him again. There was some talk of him working the oil fields in Texas, but just a rumour, no one really knew.

So Ma raised me from being just a child herself.

Granma had passed on a few years before I was born and so Ma took up the role of ranch mother. Granddaddy needed some help and it worked out just fine.

My earliest memories were with my ma, on the porch swing, her gently singing and swinging me to sleep as the red sunset lowered itself into the yellow stubby fields. She had a soft lovely voice; in another lifetime, maybe she would have been in Nashville herself, but for this life she had sunsets and farming and the company of occasional ranchers.

Ma called me her beautiful cornfield angel, on account of my white-blonde hair. She told me tales about the wonderful future I had ahead of me, she dreamed big for a little farm girl. I lapped up the attention, she was my whole world on that remote ranch in the back end of nowhere called Limestone Creek, east Kentucky, pretty much everyone who ever came didn't stay, and those that were born here rarely left, like a void in time, people lived in their community way.

I guess I was around six when Ma's tummy got huge, she had to stop cutting wood and seemed to sit down a lot. Luckily we had some help, Billy Joe Riker, a regular harvester, was staying with us and working with Granddaddy; he took over the heavy work and Ma sat by the fire and watched him with a smile on her face that she used to just give me.

He was OK, Billy, he didn't shout at me too much and I was careful to keep away from him late at night, he and

Granddaddy used to drink a lot and sometimes argue bad about politics, then I would hear doors slam and funny noises from Ma's bedroom. I buried my head under the pillow most nights and dreamed of Nashville and the grand ole opre that Ma talked about.

It was a steaming hot day and Ma was pacing the kitchen like a cat with gut rot, sweat pouring from her; she tried a weak pained smile but it was more of a grimace.

'Angel,' she called me, 'run over to town and fetch Mrs Mowbray, tell her babies are coming, be quick angel, fast as you can.'

I ran, like the wind, across the cornfields, my long white-blonde hair flowing behind; even at six years old my legs were long and strong and I flew across the land into our tiny town. Mrs Mowbray ran the local store and she had been a training nurse at the big hospital in Kentucky, she tended to all the ladies birthing in Limestone Creek.

It wasn't long before the world changed for me and the harrowing sounds of agony were followed by high-pitched screaming lungs, two of them!

Twin girls, hollering and howling worse than the wolves in the mountains.

Billy ran to the salon where Ma had birthed and Mrs Mowbray tried to make her dignified before Billy bounded in, but Ma didn't seem to mind him seeing her exposed so Mrs Mowbray busied herself with cleaning up while Ma and Billy held the girls, cooing and fussing, he bent to the floor and proposed they be married, Ma cried and said yes.

I wasn't so much Ma's favourite after that.

CHAPTER TWO

Sherrie & Angie

Angie

Three hours of gym work, a quick sauna, then wrap my body in cling film, cycle home at high speed and put the Jane Fonda workout on TV, this is my daily routine, I'm working on my body.

My face is perfect; everyone stops me to tell me I'm exquisite, my hair is corn-blonde, a throwback from a Scandinavian ancestor, thank you very much!

My eyes are so pale blue that I can look blind at certain angles, which is not a look I'm fond of, so I practise my angles for photographs for around fifteen minutes per day.

But with the right angle and light to give my butter-tan skin a lift, oh my God, even I can't stop staring at myself, it's weird, it's a perfect serendipitous arrangement of DNA, I've never met anyone who looks like me.

My mother, Rosie, is an ex-amateur beauty queen and she has schooled me in the fine art of pageanting. I came third in the Junior Miss Orange County pageant, the competition was fierce, a TV talent scout was judging, I know my wobbly body let me down, the winner was hard and toned, I felt like a whale.

My momma said it was rigged, she accused the winner's mom of fucking the judge, I've never seen her so wild and she never curses!

She says I have no wobbles, no fat on my body, I don't think she would lie, but I'm determined not to humiliate myself again, I won't take the risk.

I want to be the best, I want to win!

The next competition is part of a national major pageant, I have to be eighteen to enter, so now I can finally take part, I have four months and three days to prepare.

I have tried my gowns and bikinis so many times I'm scared they will look worn out, I've practised every smile I possess, to the point I'm starting to look like a psychopath in the mirror.

Momma has set up a small staging in our backyard and most nights we rehearse, walking, twirling, laughing appropriately for the given humorous situation, no guffaws or belly laughs for a beauty queen, refining the precise smiling aperture producing the perfect teeth–lip ratio, eradicating gummage, are the extra tweaks that make the difference, my performance is fine-tuned and automatic, my only weak area is the all-important interviewing.

So we work harder on that, we role play and rehearse every likely question, film it on our handycam and play them back to dissect every miniscule movement, facial expressions and response times, we hone it until it reaches perfection.

This is not a game, this is not silly vanity play, this is my goddamn career and I will be the best.

A beauty queen can earn mega bucks in a very short span, will most likely marry a wealthy, handsome man and live life in absolute luxury.

This is more appealing to me than working at a burger joint and dating some idiot jock from school with wandering hands and a wandering dick.

I pity the jock groupies who live and breathe the minutiae of the football team, Bor-ing, sad little bitches who will go on to lead Bor-ing, sad little lives, realising too late that their broad-backed wandering dick wanders far away after they have gained 10lbs and droopy tits from giving them children that they didn't realise would take the spotlight off them.

That's a deal-breaker for those ego maniacs.

Don't get me wrong, I'm not against relationships, marriage and family life. I hope to one day enjoy all those things. But one must prioritise life goals and mine are firmly boxed off: the husband will be of millionaire worth, he will be prepared to lavish me with the comforts I expect, in turn I will be his trophy, his ego-massaging, status-enhancing, willing accomplice and companion.

It's all been thought out in detail.

My diary is full.

The first day of my professional career.

Date: 14th June 1998
Location: Santa Fe, New Mexico
Event: 1st heat Miss American Beauty
Objective: Win; gain points for selection to Miss America heats in 1999

Date: 11th July 1998
Location: Sacramento, California
Event: 2nd Heat Miss American Beauty
Objective: Win; gain points for selection to Miss America heats in 1999

Date: 4th September 1998
Location: Austin, Texas
Event 3rd Heat – final heat Miss American Beauty
Objective: Win; gain pre-selection to Miss America

There is no other result acceptable. I received a small inheritance from my grandfather's estate on my sixteenth birthday, every cent of this money has been invested in this event and the preparation of myself to be my absolute best.

Failing is not an option.

I will not work at Wendy's and marry a jock!

CHAPTER THREE

Sherrie & Angie

Sherrie

After the twins were born, everything changed, for the worse. Ma had no time to brush my hair and sing to me on the porch swing, they took my place, with Billy up the rear. Only Granddaddy showed me a modicum of attention, in between ordering me around to do the chores that Ma simply had no time to do.

When I tried to snuggle with Ma, she shooed me away with irritation, which cut me to the core, I felt the sting like a lash.

Weeks turned into months and years, I was a ghost around the house, I went to school and did my chores, it was the loneliest time of my life. By the time I turned sixteen, my looks were getting a lot of attention; because of the heavy workload, I was very strong and toned, tall like my daddy Teddy Rae, Granddaddy told me he was near on 6ft 4in and I was looking like heading his way where physique was concerned.

I was in the store in town, at Mrs Mowbray's, she caught the sadness on me, took me aside for a cold lemonade and a pep talk.

'Hey, pretty girl, I know you feel like everyone's putting the load on you, you should come to the village dance on Saturday, help me with the lemonade stall, you could get to spend some time with your friends from school.'

That's when the tears fell; they didn't stop, pouring out like a leaky tap.

I was too ashamed to tell Mrs Mowbray that I didn't have one single friend. None of the girls at school liked me; more than that, they actively hated me.

Mrs Kneller, my head teacher, had intervened once or twice, when girls were trying to flush my head in the toilet, she was kind to me. Told me it was because of those darn pretty looks of mine, I had no way of changing them, I didn't wear any make-up or colour my hair.

It was all just natural, pure white golden straight hair, creamy skin that tanned to a light honey, perfect straight teeth, never needed a brace and the lightest, widest blue eyes, I freaked myself out many times, staring at myself in the mirror, I didn't look like anyone else I had ever seen.

I hated the way Billy looked at me, too hard and too long for a man that was supposed to be my stepfather. Ma saw it. She took it out on me, keeping me away from them as much as possible.

I didn't know what I should do, the twins would huddle around her pretending to be scared of me, then whisper about me pointing and laughing.

I truly felt like an alien being.

So I asked Mrs Mowbray if she needed a helper at the store, a little job. I needed to start planning to leave this unfriendly place and move away as soon as I was eighteen. Reluctantly, she gave me a few hours' work, worried that Billy would have something to say about keeping me from my chores, but he never did. Ma was very happy that I was spending less time around the house, my tall, slim body was driving her crazy, she had gained so much weight with the twins and never really got her body back.

Mrs Mowbray never regretted her decision, she found the store sold more and more sandwiches and lemonade to the local boys than ever before; she was delighted and increased my hours.

I put away about five dollars a week with Mrs Mowbray's saving scheme, and did every hour available for nearly a year and a half.

There were plenty of boys wanting to take me out and walk me home, I did let one, his name was Dean, he was cute and seemed sweet but next day when I got to school Geraldine Daner was waiting for me.

She screamed in my face that Dean was her boyfriend, just before she punched me. I don't know how many joined in, I was in the dirt, but I felt the kicks and blows of several girls, my head, ribs and legs were black and blue, someone's shoe buckle caught my cheek and the blood trickled into my mouth, thankfully Mrs Kneller heard the ruckus and broke it up.

Saved my sorry ass again.

After a week in the hospital, without any visitors, Granddaddy came in his truck to collect me. He had a suitcase in the back and some of my books and paints, we drove a bit in silence, not going toward the farm, he pulled the truck up at the bus depot and hugged me for the first time in years.

Gave me a ticket and a thick envelope, and told me about my auntie in Santa Fe, I was to go and live with her. Ma just couldn't cope with me and I was making the twins' life hard at school, it had all been decided.

Mixed emotions bubbled up inside me, I was feeling different after such kindness from the nurses at the hospital, to then slam-dunk into this rejection made me dizzy.

I never have seen my granddaddy cry before. He turned and drove away not looking back.

I boarded the bus and opened the envelope through teary eyes; there was $325 dollars from my saver and Granddaddy topped it up to $1000.

I'd never seen this amount of money in my life, I stuffed it quickly into my bag.

I never took my eyes off it until we arrived at Santa Fe, New Mexico.

*

Auntie Sylvia was a colourful, large bundle of fun; from the minute I stepped off the bus I was enveloped in masses of soft, warm woman.

What a contrast to the barren love of my Ma, it had been such a long time since I felt human warmth. She held my face in her hands and kissed my forehead. Huddled me up and off we went to her open-top jeep.

I felt the smile grow on my own face as the warm wind blew my hair every which way. The architecture of this amazing city blew me away, sloping walls of terracotta and sandy stone littered the roads, it felt like a another world.

Sylvia lived in a fantastic villa of several layers, like a child's sandcastle looming up in improbable angles, wow oh wow.

Huge boughs of flowering plants spilled from ironwork troughs at each window, I'd never seen anything so fertile and earthy, the farmland in Kentucky was for production only and never wasted on decoration, this was something from a film set to my naive eyes.

At nearly eighteen I finally felt that my life may just be worth living, it had possibilities!

I prayed to something above the light grey speckled clouds, for a life, a future, and if possible a little bit of love.

CHAPTER FOUR

Sherrie & Angie

Angie

Santa Fe Heat 1
21 days countdown

I have stuck rigidly to my gruelling fitness regime; the results were worth every grunting, sweaty, nauseating hour at the gym.

I am in the shape of my life, I can't walk down the street without hearing catcalls, whistles and occasional screeching brakes, this must be how Marilyn Monroe felt, invincible, superior and damn smoking hot!!!!

If I don't win this heat, I just don't know what else I could possibly do to improve myself, I have dedicated every waking moment in pursuit of this dream.

The tanning process starts tomorrow, the gym work has to cut down to half speed, then to just thirty minutes a day, to lessen the sinews and veins, it's a big no-no to look like a bodybuilder in a beauty pageant.

This is America's fairy tale, she must be a princess, like she steps from a Disney movie, not a hint of starvation, pumped-up veins or self-abuse of any sort.

Such a crock of shit! As if anyone could achieve this naturally.

Momma measures my food intake with scales and notepad in hand. Exact amounts of proteins minerals, sugars and salts, no carbs; she is an expert nutritionist, with just one client: me.

*

I'm at the final week now, my tan is perfect, my hair perfect, nails perfect, my outfits are ready, they are perfect!

We take a trip to the Plaza hotel, the venue for the heat, Momma pays and secures our room for the event, finalises the pre-registration for the pageant, nothing is left to chance.

We walk the whole hotel and gardens, making sure we know where to be, and Momma even checks the ground coverings for any potential trip hazards en route to the staging, which is being built up on the west side of the lush gardens; it's very pretty.

A tall stunning dark-haired girl catches my eye, her momma is checking the rows of flowering bushes for anything that may bring on an allergic reaction for her protégée.

We locked eyes, evaluating each other's stats; I flicked my wondrous mane and laughed cattily as if she was beneath my contempt, no competition at all.

Truthfully she made me thank the Lord that I put every minute of my waking day working on my body, and damn to hell, she did look like Disney.

Momma checked her momma, it was an atmosphere fit for the Roman coliseum, and she made this bizarre double-click sound with her tongue and motioned me away, the nut-brown steely eyes of Disney girl's mom following us all the way.

We strolled to the terrace bar and drank ice-cold water, both sitting in silence, deep in our thoughts.

'Momma, I don't know if I'm good enough.'

Momma raised her head at such a speed I thought it might snap off.

'Now you listen to me, my girl,' her face stony, 'not only are you good enough, you are a winner, Angie, I never expected you to stick with the regime, my God I stole that from the Marine Corps fitness manual!! I expected you to whine and complain at the meagre rationing and disgusting concoctions I made you drink at 5am, but you never even gagged, you worked your ass off, even when you had the flu and fever, you did your routines, so that tells me you are a winner!'

Momma's eyes filled. 'I am the most proud woman in town, Angie, I hear them talk about you in shops, "Miss America" they call you and my heart swells, you my darling are better than Disney.'

I don't cry often, it affects the skin around the eyes too much, but today in this beautiful garden terrace, with my best friend in the world, my momma, I shed two fat tears.

My inner voice piped up, *No more self-doubting, it reflects in your walk and body shape.* It was always supportive but practical and focused.

I started to believe my dreams could come true.

We made our way home and I felt the butterflies in my tummy as we passed a huge billboard advertising the forthcoming event at the Plaza. It would be televised, not live, thankfully, but after the event on Channel 42. Momma made a note to set the recording on the VCR.

I closed my eyes as we drove home and dreamed of crystal tiaras and shimmering gowns.

CHAPTER FIVE

Sherrie & Angie

Sherrie

I'd been living with Sylvia for nearly three months and she took me to town to celebrate my eighteenth birthday. It was the first time I had been inside a fancy restaurant, it was called the Terrace at the Plaza, my oh my, the beautiful tropical flowers and manicured topiary were individually lit up with tiny warm white lights, white organza canopies floated and gently billowed overhead, it looked like a fairy tale, it was a million miles from Limestone Creek, Kentucky.

When we arrived, Sally the receptionist asked if we were checking in for the pageant, we looked at her nonplussed, she motioned to the display stand advertising the Miss American Beauty Pageant on Saturday, how the hell I didn't see it I don't know, probably because my eyes were staring up at the chandeliers or down at the Italian marble floors.

Despite my pretty silk tea dress, a gift from Sylvia, I must have looked exactly what I was: a country bumpkin.

Sylvia made a daft joke about not entering it this year, too much competition for the other girls, they laughed like old friends. Sylvia had that way with her, anywhere she went, people gravitated to her warmth and she made instant friends.

Sally leant forward and said to Sylvia, 'Your daughter should be in it, I've seen most of the girls and she is right up there with the best.' I blushed red and shuffled about, I just felt like a fish out of water with all this opulence around me.

Sylvia nodded in agreement. 'Maybe next year, Sally, she's just finding her feet in this town. But I'd like to buy two tickets for the event, please.'

She beamed at me, her mischief dancing in her glittery green eyes.

So there I was sitting with my Aunt Sylvia within the huge tented air- conditioned marquee of the 1998 Miss American Beauty Pageant at the Santa Fe Plaza hotel, it felt like being on a movie set, the women, the men, so glamourous, so perfectly groomed, the dresses, the hairstyles just blew my mind, I didn't know that people could actually look like this in real life.

At the front of the marquee was the grand stage, which had been built in front of the lovely garden pavilion. Sylvia said this was usually a wedding venue, I thought if I ever married, I want it to be here.

Hundreds of beautiful people in one contained area, I realised after half an hour, no one was staring at me like an alien, ha, I fitted in! For the first time in my life, I looked normal, felt easy.

The place was buzzing with stewards, name-tagged and full of importance; they were the top people in pageant eventing, efficient, slick and in control.

I recognised faces but didn't know where from. Pointing out a very pretty girl with an even prettier boyfriend, Sylvia said she was on a TV soap that we watched sometimes, just a small part, but that's how I knew her.

Sylvia went through a 'who's who' of minor celebrities; a world of ideas flooded my mind. Nudging Sylvia I asked, 'So people actually do this for a job then?'

'Oh yes, hunny, there is big money in beauty, acting roles, modelling contracts, fashion ambassadors; it's a career, Sherrie, if you have a look that fits a brand, you can be set for life.'

She could see I had gotten caught up in it all.

'Sherrie, hunny, you could do very well in this industry, I'm not being cute, look around you, baby, do you see anyone more beautiful than you?'

I'm not vain, I don't think I'm better than anyone, but I know that I'm freaky good looking and it's a lonely place.

I loved living with Aunt Sylvia, but I didn't even get the chance to finish school, my chances of making a good living were slim, I needed to find my way in life, I was open to ideas.

The hush before the opening presentation was electric;

the hosts for the afternoon were Kelly Brocker, the residing Miss America, and a TV actor Brett Carlson, who I didn't know, but evidently everyone else did, judging by the rapturous applause and obvious appreciative looks from the ladies. Sylvia advised he played Dr Drake Mendelsohn in the number one TV soap.

The lighting changed and the atmosphere charged, the double doors of the pavilion opened, accompanied by the sounds of orchestral music. Spotlights hit the stage and two opposing lines of gliding beauties appeared from the doors. They were wearing swimsuits and silk sashes, the satin flashing from the stage lights, as they curved around the hosts coming to a perfectly timed halt, all the girls standing tall and poised with legs at angles that were elegant but undoubtedly unnatural.

My jaw hit the floor; I couldn't take my eyes off the girl with the rose pink sash with her name 'Angela' embroidered in cream thread. I looked at Sylvia who was peering and rummaging for her spectacles, she was dumbstruck too.

This beautiful, corn-blonde, tall, tanned, blue-eyed goddess could have been my twin!!

The applause broke the spell; I was staring at Sylvia who turned back to me with a look on her face I'd never seen… confusion?

The hosts waxed lyrical about the loveliness of the contestants as if we couldn't see for ourselves, we were looking at twenty specimens of the finest melange of DNA that America can produce, these girls were the epitome of the American dream.

Jeez, any of them could take that crown, they were all just perfect. How the judges could choose a winner was a mystery to me.

Sylvia said, 'Shall we try to meet Angela after the event, it's crazy freaky the similarity, Sherrie, don't you think?'

Yes I did think, I thought and wondered, how on earth will they choose? How will my doppelgänger Angela, despite her stunning looks, set herself apart from these other seriously beautiful women?

What would mark you as a winner or a loser?

But, it did become a contest after all, as the girls changed from swimwear to formal gowns, then to their chosen outfit to display their skill or hobby, it did give an edge to some and a definite shift in the odds.

Silly little mistakes like over-grinning, stuttering or brain fog caused a discomfort within us, the audience, and so we didn't like it; it was so ruthlessly simple really, one girl appeared dumb-mute, it may have only been for a few seconds, but it may as well have been an hour in this cut-throat dissection. She recognised her own error and like a row of collapsing dominoes you could visibly see her give up, I mentally judged her out!

There were four girls displaying cheerleading, predictable and pretty uninspiring, they hadn't upped their game since junior pageants, a big mistake! Four more gone. I started to get it, looks were not enough, this was a total physical and mentally controlled performance, oh my God!

I could do this, I have been walking on eggshells since seven years old, I know how to portray a second self, I'm a trained actress already!

A stunning raven-haired beauty danced a contemporary, dark, edgy movement, it was so out of place amongst this cotton-candy setting, it was so wrong, I felt the mood shift in the audience, I knew it cost her the heat. Five gone, fifteen left. What a stupid error to make!

Angela was flawless, her gown was just perfect, correct in every way, for her age, her colouring and physique, she was polished, she was shining, it was looking good for her, I felt excited and was strangely willing my twin stranger to win.

Two brunette olive-skinned beauties, Delores and Madeline, were capturing the audience, you could feel the support swell when they displayed their flute skills and harp playing, I had to admit they were incredible, the harp was played with such a delicate touch, it brought stinging tears.

One girl after another twirled and smiled, chatted and posed, I decided that if I were the judge it would have to be between Angela, Delores, Madeline and Julianne, they just had the edge. The other sixteen, for the most insignificant fails, were struck out, what a harsh critical world, but I seemed to understand the rules of it, I shared my prediction with Sylvia, who seemed surprised.

But when Julianne performed her chosen skill, she sang an operatic medley, it was painful, I wanted to shout out, 'You just ruined your chance!'

Sylvia looked at me sideways, with a slightly catty smirk, 'Glad I didn't bet on her.' We stifled a small laugh; it was ruthless, but addictive.

Finally, Angela had her chance to show her skill at ballet. Her tutu was embellished with tiny crystals that caught the lights with every pirouette, it was breathtaking, the mournful music, pure focus on her beautiful features, she was lost in the moment and that reached the hearts of the transfixed audience.

I can only describe her as other-worldly, I was open-mouthed.

Sylvia nudged me, raised her brows.

'Hmm, yep, she's a contender for sure.'

When the break came, after all girls had performed, we took a walk around the gardens, smart young waiters milled with champagne flutes and strawberry iced tea, it was heaven, several people looking confused stopped us and asked if I was Angela.

'No, I'm Sherrie, just a guest.'

'Wow!' remarked a lady. 'Well, dear, I think you should be up there.' She handed my aunt a card. 'Call me, dear.' Sylvia scanned it.

'Oh, Mrs Harris, yes I will call you, definitely.' Aunt was gushing a bit, unlike her to be flustered. 'Thank you, thank you very much.'

'What is it? Who is Mrs Harris?'

Sylvia looked pink. 'Sherrie, hunny, Mrs Harris is the biggest model booker in California, she's the top of the tree and she likes you.'

The call came over the speaker to return to the marquee, five minutes until final round, Sylvia swapped her empty champagne flute for a full one and we hurried back to our seats.

The cull had been done and a parade of exquisite rejects had to circle and wave, smiling like they'd won the darn contest, which was the cruellest part. We applauded with genuine guilt, we all knew the judges had got it right.

Four girls flanked the hosts: Angela, Madeline, Delores and Scarlet.

Hmm, I hadn't reckoned on Scarlet, but after Julianne's screeching I suppose she was the rightful recipient of the fourth spot.

The girls were dressed in daywear, smart and pretty, there was a sofa set up with a desk and chair, a bit like *The Letterman Show*.

A large screen behind them magnified the girls' faces, there was nowhere to hide!

The interview started light and easy, starting with Madeline. Brett made a few jokes about the show he was in and Sylvia laughed along with the audience, but I concentrated on her magnified face. Madeline was a seasoned performer; she was controlled and professional, like she was born on the TV screen.

Brett asked some current affairs questions, after all as ambassador for Miss America, she would need a good general knowledge. She stumbled badly, didn't know the name of her own city mayor or about the massive fundraising efforts of her community for the children's hospital. Granted, not the biggest crime in history, but it showed her as a bit uninterested in anything but herself, I mentally erased her as serious competition, three to go!

Delores fared better, she knew and contributed well to the questions levied at her, she was honest and warm. *Hmm she may have it*, I pondered, but at the last question, she started crying, Brett had asked her about her large close family and the stress of the whole event must have been too much, she started bawling, a fat tear dropping would have made us love her and protect her, but when a snot bubble appeared, that was it, *adios*, Delores!

Angela was next, Brett clearly favoured her, it was he that was actually a little bit nervous. Sylvia nudged me, he held it together but he made that interview as easy as pie, happy questioning, easy answers, opportunity for her to laugh delicately and even add to the joke. My, my, my, what a pro.

Scarlet was nice, and no real errors, she was sweet and smiley and of average intelligence, to be fair she could take the crown and do a sterling job as ambassador, but the star quality wasn't quite as bright as Angela.

I was pretty sure that my girl had the crown.

There was a break while the judges made their deliberations, we stretched our legs, enjoying another iced tea and champagne for Sylvia, there were tiny cut sandwiches and tropical fruit salads for us to nibble, it was heavenly.

Then the call came and off we went, eager to see the queen take her crown. I could hear people chatting about who they thought would win, Angela's name repeated all through this audience, I crossed my fingers and hoped so. God only knows why, I hadn't even met the girl, but I felt connected, we looked like identical twins, maybe this was my signpost, I had to meet her.

The four girls were smiling and posing within an inch of their lives, I felt the tension coursing from the stage through the floor to my toes. Sylvia took my hand and we stared at Angela, willing her on, while the handsome smooth Brett opened the small golden envelope, handed to him by Miss America.

No surprise to me at all when Angela took first place in this heat of Miss American Beauty, scoring a full ten points toward her place in Miss America 1999.

Scarlet came second, followed by Madeline, and Delores came fourth, with just two points. She looked like she was going to blow another snot bubble.

Angela showed her relief; for just a fraction of a second, her composure cracked. No one noticed, I did though.

She was radiantly accepting the crown and her arms were full of roses; she couldn't have looked more beautiful if Walt Disney himself had drawn her.

CHAPTER SIX

Sherrie & Angie

Angie

I was standing centre stage with the gorgeous Brett Carlson who had just, three minutes earlier, backstage, whispered ever so quietly in my ear, 'I'm going to marry you.'

I had won, it was my first clear win, I was on my way.

I could see my mother in the front row, she was a little crumpled and tear-streaked, dabbing furiously at her mascara, it had been a hell of a journey for her too. The cameras flashed, the cheering and clapping thundered across the audience to us on the stage, I felt something near to euphoria. I wouldn't allow myself to go there as that would be out of control and my training and discipline was too strong to let me be a snotty heap like poor Delores.

So I held myself together for another three hours, doing photo shoots and interviews with local press and of course VT shorts for the televised show later tonight.

I was whisked around from one set to another until finally at around 11pm they released me to my exhausted momma. Thank God she had booked the room; we were in no state to drive anywhere.

Sprawled on the super-king bed in our PJs, empty bottle of champagne and a half-demolished tray of sandwiches between us, we cried and beamed at each other.

'Thanks, Mommy, for everything you did to help me.'

She carefully removed the tray and cuddled me up like I was a little girl.

'My lovely, lovely Angie, my angel, I want to thank you for making my life complete, I only ever wanted to be a mom,' she laughed and said, 'well, maybe a beauty queen too, but being your mom has given me joy I never thought existed.'

We hugged for ages, tired tears spilled out and ran down my cheeks, I had earned a day of puffy eyes.

'Mommy, do you think Daddy would be proud to have me as his daughter?'

I felt her stiffen a little, she didn't talk about Daddy much, he had gone working away when she fell pregnant and gone away permanently when I was just three years old. They were very young and he was not one for staying in one place for long, but to her credit, she never bad-mouthed him, she had the right to, he never contacted us again, they were never married so Mommy just got on with the business of raising me.

She took a deep breath and told me, 'He would be damn proud, Angie, damn proud!'

I had thirty days to prepare for the next heat; there was no let-up at all. I became something of a local celebrity in our town, many had watched the televised heat and I felt the first prickle of fame. When I went to school to collect some certificates, a rush of juniors crowded me for my autograph, how crazy it felt, but good crazy, you know!

Mrs Harris had been in touch personally. She owned the modelling agency and as the official agent for the Miss America contest, I was advised to work with her for controlled exposure leading up to the finals – it was not unheard of to fall foul of rivals setting contestants up for sleazy modelling contracts to exclude them from further competitions. A candidate would be immediately barred and stripped of points for entry to Miss America if she had done any nude or semi-nude modelling, so you had to be on guard. Tanning at the beach was not a good idea, even an errant nipple could be photographed and manipulated, sounds extreme, but has happened to many. This is a career, this is an open chequebook, families have invested inheritances, trust funds for this; it can be savage.

Mrs Harris warned me of all this as I sat in her office, Momma and I solemnly nodding to her every point. I signed the contracts, my mother witnessed, we gave each other a look, we spoke without words, the journey had begun!

My first assignment was an advertising deal for a shampoo, Golden Goddess, specifically for blondes. My mother butted in, 'She won't be expected to use the actual shampoo? We make our own, you see,' she blushed, 'it's not something we can risk at this stage.'

'Of course not,' Mrs Harris laughed, 'we wouldn't expect Angie to deviate from her regime, it's not a requirement of the contract.' That settled, we quietly agreed on the fee, $23,000 for the three days filming and a twelve-month buyout for all media usage. We smiled and nodded as if we received this sort of money every day.

'Yes, yes that would be quite adequate,' said Mommy.

I saw her feet cross, she was bursting inside.

When we got home, we laughed like loons.

'Oh my God, Mom, we did it, we did it!' We danced around the kitchen like loonies, prancing about like models on the catwalk, she really was my best friend, I didn't need my stupid father, I had my wonderful mom.

I had to rest for forty-eight hours and then train for six before the shoot on the Friday. This was my routine and the late nights, champagne and carb pig-out was noticeable, not to the naked eye, but to my internal gauge, I could detect a fraction of weight difference, so I got myself into my favourite PJs and snuggled down, soon dreaming of Hollywood, film sets, handsome men and filthy money.

CHAPTER SEVEN

Sherrie & Angie

Sherrie

Aunt Sylvia had tried to get a pass for backstage, but no one could get through; it was jammed tight as the cameras were still rolling for the later show. She had so wanted me to meet the winning girl Angela, who was my doppelgänger, Sylvia had tried every way to get us a pass, but to no avail.

A few of the TV crew had taken a double look at me and Sylvia; they were not sure if Angie had slipped away and was strolling around with a large, brightly dressed lady, but of course it was me, not Angie. One cameraman trailed me for about five minutes, before he was redirected to the winners' set. This was incredible, I didn't want to leave, but eventually we made our way out of the hotel and stopped by reception.

Sally was on duty, did she never get a day off? She greeted Sylvia with a beaming smile, Aunt Sylvia leant in.

'I wondered, Sally darling, can you possibly get two tickets for us for the next heat in California, and a room?'

Sally made a phone call to the California Plaza, reserved us a room and tickets and VIP seats. I was ecstatic.

'Let me pay for this, Sylvia, you have done enough for me already.'

'Nonsense, child, I haven't had so much fun in ages, I'm going for the free champagne and strawberries. Now we must get home and start thinking about the dress you are going to wear.'

We chatted and chuckled all the way home, dissecting the contestants, making catty remarks and belly laughing, I had never felt so happy. I didn't want this to end.

I thought about my ma that night, my eighteenth birthday had passed without a word from her. Granddaddy sent a card and I could see his writing had gone spindly and frail, it wouldn't be too long before he joined Granma.

I decided from that day, I wouldn't ever use the name Sherrie Lynne Tammy Rae Boutine; my new name was Sherrie Rae, it was enough.

I needed to find my way in this fierce world.

CHAPTER EIGHT

Sherrie & Angie

Angie

Mrs Harris, Pamela to her friends, was holding her usual breakfast meeting with her associates. They had 8 x 12 photos of each of us finalists they had signed to the agency, duplicate photos were placed on a huge cork wall.

Surrounding the photos were brainstorming notes firing from the head of each beautiful face. Shampoo, perfume, clothing brands, big names had all been sent the photos and stats of each new model, all the agencies fought tooth and nail to secure contracts with the large brands, the commission was fantastic.

Four new faces from the Santa Fe heat were the focus of the current push. My face was firing many more arrow ideas than the rest because I was the heat winner and Pamela announced I had already signed as the new girl for Golden Goddess shampoo. A small burst of well-practised applause ensued. Pamela cut it dead with a stiff momentary smile; she didn't like to waste time.

The video of the event silently played on the large screen behind her at the head of the table. Sasha, Pamela's assistant, noticed something odd.

'Look at that!'

Sasha grabbed the remote and rewound as Pamela swivelled to see the screen. There it was: me being interviewed by Brett and at the same time me walking across the set. Not possible!

The video was rewound several times. Yes, the dress was different, but that was me! It took a while for Mrs Harris to remember, she exclaimed like a scientist discovering a cure for cancer.

'Ahhh, yes! The girl with the colourful lady, I gave her my card, she was a dead ringer for Angela, stunning skin, completely unblemished, like butter.'

Everyone returned to their notes and continued processing the new girls, nothing more was said.

I, of course, had not been aware of this doppelgänger at all, I had hardly had time to breathe, with all the filming and photos after I was crowned, I hadn't noticed my identical twin wandering around.

CHAPTER NINE

Sherrie & Angie

Sherrie

Sylvia and I went shopping, and what an eye opener. Back in Limestone Creek, if you wanted a new dress, you basically had to order some material and sew it. If you had enough money you could order from the catalogue at Mrs Mowbray's store and wait three weeks or if you were very lucky, catch a ride into Bulls Head, the big town, which had three dress shops and maybe find something there; but the styles were always for older women, the young fashion was snapped up the moment it arrived. We wore hand-me-downs or people's jumble-sale throwaways.

When you lived on a ranch, pretty dresses were not so important. Ma never suggested I do anything to improve my appearance, I understood why. I just found life easier if I looked as boring as possible, but truth is even if I wore a dirt sack, I still looked like the prettiest girl in town, it was so lonely.

Mrs Mowbray was the nearest thing to a friend I had.

So when Aunt Sylvia paraded me around Santa Fe mall like the proudest mama in the world it was a warm and fuzzy feeling that brought me to tears. This was the companionship, the warmth, and dare I say love, I'd lost when my twin half sisters arrived. I hadn't realised I missed it so much.

In one store, I had to hide in the cubicle to have a little cry, I saw the curtain pull back a little, Sylvia passed me a tissue and said, 'Now don't cry, child, you have the world at your feet now and only laughter and happiness to look forward to.'

She always knew what to say, she was never awkward faced with emotion, it was a rare quality. I wanted to make her proud of me after all her support.

We settled on two pretty day dresses and a cocktail dress, it was off the shoulder in pretty swooping frills, then tightly fitted all through to just above the knee, pure white.

When I stepped out of the cubicle, three sales assistants stopped talking and walked to me and Aunt Sylvia.

A beautifully groomed assistant, Marta, whistled loudly and clapped her hands.

'Oh my Gawd, this is the most perfect dress for you, I've never seen it look so right on anyone.' She got a digital camera from the counter. 'May I take a snap? The store buyer would love to see this but he's on his lunch break.'

Posing a little I let her take a few snaps and we all decided it was my perfect killer dress.

My Aunt Sylvia was plotting something and I bugged her to tell me what she was up to, but even through lunch and the drive home, she just said, 'You wait 'n' see my girl, California may just change your life.'

And it did!

CHAPTER TEN

Helena

The steady blip of the machine keeping my husband Daniel alive is the signature tune of my life, the constant even tone marks the past eleven years of my existence.

I hear it in my sleep, it never lets me forget, a constant reminder that I am a married woman, with a husband alive, albeit mechanically.

It feels at times like a prison. Just the simple sound of a blip fills my world with mental chains, resentment, guilty feelings that I just can't reconcile.

No one has ever uttered the word 'guilty' at me, they don't need to, the 'blip-blip-blip' tells me every second of my life.

I am Daniel's wife, stepmother to his children, Katie, twenty-three, and Nathan, twenty-six. They don't look at me like they used to, or maybe they do but the blip has addled my brain and sent my cognitive processing askew, I can't know which, because I can never open the conversation about their father's accident.

I am guilty, blip-blip-blip-blip.

It's my fault.

I am a bad person, blip-blip.

I attend to his personal care as much as possible around my work schedule .I sit and read to him, play his favourite music and talk about my daily experiences, of which there are very few worth noting, but after eleven years of one-sided conversation, I'm not sure that it matters anymore, to Daniel or me. I think I'm just perpetuating the image of the loving, caring good wife, I suppose for the sake of Daniel's children and my corrosive guilt. Certainly not for the medical staff here at the hospital, they know very well Daniel is unlikely to ever come out of this coma and if he did he would be severely brain-damaged. I will never have a conversation with my husband again, I will never be able to apologise to him.

Many nurses have come and gone over the years, they read the notes and start off their duties with bright enthusiasm and optimistic anecdotes from previous coma cases. I smile and thank them and looking back maybe those young girls with their strong legs and sensible shoes have kept a tiny bit of hope going inside of me, allowing me to continue with this life of purgatory.

My faith in God left me a long long time ago, I'm sorry to say.

My friends have slowly slipped away into lives that don't involve me. I can't blame them at all, how many times can a dear friend ask you, 'Any news? Any change? How are you coping?'

The answers are always the same.

No, none, OK.

It becomes so that you actually don't want anyone to call you or enquire, because the response is as depressing and boring to yourself as it must be to the loyal friend.

So you avoid calls and anything that comes close to a get-together. It becomes a battle. Friends feel obliged to keep trying; you do your best to be rude sometimes to bring about the inevitable break-up. I'm alone with my burden and that's how it should be.

I know exactly why Daniel was driving like a manic on that rainy night. I am guilty, it is my fault, I must live with it. There is only one place that I get peace and respite from the blip, where I can stop appearing to be a devoted wife.

I'm going there now, my duty is done, I've read the autobiography of Rod Stewart to Daniel this week, he loves his music and I enjoyed the read, even if Daniel didn't catch a word of it.

It's a bank holiday weekend, I have two days to myself and I know where I must go, I've packed my overnight bag, wet wipes, pyjamas, some bottled water, biscuits and my make-up bag.

I'm driving to the shittiest part of the city, a horrible rotten hole of poverty and crime, the most prolific display of debased humanity I can find. Dr Gerry, as he calls himself, lives here. He has the only cure I know of to remove the blip. His medicine is heroin, not enough to kill me, but enough to let me reach oblivion for sixteen to twenty hours, depending on my metabolic rate today.

I arrive and park in the usual spot, in the far corner of a supermarket car park. I'm always careful; even though I'm unlikely to bump in to anyone I know around this neck of the woods, I don't want anyone asking why I'm here.

Wearing a cheap track suit, trainers, baseball cap, scraped back hair and an air of despondency, I blend in OK; nobody takes any notice of me, I'm a nondescript forty-four-year-old loser to the naked eye.

The smell hits you before you arrive at the stairwell of the high-rise tower block. No point in checking if the lift works, it doesn't, and to be honest it's more accurately described as a urinal than a lift; filthy walls, wet, piss-covered floors. I never touch the handrail, which I do find ironic considering what filth I'm about to shoot into my veins.

I used to bring a sleeping bag with me, but it got so messed up I was scared someone would see me walking back to the car. Often it had vomit or shit on it, I couldn't think of an excuse to cover that.

Dr Gerry charges an extra £5 to provide a clean duvet cover, I think he actually just sponges it off and sprays Febreeze on it, the stains tell stories that I know too well, but to be honest with you, I don't really care.

When I'm so low and need to come here, I barely care if I live or die, so the laundry matters so very little.

Five flights of stairs, I run up them, it's better not to dwell too long on these stairs, lots of scallies and dealers are around. I come in the morning and leave in the morning, you don't want to be here in this concrete jungle in the night-time, it's like Beirut.

I knock and announce myself as Kelly. No real names here. He asks me the name of my cat, I say, 'Ginger.'

Eight deadbolts from base to the top of the door slide back. I enter the den, it's quietest at this time, only one or two other users, comatose on sofas, I see one young lad about mid-twenties, laying like Jesus on the cross, his breathing is shallow, his skin pale and a light beading of sweat covers his brow. I'm not sure what he's taken, we don't talk about these things, it's not like a ladies' lunch where we compare lipsticks or shampoo, nobody wants to know your problems here, they just solve them for a short time for a wad of cash.

I take my shitty trainers off and peel back the sole. Inside, wrapped in a plastic ziplock, is sixty-five pounds, he takes the five and puts that in a tin in the kitchen. 'For the laundry,' he says.

Same routine every time, he reappears with a Thomas the Tank duvet cover and pillow, they match and I try and make a joke about getting an extra star rating. It falls on deaf ears, it's not that Dr Gerry doesn't have a sense of humour, but he doesn't like to be friends with his customers.

One of his rules.

I go through to the box room. It's an agreement we have had since I started coming here: I wanted a room I can lock, he has a key, he assures me he will check on me twice or if he hears anything too noisy, but other than that I will be left alone for my session.

I go in and change into my pyjamas, I will sweat so much over the next twelve hours that I reek when I leave.

The wet wipes are essential. I arrange my things neatly on the table next to the bed, and lay down, ready for Dr Gerry.

His method is as safe as it can be, he uses a sterile needle each time, I watch him break the steripack, he heats up his burner and sets the crystals in the spoon, and it soon starts bubbling and melting into syrup, I'm sweating already in a sort of pre-emptive high, knowing the ecstasy of peace that awaits me.

In a funny kind of way, I'm a posh junkie, this is five star compared to the users living rough, sharing needles. I have experienced top quality heroin and deep down inside this is probably one of the biggest motivators I have to get my ass out of bed and go to work and earn money. I couldn't bear the thought of having to go to the railway arches to beg a hit from some infected user and I will not use my inherited wealth, Daniel's insurance money, for this shit.

I am ready, Dr Gerry has the syringe primed and my vein is up, the tightness of the rubber strap is causing a throb; he works his needle like a hospital phlebotomist, expert and almost painless.

Immediately my head lolls back onto the pillow and I'm vaguely aware of Dr Gerry leaving the room, I hear the key turn and that is my final conscious thought.

*

Everyone experiences heroin in a different way, depending on their psychology and physical health. As I'm wrought with the agony of my guilt I seem to start my floating process from above the scene of the accident, which is odd as I was not there. I can only assume that, from the information given to me by the police, ambulance guys, witnesses and medical team, I am desperately scouring the scene for any fragment of evidence that would absolve me from the guilt.

But so far I have never found it.

I'm watching from the trees as Daniel speeds along the road, it's raining heavily, he's got his wipers on full and his headlights are shining, the road is familiar to him, he picked me up many times from that bar, I was a barmaid for years when we were students and he knows about that bend, he knows that there is a patch of adverse camber that can tilt you and make you lose control if you're going too fast.

A few young men have died on that road, it's notorious and that also helped my defence, because there was almost an attitude of, 'Damn it, that road has claimed another.'

But then I flash forward to me at the bar, somewhere I never should have gone, not after what had happened there. You see, I was pregnant with Daniel's baby but at the time but I wasn't sure if it was Daniel's or my ex-lover John's. He owned the bar and we were always close. Truth is I was close to him, but for him, I was just a friend-slash-barmaid with benefits.

When I discovered I was pregnant, Daniel automatically assumed it was his child, of course – he was a decent, loyal, faithful human being and so he wouldn't think I could have been fucking John, why would I? Daniel and I had the perfect life, he worked hard and provided a lovely home, his children from his first marriage came and stayed with us at weekends and we all got along great, it was happy, healthy, secure, we had got married just six months earlier and no one on the outside would ever have thought there could be any problem with us.

Daniel and Helena, they are a great couple!

But as soon as I fell pregnant, I had the strangest reaction, it was like everything was closing me in, I felt like I had no choice, no options left in my life, good old-fashioned fear, I suppose. My mother had died when I was young and with no sisters or female family members to talk to I was terrified. Had the whole thing been a huge mistake? Was John the man I should be with? I mulled it over and over, my erratic behaviour troubled Daniel enough to take me to the doctor, who duly felt that it was normal anxiety and exhaustion after the busy year marrying and moving house, new job and now pregnancy, he prescribed a mild anti-anxiety pill and recommended yoga for mummies, which Daniel thought was a great idea, great way of making mummy friends. It probably was, but to me at that time it just felt like another loss of my identity, a forced new me, I didn't like it at all, I went a couple of times and then I did a stupid thing.

I skipped the yoga class and drove along that road to John's bar, it was around six thirty by the time I got there, I should have been home at least an hour before.

The missed calls on my phone and texts flashing as I turned it to silent and dumped it low in my bag told me that Daniel was worried. I didn't care. I sat at the bar and drank soda with lime and lemons. John made a fuss of me at first and congratulated me on the bump.

By about seven thirty the bar was warming up and a couple of pretty girls took stools at the bar and were flirting with John. I laughed at first like a buddy would, but then feelings of insane jealousy flashed into my conscious thoughts. I visualised myself walking casually up to the girls and knocking their white teeth out with a hammer.

I shook my head and dismissed the horrible thought, but more and more flashes came flooding through: I was burning them, I took a chainsaw and cut them up, I boiled them in a huge vat. It was mental. It was crazy.

I was trembling and dizzy, John finally noticed I wasn't OK and dragged himself away from the girls.

'Hey Hel, what's up, you should go home, hun, you're not looking too good, shall I call Daniel?'

His normal voice had morphed into a sing-song in my brain, that moment I can't tell you really what happened, I looked at John and tears were rolling down my face.

'This baby is yours, John,' I whispered.

I have no idea what reaction I hoped for; I can barely understand why I uttered the words as I didn't honestly know who the daddy was.

He reared back and the look of horror sent me spinning.

'No way, Hel, no fucking way, you out of your mind? Go home Helena, sort your shit out and leave me alone.'

They call it a red mist, it's absolutely accurate, like blood fills your eyeballs and everything goes weird.

The girl with the white-white teeth sneered at me.

'Sweetie, don't you think you better get off home and leave my Johnny alone? You are hardly in a condition to party, honey.'

I flew off my stool like a scud missile, I don't know who I hit first, white teeth or her unfortunate friend, who was just in the wrong place at the wrong time, but I heard the smash of bone, someone's nose was broken, I ripped hair out, pummelled flesh with my fists and didn't stop until I was physically hauled off her by John, so I vented more on him, scratching at his face and neck, screaming and calling him every kind of bastard.

Three guys, one of whom was an off-duty police officer, pulled me unceremoniously off John and restrained me with duct tape, harsh but I was a psychotic, dangerous woman at that point.

The phone call they made from my mobile phone to my already frantic husband Daniel was the catalyst, they just told it like it was.

Mad, violent, crazy, attacking everyone, accusing John of being the father of her baby, attacking his girlfriend.

I was barely coherent myself, no way to control anything, I was past caring, but Daniel, who actually loved the bones of me and our unborn baby, jumped in his car and drove like a maniac and the adverse camber spun him off the road, into the tree that I was floating in, and left him brain-dead.

There was a police report following my deranged attack. No one wanted to press any charges, John was more than glad to just get me away from his bar. I was not charged with any crime, the girl with the broken nose was convinced by John to let it go and he would compensate her from his insurance.

I was told off like a child, officially cautioned and reminded that I am indeed a lucky young lady.

The police officer drove me home, I actually passed the scene of the accident, barely noticing the ambulance and the crumpled car off the road. I must have been in another realm not to recognise it was Daniel's car, it just didn't register in my mind, only when the police arrived at our house later that evening did I know what had happened to Daniel and realisation kicked in as to what I had done.

It was deemed that I wasn't responsible for his accident; ultimately he was driving very fast and hit that bad patch of road at nearly double the advised speed limit, I was advised again that I had been very lucky not be charged with the assault. The fact I was pregnant may have helped and no charges were made.

So I can't ever expect to find that new piece of evidence that will absolve me of the heavy guilt I carry. It doesn't exist.

I am guilty.

I aborted the baby three weeks after his funeral and I believe that I'm guilty of murder twice.

So this is my penance.

Nobody knows what I carry within; I don't understand where that craziness reared up from. I stopped taking the medication and swapped over to a heavy tranquillizer. The doctor was sympathetic after what I had gone through. But it stopped taking the edge off a very long time ago.

I'm keeping going for Daniel's kids, but I made a deal with myself; when they have both moved on with their lives and have loving partners to support them, I will end my life.

I'm really hoping Katie will meet someone soon, I don't know if I can hold on much longer.

CHAPTER ELEVEN

1978

Carmella

'Sit up straight, Carmella,' my mama clicked her tongue sharply. I straightened myself against the hard dining chair. We were learning the etiquette of dining, I was eleven, bored and getting really pissed off at this too-fussy dress in a too-hot dining room, with a too-strict mama.

The midday sun in Rome was relentless, I wanted to play at the lido with the local children, but Mama said it was forbidden now I was nearly a woman. I wanted to splash the crystal clear cool water all over my head and dunk myself deep into the cold depths. If I stayed in long enough, I couldn't feel anything.

Numb! That was my favourite feeling.

My name is Carmella Maria Isabella di Rosa.

My mama is a professional bitch and my papa is a very important man, Mama tells me at least twenty times a day.

She has no life and no imagination, she is a robot of society and I hate her, but I obey her!

After our lesson I am allowed a break of thirty minutes to change into a suitable day dress to sit with Professor Arro; he is teaching me piano and English language. I don't mind this too much, but Professor Arro often smells like brandy and acrid cigarettes. He can swill with peppermint tea all he likes, he still smells. And I don't like his breath on my neck when I'm playing a difficult part of Chopin, it doesn't help at all.

He says I speak English like an aristocrat. I don't know what that means, but Mama is always gushing and silly when he compliments me, as if she did the lesson and read Dickens, *Jane Eyre* and Shakespeare every night before bed.

After piano I can go and play for one hour before returning for cooking lesson with Mama and her housekeeper, Maria. This is what I live for, this precious hour that I can be myself. I have one hour to think my own thoughts and dream of castles and dragons, fairies, kittens, puppies and chocolate cake with sugared cherries and ice cream. I can only dream of this now as my mama doesn't allow any food that might cause me to be fat; she says I won't get a good marriage if I'm fat as a pig.

I don't care, I don't want to be married, but I obey!

My future husband is already decided anyway, Massimo Gaetano Matteo. He is thirteen, the son of a very important man, a friend of my papa. I have no say in this matter, it has been decided at my birth almost, the two families have decided my future, so I live for the hour a day I can feel almost nothing, it helps.

My papa says I'm his beautiful little princess, he kisses my head and carries me high on his shoulders; it's fun and I love Papa when he is like this, but he only does it when Mama tells him I have been a good girl, a perfect young lady and a diligent scholar, so I obey.

CHAPTER TWELVE

1988

Carmella

Today I married Massimo. The whole of Rome it seems, attended my wedding.

The day seemed to last for a year, relatives, friends, business associates visiting our home, more and more came, an endless stream of grinning faces, many complete strangers to me. The women clucked and cooed over how gorgeous I looked in my hand-sewn Valentino wedding gown, it was beautiful, any girl would feel like a princess.

The families had spent a lot of money, extravagant money, dressing the manicured gardens of our enormous villa, antique pergolas decked with budding pale pink and white bougainvillea flowed south from the ancient steps of our grand balcony down to the creamy silk marquees, held up by plaster columns fit for the coliseum. It was a sight and poor Georgianna from *Bella* magazine who had won the tender to be the official photographer worked her perfect ass off, buzzing like a wasp capturing every celebrity, every politician and famous face, of which there were many.

She took private photographs of Massimo and me kissing and staring at each other with what was supposed to be deep meaningful love. We played our part, Massimo has been trained for this, just as I have.

Not many words passed between us, we didn't really like each other that much, but at least he was good-looking; full-mouthed and broad-chested, he looked perfect in each photo. Mama was gushing at full steam, Papa was laughing with a table of men, the band played, the sun shone and our mission was accomplished.

My new life as Mrs Carmella Matteo would be endured at our fabulous apartment in Rome, overlooking the Trevi Fountain. A wedding gift from my father-in-law, this sophisticated address was to be my home, I wasn't exactly excited but keen to get away from Mama, that at least would be a relief.

It was very late and the guests were kissing each other and hugging and crying. A lot of champagne had been enjoyed. I found a passing waitress and motioned for a glass; she opened a fresh bottle and poured me a long stem, I drank it down like water, unblinking. She stayed by my side and topped me up.

'Dutch courage for tonight,' I waffled at her, she smiled and blushed. It had dawned on me: I was going to have sex with Massimo tonight. Grabbing the bottle, I retreated to the pond at the back of the marquee. Lovely to be alone, away from the unrelenting guest invasion. The champagne was excellent, of course, no cheap plonk for the di Rosa-Matteo families. Feeling giddy and sharp, I let my thoughts linger on Massimo. *How would it be?*

A surge of electricity coursed through my body, landing squarely at the sweet spot, I was certainly ready. Masturbation had been my only sexual experience, fraught with guilt and fear of Mama discovering my secret pleasure, my experiences were hurried and borderline painful.

It was forbidden to discuss sex with Mama, but Nonna had taken me aside one day and told me with a face that looked like she had endured ten wars, 'Never deny your husband his right to your body, Carmella, you are his wife and it is your duty to lay with him when he desires, keep clean and ready for him at all times.'

She made me think I was supposed to be some kind of whore! Or a wedded slave from the history books I'd read. That thought tumbled around a while. I couldn't decide which, so I put it to the back of my mind.

What does an old woman know about modern marriage? I was about to find out for myself.

I had wanted to explore a man, to know sex, from about the age of fifteen. Watching the gardeners work in summer was as near to sex as I had ever been. One very hot day, I had been asked to take cold water to the gardeners and Piero, son of the head gardener, looked at me like he could eat me. I couldn't take my eyes off his bare chest, it was a fleeting two-minute encounter, but it fuelled my guilty self-pleasure for months, like a good book you keep rereading. Piero was well thumbed.

Intrigued to experience that powerful animal thrusting, the sense of being somewhere else other than in your own mind, it made me tingle. Nonna's words confused me, male dominance frees all inhibitions according to battle-weary Nonna.

'A married woman can live sin-free in the eyes of God, she is weaker than her husband, powerless to deny his pleasure, this is your duty as a good wife.'

I nodded as if I understood her, crazy bat!

I wanted to know the capabilities of my own body, to open myself to a new world of womanhood, 'carnal knowledge', they call it, I like to learn, I am a diligent scholar after all. 'Hah!' I burst out aloud.

The champagne was making me silly, laughing to myself, fantasising, about Massimo, my husband. My lover!

'Lover' is a strange term, not really fitting for this forced union. I don't love him, he doesn't love me, but maybe this new life of having a husband, living away from my overbearing mother, and discovering the pleasures of sex would answer all these questions I have.

And hopefully love will come!

We arrived in our lavish twelve-room apartment; it was a stunning building, no doubt as to the net worth of a resident here. I could feel the attitude shift of the doorman as he held the door. Being the wife of an important man, or at least the son of an important man, changed everything.

I am a beautiful young woman, don't think me vain,

I have been designed that way by Mama, my appearance has been her full-time job for the last ten years, taking no chances that I would be unworthy of the son of an important man. No more sly lecherous glances from drivers or doormen. I was treated royally, not sure if I liked it, but the choice was never mine.

Still in our bridal costumes we were greeted with gusto from the foyer staff. Massimo played his part at the threshold, picking me up and whisking me through the heavily carved oak doors, our paid entourage discreetly disappearing like ghosts. Kicking it closed behind him, he set me down in our lavish hallway. We were home.

We silently wandered around the rooms. Massimo's mother, Francesca, had employed the best interior decorators in Italy, everything was decorated in muted champagne colours, bringing the grand marble fireplaces forward, making a statement of their own. Heavy gilt mirrors and paintings adorned every creamy wall, and golden velvet sofas with hand-painted silk cushions filled the wonderful salon. It was a beauty, and despite my not being party to designing or furnishing my own home, I felt I couldn't have put this together, it was stunning.

I decided to be appreciative of all I had; maybe this life would be wonderful? Churlish to dismiss everything simply because it was not of my choosing. A little faith in God was needed, I firmly intended to try and enjoy this marriage and to love my husband.

Massimo crept behind me and lifted my dress, pushing me over the arm of a beautifully overstuffed fireside chair. I was shocked, he roughly parted my legs and pulled my white lace thong down to my ankles. Despite the lack of romance, I felt the burning heat and excitement reach my labia and the slick wetness enabled him to drive into me with ease, so easy that I couldn't feel much, I was bent over the arm, with masses of dress over my back, I faced forward like a startled swan, not sure of what to do. I wanted to ask if he was inside me, I actually couldn't tell, but I wasn't sure if I should.

Three or four seconds later, I felt him grunt and shudder, then a wet sticky dribble ran down my leg.

He was gone; I heard the shower running in the master bathroom.

Was that it?

Is that what Nonna had endured for fifty years with Grandpa?

No, no, probably he was exhausted after the party and it's our first time. So I didn't want to make any unfair judgement, but I was really disappointed.

All the movies I had seen and books I had read talked about this moment like it was the pinnacle of romantic passion and love, a bonding of two souls. Even though our marriage was manufactured, this episode was not that, nothing near that, for sure.

I used the guest suite shower, cleaned myself and when I got to our bed, he was snoring like a hog. I padded back to the guest suite and slept with an ear open for the sound of Massimo.

He never came.

That was our first and only night together, it was the only time he intimately touched me throughout our marriage.

CHAPTER THIRTEEN

1992

Carmella

It was the very hot summer of 1992, Rome was burning up and people were even more highly strung than usual. I could hear the distant sounds of couples fighting furiously and making up late in the evening, cooling themselves at the fountain, the sheer relief of the cool, moist air.

The national average for road rage incidents involving physical injury soared; it was like people were insane between 10am and 7pm.

But I was feeling this madness even in the cooler weather. The last four years had been impossible, I couldn't bear it any longer, the misery of my loveless, sexless marriage was bad enough, but to have the sweating, sulking, fractious Massimo around the house all day was just too much.

Many of the equine and motor sport clubs he frequented had ceased to operate until the temperatures were lower; tarmac was melting and horses died in this extreme heat. I don't believe it was the lack of riding horses that was putting Massimo in this foul demeanour, but the general lack of escape from me that he hated.

I had spent the first two years trying every approach known to man to engage him in a relationship, sexual or otherwise. He wasn't interested. We attended gala dinners, the opera, the ballet, we were patrons of many of the arts in Rome, a family legacy we were obliged to keep up. I enjoyed it; despite Massimo and his dreadful mother who nearly always accompanied us, the events were wonderful. I had gowns made for all the charitable balls we attended and it was a luxurious lifestyle, but at home it was oh so boring and so unfulfilling.

Many days I would take coffee at the piazza and watch the young lovers kiss and touch each other without inhibition, their passion and love acting as a shield to the rest of the world.

How must that feel?

I envied those skinny, carefree girls in their coloured capri pants and skimpy tops showing glorious toned stomachs, no doubt from sexual keep-fit, not the vile gymnasium I attended four times a week. This was not my choice; I was still under the shackles of a mama, but this was Massimo's mother Francesca calling the shots.

The gym membership had been sent by courier the day after a fitting for a gown for a charity event. I had gained around 1kg, a massive crime in her eyes. The tiniest difference in measurement was discussed between the seamstress and Francesca, like I had committed the most heinous act, circling and scrutinising me with no consideration for me as a person. Yes, I had gained a tiny bit of fat, I was alone and bored, no husband around to keep me interested, I had taken to enjoying a little *torta limone* with my cappuccino at the piazza, I was clearly fit for hanging.

That, of course, had to stop. Francesca spoke to me like a five-year-old child. Espresso and water, not even a tiny bite of cantucinni biscuit, could be my pleasure.

I wondered if it was all worth it really, I would gladly trade with the young girls and their cheeky boyfriends trailing them on mopeds while they acted indifferently. Ahh, it was a great charade to watch, old-style Italian courtship. She has to look so disinterested and even disgusted at the mere thought of talking to the boy. He takes her insults with a smile and a shrug and, like a loving puppy, relentlessly pursues her with declarations of *amore*.

If you watch for long enough, you can see the final result: she reluctantly gets on his bike and her arms cling tightly to his young torso, her head against his back.

She would fight like a lioness if another girl sat on that seat, it's all a farce, but done so beautifully; both sexes know the rules, the lines and the limits.

Love is a many splendored thing, apparently, though I'm yet to discover that! The string quartet often plays this song for the tourists in season, they were playing its easy, sweet melody today as I entered the square. It hits me hard sometimes, strolling alone around the fountains, how lonely I am, without a purpose. Would it matter if I didn't exist?

I often plotted fantasies about being kidnapped and held hostage for ransom money, but falling in love with the mafia boss, secretly having wild sex in the safe house, and after the millions were paid, faking my own death and living with him on a private island. Fanciful, childish thoughts, I know, but loneliness sends you deep into yourself; sometimes it's hard to know reality from fantasy, I was feeling that more and more.

I was having one of these spells, as I like to think of them, while sitting at a shady table in the piazza, which was why I hadn't noticed the gentleman asking if he could join me. His polite cough brought me round to this reality.

'Oh yes, of course, please do, I'm leaving shortly.'

'Please don't go on my account, I would hate to send you away and spoil this moment, you looked so far away in your daydream.'

I blushed and realised I must have been away with my spells again. *Oh gosh, I must control this in public.*

I felt highly embarrassed and motioned to the waiter for my bill.

He attended in a second; he was aware of my status and the boss had told him to watch me continually, it was very good for business to have wealthy, important and beautiful people at the café.

The gentleman caught his attention before I could speak.

'Please bring us cappucino and *torta limone* for two.'

I started to protest; the waiter looked frightened, not knowing who to obey.

I didn't realise but this gentleman actually out-ranked my high status by several notches. Seeing the boy's distress, I relented and smiled.

'That would be lovely, thank you.'

Manners maketh the man, my mama instilled in me: be anything and everything but never be ill-mannered.

So we sat in the dappled shade and watched the young lovers parade their youth and beauty, in silence but not discomfort. It was minutes before the owner himself, Giuseppe, appeared with the tray.

He greeted the gentleman with deference.

'It is a great honour to have you patronise my little café, I am at your service sir, madam.'

A little bemused, we reached out to the coffee and bumped hands. The electricity jarred me physically; for a split second I lost my breath.

'Allow me,' the gentleman took control and I was served beautifully.

A troubadour was making good money entertaining the tourists with his trained monkey. We laughed as he performed a trick with a little girl, her mother watching the monkey with apprehension, but it was joyous, he played an old accordion while the monkey flitted from one side to another, presenting the little girl with flowers and lollipops, but whisking them away just a moment before she had hold. The little girl laughed and jumped for joy, the tiny monkey finally dropped to his knee in front of the little girl as if he was to propose marriage, holding a little velvet box to her. With wary humour she reached for the box, with a flash of fur it became an ice cream cone and then he gently gave it her.

The crowd applauded and many coins were thrown to the troubadour's hat. As I turned to my companion to see if he was laughing, I found myself facing his lovely, serious face.

I couldn't return my gaze back to the monkey, this stranger's green eyes held mine, it felt like he was tunnelling deep into my soul, reading my loneliness, feeling my sadness, a spell, a trance, I can't say what it was, but something changed that very second, I think I fell in love.

The spell broke as a large American man in khaki shorts and a Hawaiian shirt backed into our table; he was trying to photograph his equally generous and colourful wife with the monkey.

We both grabbed the table edges to steady it and his hand fell onto mine. The tourist apologised profusely, but was watching his wife with such hilarity it was understandable. The little monkey was perched on her shoulder and every time he shouted, 'Say cheese!' the monkey reached down to one of his wife's bosoms and squeezed it with a huge toothy grin. Oh my word, we openly laughed together, this lovely gentleman and I.

His hand stayed too long over mine as the tourist had moved away. I didn't want him to remove it, the touch of a warm male hand over mine felt so good.

Finally the crowd dispersed and he passed my coffee.

'Don't let it get cold, cara.'

Now, correct etiquette dictates he shouldn't address an unknown woman of status as 'cara'. It's impertinent, if you want to be precise. Not to my ears, though, it was a sound I'd longed to hear.

Cara, darling, sweetheart, my love, it conjured all that was missing and that I had wanted and needed to hear.

He abruptly stood and left a card at my hand.

'Please forgive my familiarity, I just feel like we know each other well, maybe from another life perhaps. Would you care to meet again for coffee tomorrow?'

I caressed the expensive card, the thick embossed paper, the raised gilt wording: *Roberto Carlutto, Collector of Fine Art, Rome.*

I locked eyes with this gentleman, Roberto Carlutto, collector of fine art.

My conscious brain did not answer for me. My heart and possibly my vagina did all the talking.

'Yes, Mr Carlutto, that would be lovely, same time?'

'Yes,' he bent and took my hand, kissing it gently on the back. He told me to call him Roberto, with that he was gone, and my life changed forever.

When I walked home, I felt like one of those young beauties in turquoise capri pants, I may have even swung my hips a little like they do to keep their boys trailing them, I certainly smiled all the way.

Two old head-scarfed ladies on a stoop next to the piazza smiled and one called out in old Italian dialect. 'Ahh, the beauty of love,' they grinned at me, I beamed back.

My sleep that night was disturbed, dreams looked like fairy tales from my childhood, flashing images of princesses with tumbling hair, handsome chisel-chinned knights on white stallions jousting to win my hand and claim the kingdom. I woke several times, checking where I was; my mind was all over the place. I had a sharp word with myself at 4.32am; eye bags are not the look I wanted for my next meeting with the handsome Roberto, my subconscious understood and I enjoyed a deep five-hours sleep and woke lazily, before the conscious brain shouted, *Move it girl, you look like hell and you have a date in three hours!!*

I jumped like a cat with burning feet into the shower, to let the process begin.

It was 11.30am and I had twenty-five day dresses flung across the bedroom. Massimo had called for me to inspect his new watch that had arrived that morning. I ignored him, I could feel the defiance in me bubbling.

He appeared at the door, his mood foul.

'I asked you to come, Carmella, what is so important that you have to do in your pathetic life that you defy your husband?'

I had heard this nonsense from him many times, speaking to me like we were in some historical play, his constant criticism of my every action; I had let it roll off me over and over, chipping away at my self-esteem, but today, I wasn't taking his shit.

'Go away, Massimo, leave me alone.'

He approached and stood just inches from my face, I could smell the coffee on his breath, and the underlying alcohol from the previous night.

'I won't go away, Carmella, I'm your husband until death us do part, don't forget this, you do as I say, this is my house, you are nothing without my family name, don't ever forget it, and clear this mess, you look like a village washer woman, with clothes everywhere.'

He turned to go and I was just putting the V-sign up to the back of his head when he sharply turned and caught my two fingers, crushing them tightly. I shouted out in pain, I saw the flash of pleasure on his fleshy face.

Everything changed that day.

He dropped his hold and I instinctively held my own hand, the pain was fierce, involuntary tears sprung and rolled down my face, a tiny flicker of panic crossed his features. He was not remorseful that he had hurt me, but concerned that I may seek medical treatment and an explanation would be needed.

He spun around and left my room. I heard his plethora of threats and insults through the hall, finally silenced as the grand door to our apartment sealed shut.

The sound of the ancient solid oak door of this architectural beauty echoed my own feelings living here, heavy and sombre. The pleasure of living in such splendour takes some of the melancholy from the soul, but after nearly four years of this isolation, even the stucco cherubs can't raise a smile anymore.

I cooled my fingers under the cold tap until the numbness took the pain away. I could see some bruising coming but thankfully a little movement in the fingers assured me they were not broken.

This limited my dress choice: no way I could manage one-handed with the tiny buttoning on the lavender sundress, so I chose a yellow silk 50s-style favourite that I managed to slip over my head; I wrangled my breasts into the pre-zipped dress.

It had tiny cream roses embroidered across the hem and bodice. My tan was nice and even and it brought the green flecks out in my hazel eyes. Yellow makes me happy, it doesn't allow any self-negative thoughts; this wise mantra had been given to me by a very glamourous singer, Freya Marzari, who frequented the gym. I saw her working out in a bright yellow tracksuit and had commented on its fabulous colour.

After that I bought several key pieces in shades of yellow, the acid tones didn't work at all, but the buttery, creamy yellow that is easily found in silk fabrics works wonderfully with my colouring.

I chose a relatively safe pair of cream pumps; I was walking to the piazza and with this heat I couldn't risk blisters today.

Of course, my driver would take me anywhere I desired, even twenty yards up the road should I require, but I like to walk, it gave me the tiniest feeling of independence and freedom.

There had been times early in our marriage when I had felt like I was under surveillance. I talked to Massimo about this and he confessed that, yes, as a representative of his family, it was natural that his mother would employ a detective to monitor movements. My life had proved to be so extraordinarily dull that after a year of the detective stalking me to the gym and the piazza, where I was always reported to sit alone for no more than one hour before returning to the apartment via some unremarkable shopping for items I didn't even need, mostly the florist's to buy a few stems for my room, Francesca ceased the surveillance, satisfied I was the compliant dullard she had hoped I would be.

Because there was a florist on contract for the apartment, I couldn't even have the pleasure of arranging my own floral décor, which was a loss to me as I had enjoyed doing this for the church for years as a girl and had quite a flair for wedding arrangements.

I will never forget the time I purchased flowers and arranged them in the entrance hall; I said nothing to anyone after removing the contract display and replacing it with mine. I listened from the bedroom to Massimo's mother declaring what a stunning display it was. I swelled and beamed. A little headway maybe?

It was at dinner that I confessed my little ruse and her face shifted to a cold mask.

'Carmella, we all have talents in life, although we are yet to discover yours.' Massimo sniggered at his mother's caustic barbs. 'But I assure you, dear, floristry is not one of them, the display is crude and vulgar, not fitting for a building and a family of this importance.'

She summoned the maid to have the offending display removed.

I bit back the tears; the satisfied look on Massimo's face made me want to throw my wine glass at him! Humiliation burned me from top to bottom. I excused myself from dinner and wept in my bedroom, this was not the life I had imagined.

I hadn't dared to expect a great love, I hadn't dreamed of a joyful, carefree life, but this barren, endless, cold, scathing nothingness was beyond my nightmares. I wasn't sure I could survive much longer.

I had endured enough.

So I walked to my rendezvous with Roberto with my head held high, my high ponytail swinging behind me. The heat made it impossible to wear your hair loose, I almost envied the old ladies with their heads covered. In this heat, my hair multiplied in volume by enormous proportions. To try and maintain a groomed appearance in the daytime heat, it had to be up on your head or heavily plaited in a high ponytail.

I had put it up at first, and loved the Audrey Hepburn feel with the full-skirted 50s dress, but it looked too much of a cocktail, pre-dinner style. I didn't want Roberto to think I had no etiquette, so I smoothed it with salon crème and plaited it all the way. It took three attempts with my sore fingers refusing to grip, but finally I secured it with a rose clip and off I trotted to the piazza.

It was impossible to ignore the admiring glances from the men, and some hostile looks from the women. Only the older ladies clucked and smiled with warmth as I passed by. I chuckled inwardly as I heard a fight kick off behind me, a woman accusing her boyfriend of staring at me with an open mouth like he was watching an ice cream walk by. In true Italian style, she stood feet wide apart, one hand on shapely hip, the other slicing the air between them like a knife, simultaneously verbally blasting him with every venomous insult she could muster. Others sniggered and I had to quicken my pace before I let out a laugh.

The strains of the quartet alerted me to the nearness of my rendezvous with Roberto. It was baffling that I had no doubts or confusion about meeting up with this stranger, even the pain of my fingers disappeared.

I believe, looking back, this could have been a subconscious act of survival, survival of my spirit as a woman!

I scanned my favourite table, the dappled shady one, under the giant olive tree. It had a little cardboard sign clipped to a tall steel prong: 'Reserved'.

Ahh, oh no, I couldn't see any other seat, no sign of Roberto.

At that moment Giuseppe appeared at my side and escorted me by my elbow to the reserved table.

'Of course, madam, Mr Carlutto made arrangements as he will be a few minutes delayed.' I wasn't sure if we had even set a firm time, but it was a considerate act.

I settled myself in, taking a glass of iced water to cool me, then a familiar voice from behind said, 'May I join you?'

Roberto.

I stood for some reason, perhaps the involuntary jolt of electricity from hearing his voice shot me upward.

We kissed on both cheeks and I saw him appraise my figure, subtly and practised, but I saw the curve of a smile on his nice upturned mouth.

'Bellisimo, cara, you are a vision to make Audrey Hepburn feel drab.'

I blushed as I recalled looking in the mirror and calling out to no one, 'Audrey eat your heart out.'

Can this man read my damn mind?

Without any ordering needed, a tray of our favourites arrived, *torta limone* and cappuccino, accompanied by tiny cantuccini and ice-cold sparkling water.

'You will make me fat, Roberto.' I headed for a bite of that sharp but sweet pastry and a sip of excellent coffee.

'Carmella, cara, you could be the size of an elephant and my heart would not feel anything less than I do already.'

I laughed and told him gently that as much as we girls appreciate that kind of lie, I can't gain weight without sending my seamstress in to cardiac arrest. I neglected to mention Francesca.

'And Roberto, may I ask how did you discover my name?'

'Well, that was easy; you see the tall arched windows high up on the west side of the piazza?' His long fingers pointed toward a stunning building.

'Yes, I see.'

'That is my office. I have watched you have coffee here for the last four years. My heart has grown daily. I don't wish to make you think me some kind of stalker, but the days you didn't come, the days I was working away, I felt empty. Three years ago, I telephoned the Cafe Giuseppe and asked him the name of the most beautiful creature sitting under the olive tree. He knows, as many know, you are the wife of Massimo Matteo. I was determined to stop this boyish obsession with you as you were married, but...'

I rushed to fill the awkward silence.

'Roberto, you must tell me about your art collection, I am very interested in contemporary work.'

'I know, Carmella. In fact you and your husband attended an exhibition recently, my company supports artists internationally and I confess I watched you that night; my God, perhaps I am a stalker!' he laughed shyly. 'You were engrossed in the work of a young Russian artist, Vasille Zaharov, do you remember?'

'I didn't see you there that night. I would have remembered you, I'm sure.' I gave him a flicker of flirtatious smile to let him know I wasn't put off by his stalking.

'I was tasked with curating and showing the private collection. We see you but you see a grand mirrored wall, these are the hidden treasures of the art world, rare and sold very occasionally and very privately.'

I was a little taken aback, not sure how to take this romantic attention; he seemed so easy and straightforward, not creepy or odd, but I wasn't used to anyone taking any interest in me other than paid staff. This feeling of being important to someone, it was all a bit of a shock.

The artist he talked about was clear in my mind though; such passion, such use of colour and dangerous imagery; a stark contrast to the calm serenity of champagne satins and creamy linens of my world.

I remembered thinking I wanted to buy a work, but where the hell could I place it in my home? It would stand out like a bloodied carcass.

'Yes, Roberto, he is an amazing talent, I felt connected with him. Just looking at his canvas made my blood pressure rise. I'm not an art connoisseur but I believe that it should evoke some emotion in the viewer and Vasille's work certainly does.'

'Carmella, that night when I saw you entranced in the wonders of art, my world, my passion, my business, I knew for sure that this emotion I have for you was not some schoolboy crush. I held back so many times. I wanted to rush over here and join you, but I am an honourable man, knowing you were married always rooted me to my seat. I'm a man not a boy, but I have never been able to clear you from my mind, my heart even.' He looked at me so sincerely, I couldn't take my eyes away from his lovely face.

'I believe in fate, Carmella, and that two people cross paths for a real purpose. You have been here in the piazza alone for so many years, I alone in my office wishing to be with you, I had to act on my feelings, I'm sorry.'

'Sorry for what, Roberto? I'm deeply flattered and you have brought something to my life, just in these last forty-eight hours, something that I knew I was longing for. I'm glad you came to join me, Roberto.'

'Wait, cara, I must tell you something, you may hate me...'

I stopped open-mouthed, I was used to being hurt verbally from Massimo, my survival instinct kicked in and I stiffened waiting for his words.

He emitted a deep sigh.

'That night, at the art exhibition, I discovered something, Carmella. My selfish side got the better of me, call it jealousy, manipulation, whatever you will, I had a suspicion and I acted upon it to prove a rumour.'

'What are you talking about, Roberto?'

'I asked a very dear friend, who is openly homosexual, to make a subtle advance to Massimo. As a man, I had my doubts about his sexuality; I had heard talk, but again, not my business. But Carmella, I did this dishonourable thing.'

'You better tell me, I'm not as fragile as I look, Roberto.'

I couldn't believe what I was hearing, this lovely handsome man was saying things I didn't know if I wanted to hear. Should I stop him talking and leave? What was the bloody etiquette for this situation?

'Roberto, are you saying to me that you set Massimo up on a date with a man?'

'Well, yes, Carmella, I did. Giorgio is a well-known openly gay friend, he is an extravagant socialite with a large circle of artistic, bohemian friends, many men and women, of every sexual orientation. Massimo was not obliged or cornered in any way.'

I took a sharp breath. 'Go on, Roberto, tell me the end of this sordid tale please.'

'Giorgio told me that he only gave the merest hint of flirtation. In other words, you would need to be a gay man to have read the undercurrent. You may not realise, Carmella, but for centuries many public figures have had to hide their homosexuality for fear of hostility and in many cases losing their jobs or businesses, never mind their veneer of family life that has screened them, a language of their own became the way of allowing relationships and liaisons to occur, you get where I'm going?'

'Yes, Roberto, I may look naive, but I am well read.'

He laughed softly, without a hint of sarcasm or nastiness, he was not Massimo.

'So Giorgio did what? Had sex with my husband?'

I couldn't believe I just said those words out loud to a man I barely knew and was as cool as a cucumber. Perhaps it was the confirmation of the deep thoughts I'd harboured since my wedding night. Better this than the other option, that I was so repulsive to men that even my husband couldn't touch me.

Roberto exhaled and looked deeply into my eyes. I think he was trying unsuccessfully to read my emotions, but I've learned to mask any weakness so deciding to finish the task he set out to do, he said,

'OK, Carmella I will finish this sordid tale and I hope that you will not shoot the messenger. I think you understand my hopes. Your husband took Giorgio up on his hint; he arranged to meet him on the roof terrace of the gallery, which he did. There are service stairs leading to staff rooms and Giorgio suggested they be alone for a moment, to talk. Massimo didn't hesitate, he urged Giorgio; if you saw Giorgio you would understand, he is a magnificent example of Adonis, I confess that is why I asked him.'

'Go on,' I urged him. Without any hint of sentiment, Roberto spoke like he was reading a witness statement in court.

'Once alone in the staff room, Giorgio asked him was he bisexual as he was aware Massimo was married. According to Giorgio, he just laughed.'

A look of concern flashed on Roberto's lovely face.

'Sorry, cara.'

'Go on, Roberto, I'm not hurt, I just want to know.'

'Giorgio told me that Massimo declared he is totally gay, the thought of a woman disgusted him, he said he was married in name only, forced, arranged, whatever you like to call it, but it was a paper marriage.'

I felt nothing, not even humiliation. Just a bit nauseous. 'And… ?'

'And, Carmella, Massimo and Giorgio have been having an affair since that night. Giorgio confessed that he took things further than I had asked him, but Massimo was driving things fast and furious, he has rented an apartment here in Rome and Giorgio moved in last month. I have the address if you want to know.'

My cappuccino had gone cold, I casually attracted the waiter and reordered. 'And a bottle of your most expensive Cristal, please.'

Roberto looked a bit taken aback. 'Are we celebrating, Carmella?'

'Yes we are, we are celebrating my release from prison.' He couldn't know the hurt and humiliation I had felt through four years of being rejected, insulted, criticised, bullied and downright abused by that bastard and his mother. I felt vindicated, I was not the ugly, sexless being he made me believe I was; it was him and his predilections for men that made our marriage this living hell.

It was a relief, a giant weight off me.

'Roberto, you have helped me, not hurt me, I want you to know that; please let us not talk of this horrible matter again, I will take matters into my own hands now.' The relief on his face was clear to see.

So we drank and chatted and he talked about the artists and the hopes he had that I would get involved in his world. I felt like this man, this lovely patient stranger, was the man I had been looking for all my life.

Giuseppe popped the cork and ceremoniously poured the effervescent bubbly.

'Here's to the future, cara.' He raised his flute. 'Wherever it takes you and whatever it holds, I wish my heart and soul to be with you in its journey.'

'To the future, to my new life and thank you, Roberto, *salute!*'

Thankfully the apartment was empty when I got home, my fingers were throbbing and I took a long bath, the champagne had relaxed me. Lying there in the opulent bubbles from the finest hand-crafted bath crystals in Italy, I processed all the information Roberto had given me about Massimo.

It explained why he had been in such a foul mood; it wasn't the heat or the cancelled equine clubs, it was the fact that his great love Giorgio was away with his other lover, living it up in New York, while Massimo was stuck here with me.

Evidence was what I needed, a cast-iron defence for when the shit hit the fan, which, knowing his mother, was sure to happen.

But I didn't want to cause an almighty fire for Roberto, I had to keep him out of this, get my own dossier on the goings-on between Massimo and Giorgio.

I couldn't risk hiring a detective in my name; no matter how modern-day women were empowered, this was Italy,

Matteo's family were a big deal and I for sure would be ruined. I must be sure to have my ducks in a row, this quaint English saying that I learned from my literature studies always made me smile. That was it: England!

I had read about beautiful Cotswold villages with streams and rivers, lush, green abundant gardens swamping the ancient thatched cottages, the slow and easy pace of rural life. Thinking about this fresh landscape seemed to cool me in the heavy oppressive heat.

I would take a trip to England, rent a cottage and think for a bit, plan, work things out; I'd tell Massimo I was furthering my literature and Shakespeare studies, nowhere better to hatch a plot.

He wouldn't care anyway!

CHAPTER FOURTEEN

Carmella

Having made the firm decision to make my escape to England, I slept well that night, apart from the occasional pain in my fingers. I was planning my own future for the first time in my life; how bizarre that such horrendous news about my own husband could feel like a prayer had been answered.

Maybe I have a cold heart, I mused, no capacity to care anymore? But that was at odds with my fluttering chest when Roberto was near me. His touch alone sent sparks; that at least was a sign that I was alive. Passion does reside in me; it's just buried very deep.

When I walked to the piazza yesterday, I saw the most fantastic double-headed tea roses, the muted, dusty, creamy pink leaves looked so romantic and English! That was surely an omen. Time for me to liberate myself from this prison; I'm sure there are private detectives in London.

I slipped on my gym gear and jogged toward the piazza. Maria was on the step getting some respite from the moist air of the florist's shop.

'Will you put aside two dozen of those beautiful blooms, and some greenery? I'm treating myself to a touch of England.' A suppressed chuckle failed to reach the air, but it lifted my spirits, just knowing I would be getting the hell out of here soon, away from the oppression and escalating temper of Massimo.

'I'll get them on my way back, OK?'

She nodded and shook her head a little. It was no secret that my floristry had been ridiculed by Massimo's vile mother.

Maria's cousin Maria – there are many! – was a cleaner in our apartment building and she simply couldn't let my fabulous display be trashed. Little did I know it ended up at the church and was remarked on by all that visited.

I reached the gym and almost crashed into Freya. She admired my butter-yellow velour suit.

'Ahh, Carmella, good to see you out of black for a change, it should not be worn for anything but diamond theft and funerals.' We laughed as we entered the lower level entrance, into the ice-cool, perfectly air-conditioned lobby; it was worth every penny of the exorbitant membership fee paid for by Francesca.

Every facility existed in this hidden sanctuary, very private, discreet and if you ever saw a beautician or trainer out in the street, they only acknowledged you with a polite nod – it was spa policy. The great and good of Rome did not want the world knowing she had to work at her beauty, her body, her moustache even, oh no, we were supposed to be natural goddesses. Well, I knew from raw experience, Mama's acid tongue and sharp rules, that extreme beauty was rarely natural, even those young street girls spent hours in beauty shops perfecting curls, figures and sex appeal. It's our favourite currency, after wine, fashion and great food.

I had come for my appointment with Shakir, a Middle Eastern young man, a magician when it came to managing my hair in this heat. He blended his own oils to tame the frizz and leave it sleek and flowing. He had fled his oppressive country because of his sexuality; it had taken his eldest brother Nizar to advise him that he was no longer a member of the al Habib family unless he married and followed the Quran to the letter.

Nizar had witnessed Shakir with another young man in the souk, he knew instinctively the way they looked upon each other that they were indeed lovers. There had been odd remarks made about his young feminine brother at college, which he had immediately quashed, but the worry was growing. His mother had asked him too many times now if Shakir had a girl in mind for marriage; he had nothing to tell her and his mother's shrewd, dark brown eyes gave up a fear she had been harbouring since her little boy was about twelve years old. She muttered a well-worn prayer a few times and went back to her cooking, but the steady look she gave Nizar told him he must act before his father made a decision that would finish Shakir's life. If not death, it would be as good as.

Nizar arranged for Shakir to take a job on the cruise lines; their uncle had been a chef in the American-owned cruise company Royal Caribbean and as far as Nizar was concerned, it was as far away as he could possibly get him, safer for him and the family would not be disgraced.

Shakir complained to his brother.

'But Nizar, I don't understand, I don't want to leave here. I'm happy here, I have my friends.' His teary sniffling made Nizar's fists clench. He was torn inside. He grabbed him by the scruff so they were eye level.

'Brother, trust me when I say to you, I'm protecting you, don't disobey me! Things will be very bad for us all if you stay, your ways are not acceptable to our family, you know. You will kill Mother from shame and father will kill you.'

The tears stopped immediately. The bare truth wiped them away in a flash. He knew... Nizar knew...

'Yes, brother, I will of course go, when should I leave?'

'It is arranged for you to fly to Miami on the 11th.'

'America?'

'I don't know any other Miami, Shakir. Uncle Abdul will meet you on the 15th of next month when his ship comes back to dock. Uncle has secured a position of salon assistant in the male spa. He knows you are light and fast, that is what they require on the ship. You don't take up too much space, can run like a cat and work hard, you will have a new life. Don't you bring shame on Uncle, either; he has risked a lot to get you a work visa, called in every favour!'

It was the 9th of the month already and Shakir decided for once in his life to follow orders, because he was not so stupid to ignore this warning from his brother.

And so his life changed, surprisingly for the better. He started his work and very quickly realised he had a skill for hairdressing, working on the hair of the many overworked, exhausted girls who cleaned, cooked, served and skivvied relentlessly. Too exhausted and time-starved to wash and set their hair, better to give a few dollars to this girly boy who worked magic, sending them back out on duty looking like they had been to Paris for their hair appointment.

It wasn't long before he was poached over to the female salon and he quickly gained his qualifications as hairdresser. It was a revelation to be so open, no one asked him if he was gay, it was simply accepted, as a male hairdresser it was almost expected!

Life was fun and busy, all the girls loved Shakir, he was working on the crowns of wealthy ladies, celebrities, gorgeous escorts, models, businesswomen and in particular a wonderful Italian actress called Sofia Loren, who had despaired of her thick hair in the middle of a Caribbean swelter. His first encounter with his idol was when she marched into the spa and demanded somebody either shave her head or fix this fucking nest!

It was the petite, fast hands of Shakir that took charge of Ms Loren's famous bouffant, but not only that, he treated her like the royalty that she was. The young girls in the spa didn't realise what an icon she was; thinking her a has-been celeb, they didn't treat her quite right.

Shakir, however, loved Ms Loren. As a young gay boy in Abu Dhabi, the only poster in the cinema that ever took his breath away was this queen of sexual allure, Sofia.

She was advertising her role as a sexually liberated Italian woman, playing the leading lady in the old 1964 film called *Marriage Italian Style*. It was quite a find for the small local cinema, they must have got a bit carried away having seen her in that sheer black negligee. If you looked closely you could just make out her nipples despite the strategically placed embroidered spiders. It hid nothing at all, in fact it accentuated her amazing body, totally inappropriate for a Muslim community, a moment of madness on the part of the proprietor. The reason he had run to the cinema that day was the huge uproar from the mosque about that very image being on display. It lasted approximately forty-five minutes up on the wall of the cinema before an angry crowd ripped it to shreds.

He caught a piece of the poster and stuffed it in his pocket. It was a scrap of about one inch square, just half an eye, but the power flowing from that segment of eye had more energy than any woman he had ever seen.

He fell in love with her that day aged thirteen. Unfortunately for his mother, it was a love of her abject feminine prowess, not a heterosexual love.

She was here in his salon, his hands working his argan crème, blended with almond oil and a secret ingredient that he never divulged. He skilfully massaged her scalp, calming her effortlessly, and she was putty in his small, strong hands.

Ms Loren would have no other touch her crown.

After Ms Loren departed from her cruise holiday, she sent him a letter of invitation to attend at La Salon de Roma within the very exclusive private health club, a ticket for his flight and five-star accommodation at Travisia de Roma, along with details of his chauffer and credit account at Versace. As if this wasn't lavish enough, he opened an envelope with a bank draft for ten thousand lira. It was an unbelievable offer.

He didn't know Sofia's multi-millionaire husband owned the health club and had been more than happy to poach this young man who had basically saved him from hours of angry outburst from his beloved wild woman. He understood the importance of her image as she was ageing; he still saw the young goddess she had been when he watched his wife dress, but naturally she didn't see the same and batted away his reassurances. Age and beauty are not good bedfellows for any woman, especially this Hollywood icon.

He had hardly time to say farewell to his colleagues as he packed up for his trip. His uncle was so proud of him and the head of personnel was sorry to see him leave, but assured him that if it didn't work out he would renew his contract without hesitation, and so with an opportunity like that on the table he had no reservations. Off he flew to his love, Ms Loren, and his new adventure in Rome.

Shakir al Habib became senior director of hairdressing at the Salon de Roma. He was the youngest person ever to achieve this position and his favourite client was, of course, Ms Loren, who frequented at least once a week. Today, however, he had a session booked with me, or as he put it, 'the most delectable lady in Rome, Mrs Carmella Matteo.'

Always a pleasure to have a session with Shakir, it was a superb quality treatment and a lot of fun. We're not exactly friends, but more than client–stylist for sure, but I was stuck how to ask the questions without giving up anything.

Shakir bounded out to greet me, we kissed both cheeks and I settled in to the sumptuous leather chair. Shakir reclined it and started with a relaxing Nepalese massage: scalp, temples, cheeks, neck and shoulders. A tiny snore emitted from my gaping mouth and Shakir left me for twenty minutes until I revived from my nap, feeling refreshed and a little sheepish.

'Oh God, you are like a hypnotist, Shakir, I wasn't even sleepy.'

'No, Carmella, but your mind was wishing for a little meditative restoration, so we gave it what it wanted. How do you feel?'

'Amazing, actually!' I decided I must approach him; he was the only gay man I knew and hoped I could trust.

'I need to talk about something, it's very private, I need your help, Shakir.'

Our briefing lasted no more than five minutes, because humiliatingly it was common knowledge in the gay community that my husband was, shall we say, extremely active on the scene. Shakir agreed to be my spy, just to keep me aware of the men he was out and about with, parties he attended and with whom he left. I needed to build my dossier.

I saw his genuine sympathy at my sadness and embarrassment, I felt sure that he was in my corner. He kissed the top of my head and continued like I hadn't asked him for anything more than a glass of water.

Working his hands thought my heavy plait, loosening each strand, taking care not to damage the glossy mane once it was free, a silent petite Asian girl, Suki, appeared and motioned me to the back wash. This area was a serene waterfall tumbling over natural unpolished marble, forming a shallow heated pool that was underlit with soft, undulating lights. I undressed and slipped on the silk kimono, laying down on the pure white terry cloth bed that overhung the pool, my hair dangling over the waters. Suki silently knelt in the pool. Using a clay urn, she washed my hair with the natural mineral waters flowing from the rock face. These fortified waters were magical in keeping the thick Italian hair strong and grease-free; only natural organic cleansers were used, a process of washing and rinsing very gently in rhythm with my breathing.

No detergent ever touched the hair of a lady at Salon de Roma. We were treated like queens, I felt like Cleopatra herself.

I nearly fell asleep again. Suki was so serene and gentle, I felt all my anxiety flowing away with each rinse. She wrapped my cleansed hair in warm terry cloth and led me back to Shakir, who was ready with his secret weapon, but before he began, another tiny Asian girl, Mia, applied a light moisturising mask to my face, blending away the tiny few tears that had spilled as the tension had left my body.

This was undoubtedly the most luxurious, relaxing hair appointment in the world!

CHAPTER FIFTEEN

HULYA

My life is wonderful, I am married to a smart, funny, handsome man, we have a lovely home and my husband has a great, well-paid career. We are truly blessed by Allah in every way, we practise our faith as a family, we are a close, noisy, funny, crazy, warm Turkish family.

All those statements have been true at one moment or another in our lives, but rarely at the same time!

When our families came together to discuss our union, I was so happy. Mehmet was a gorgeous, serious, educated boy, shy and handsome. I fell in love with him at our first chaperoned meeting. We were so lucky, we have love and deep respect for each other, we recognised straight away that we could build a very good life together, sharing the same values, same upbringing and our families matched well. In our Muslim faith it is very important to be compatible with each other's families because after our marriage, it becomes one bigger family. My mother-in-law was very warm and loving, she approved of this union and that meant our married life would be easier.

Mehmet's father, Kubilay, is an Imam. He is an important religious figure in our town, respected widely, and his wife, Senem, strictly manages her children's lives to reflect well on her husband's reputation.

My father was very proud that his daughter was marrying the son of the respected Kubilay. Life was good; life was blessed for us.

Our marriage was set for the year after Mehmet finished university. Three glorious days of celebration were planned. Myself, my mother, Berrin, and my future mother-in-law, Senem, spent several weeks shopping and planning and as the date approached, I felt like the luckiest girl in Istanbul.

Our wedding was exhausting but amazing. You can imagine that everyone that knew our families wanted to attend, the kudos of an invite to the Imam's son's wedding was something to be bragged about in our culture. It was a wonderful frenzy of dancing, laughing, eating, kissing, more dancing, more eating, more kissing and finally, the money!

We have a funny saying here: marry the biggest girl you can find, so that you are made rich by the covering of the dress with money. Ha, well, we were not exactly rich, I'm too petite, but it was a great start to our lives. With financial gifts from our families, we had enough to start our married life well.

Having been educated at university in Maritime Law, Mehmet decided the next logical step would be to try and get a position in Europe; he had studied Spanish and English and was fluent in both.

He researched and found that if he did one more year at university in England, this would mean he could get a position for an international shipping firm as an in-house lawyer; London was a likely starting point as the city has many trading links with Istanbul.

It was all a bit of a whirlwind. Although my family is modern-thinking, I have been raised to be a support to my husband in the traditional way, meaning his career would be his priority and the home and children mine, and even if I was a little anxious about moving away from our families, I didn't fuss about it. We were young, this was a stepping stone in our life, so it was arranged and off we went. Mehmet had no trouble getting a place at university, he was a serious scholar and we arrived at Heathrow in the early hours of a freezing cold January.

I had studied English language to a reasonable level, but I found myself a confused dumb mute when we arrived, because no one here sounded like the American English tapes I had studied. This strange accent and slang threw me, we may as well have landed in Hong Kong.

Mehmet had more skill and we managed OK, took a cab to our uncle's flat in a tree-lined, frosty street in north London. We were blessed with having one of Mehmet's extended family already here, Uncle Zafar. He was a bit of a character, his mother said he owned three Turkish restaurants in London and that made him akin to Sir Alan Sugar in her eyes; how she bragged about her son's business acumen.

The truth was, he clung on by a thread to a small share of the last business, which was the grottiest kebab house takeaway in the area; you wouldn't eat from it unless starving or drunk, but it appeared there were many drunk, starving people in that area, so he did OK.

He had lost the rest of the businesses, two other grotty takeaways, to his partners through gambling. He was not a good Muslim at all, he had a string of blonde girlfriends and liked a tot of the old whiskey. A tot apparently means a bottle, judging by the recycling at the steps, but we tried to respectfully ignore that and not judge; he was family and helping us, we must thank God and Zafar for his kindness.

We had the attic flat in a terraced Victorian villa that had been dissected at every turn to maximise the capacity for rentals. Fifteen people inhabited this ancient house, including Zafar in the tiny basement studio. I discovered that Grosvenor Road had been a prestigious address back in the 1800s, but these days it was a cheap rent area for London, people crammed in like sardines. Despite his mother assuring us that this mansion was her son's property, the truth was that it belonged to his partner and he earned a bit of commission and free accommodation renting the rooms out and collecting the cash. It was sufficient for Mehmet and me in the short term, it could never be a home for us to raise children, but that was years ahead anyway and I was sure we would be long gone before the patter of tiny feet was heard.

Mehmet was halfway through the Uni year and I was getting very bored and homesick sitting in our tiny attic day after day. My English was coming along, listening to the radio, but it wasn't easy, just the speed of the words flying at me left me dizzy.

I needed to get out more and listen to the rhythm; I did take a few walks around the area but was so worried about getting lost.

One day I found myself at the other side of a large park. It was a lovely sunny day and I was distracted by the flowers and children playing, I walked and walked and couldn't see my route back. I panicked and ran around until I found a red phone box and called Zafar at the Topkapi kebab house. Twenty minutes later, he picked me up, I was so pleased to see a friendly face.

But Zafar didn't drop me home; he was rushing to the cash and carry food market to buy stock, a busy bank holiday weekend coming up, so I had to go with him.

We chatted in Turkish and I realised that his dialect had become strange and not easy to understand. I wondered how anyone could lose their mother tongue, but of course Zafar had been in London for more than thirty years. Only the chat of the guys at the Turkish community coffee shop, or gambling den as it really is, kept him in the loop, but talking to a bunch of gamblers every day and shouting at the young lads in the takeaway exercised probably 5% of a full vocabulary. He didn't have the time or inclination to sit with educated men at the mosque and discuss theology, religion or current affairs, so those words had been lost to him. I thought about Zafar's situation, how back home people assumed he was living like a lord in England; it couldn't have been further from the truth.

I assumed that was why he had lost his faith, gambled and drank himself through each repetitive week but I never once heard him complain. He was a perpetual optimist. His eyes rheumy and tired from all-night poker, he still managed to maintain a bright and almost excited outlook for the coming weekend – amazing resilience!

We walked around the cash and carry, several fellow Turkish caterers shouting greetings and a few obtuse remarks that I couldn't understand, but clearly relating to some debt unpaid or a recent argument.

It seemed there was a lot of discontent between the Turkish men in the coffee shop. It wasn't uncommon to find one sleeping there having lost the rent money on a card game, which meant he had better not go home to face his furious wife, so he stayed in the coffee shop hoping to borrow money from a sympathetic fellow and win on the next game, take his rent money back and scuttle off home.

Not the healthiest place to be, but it was a central hub where tea was always hot and a fellow loser was always on hand with a sympathetic ear or a sob story much worse than yours to make you feel less of a loser, but never any real financial solution. Dreams were discussed without embarrassment as every one of the guys in the coffee shop was here for the same reason: to make their fortune and return to the homeland to support the families depending on them.

Money went around the regulars like 'pass the parcel'. The coffee shop owner made a tiny percentage on the games, sold tea for a little profit and gave a touch of home culture for the expats. It was an oasis for many.

In the market, I was reading a promotional poster, struggling to pronounce the English word 'discounted', and Zafar laughed.

'Yes,' he said, 'good girl, keep your eye out for that word, most important word here!'

I probably looked silly, walking around reading the words slowly, but it really caught my interest. Much easier to learn the words in context, so a bag of something had a picture of what it was and the word in large lettering, hah, such a simple way to learn, like a giant child's English storybook.

Just two hours in the store and I felt I had taken my understanding of the English language up another level; it cemented some grammatical rules which hadn't made any sense before, and it was starting to click into place.

We agreed that I would go with Zafar twice a week to the cash and carry. I was elated, had the best day and was smiling like your proverbial Cheshire cat when Mehmet got home, not least because I had got some swordfish heavily discounted and I had made a traditional lentil and fish soup for our supper. The smell made him hungry and a little nostalgic for home. We made love with extra warmth that night, I felt I had turned a corner in accepting my new habitat.

I excitedly told Mehmet about the cash and carry arrangement. He was still and silent for a while, then he surprised me when he said no, I wasn't to go with Zafar again. We had never disagreed before. It stung a bit that the reason for my obviously uplifted mood was dismissed so readily.

I tried again to explain the importance to my life of being busy and productive and improving my English so I could hopefully gain employment here and start to save for a nicer home.

For the first time in our married life he shouted at me: 'NO, Hulya!'

I quieted myself on the matter and said, 'OK,' I placated my husband, said, 'I understand,' and 'Don't be angry, it's fine, no big deal.'

But I wasn't fine, I was shocked. What was I supposed to do here in England, sit in a flat for the next five years?

I didn't sleep much that night.

Mehmet slept fine and was normal in the morning. Oblivious to my brooding, he went off to university for the day. He should have been on summer break but there were extra studies for overseas students and he attended every one. The serious scholar I married was exactly that, driven and competitive, to the detriment of everything else. Sunday was the only day I had to enjoy some time with him, but he was usually too tired to do much more than a short walk in the park, then he would be at the mosque for the rest of the afternoon.

So when Zafar beeped his horn and waved me to get in the car, I did.

We drove along, chatting about nothing much, then he said, 'OK, what happened?'

'Nothing happened, I'm OK.'

'Hmm, are you sure about that? Because there seems to be a huge elephant in the car.'

'What?' I stupidly swivelled around to inspect the back seat. What I would have done had there been an elephant in the car I'm not sure, but he laughed heartily.

'An English saying, Hulya, means we are ignoring something as huge and un-ignorable as an elephant in the car and yet we hadn't noticed it.'

'Ah, ha-ha, English humour is bizarre.'

'Bizarre yet so accurate. So, what happened?'

I told him, he stopped the car.

'Shall I take you home, Hulya? It's not a good idea to go against your husband's wishes, I don't want to cause any upset between you.'

I thought for a moment. *Maybe he is right; am I being a bad wife, ignoring his word?* But inside of my brain a little voice said, 'Go!'

My mother always taught me: do not complain until you have exhausted all possible remedies for your complaint. I chuckled at the memory; I never once complained to Mehmet, I must sort myself out, solve my own misery.

Mehmet was probably tired and didn't realise how much the trips out helped me or how lonely I was, alone day after day. So off we went and I enjoyed the trip even more than before because the fishmonger gave me some lovely queen scallops for half the price. I knew exactly the dish I would make for Mehmet and he would forgive me immediately.

How naive a newly married woman can be!

We chatted to many people in the market and I was amazed to hear Zafar switch from English to Turkish to

Italian to Armenian to Spanish, all the languages of the regulars at the market. He gave me a running commentary about the fellow caterers. Pointing to a small, compact, attractive man, 'That's Giovanni, he owns Don Marco Italian restaurant just off the square.' A statuesque blonde lady in her fifties strolled past, giving a coy smile to Zafar. He coughed, 'That's Melanie, she owns the coffee shop near the park.' There had clearly been some liaison between them, but I didn't pry.

A broad, muscular, serious-looking man passed us, nodding at Zafar. He told me, 'That guy, Bahadir, has three Turkish restaurants, he's very wealthy, he started as a washing-up boy thirty-two years ago, so he earned everything he has with sweat and hard work. You don't want to get on the wrong side of him, he's known for his temper.' I turned back to look at the man Bahadir. His massive back told of his hard physical labour, he looked tired but determined, even his walk told a story.

'That man,' said Zafar, tipping his head left toward a small, thin, beady-eyed man, 'Baris, is a bad one. He ripped off his English wife to get his restaurant. He was already married back home. There are a few you shouldn't say hello to.'

I nodded. It was a lot to take in. the market was full of interesting characters. As a single woman in Turkey, I didn't get too involved in knowing the local men, it wasn't proper to do so, but here in England, the men and women worked alongside each other, all nationalities here, chatting, nodding, all with the same goal: to make money. It was quite an eye opener.

I complimented Zafar on his languages.

'Well, Hulya, in England, the restaurants are mostly run by foreign people. You get to work with most nationalities, you pick bits up over the years. I never had a sushi bar though so I can't help you with Japanese,' he roared with laughter at his own joke and I just laughed along. He was a funny one, Zafar.

We were lucky with the traffic and were at the Topkapi takeaway earlier than normal, so we unloaded the stock ourselves, the staff not due for another half hour. I cringed at the state of the fridges as I stocked them up.

When we were done, Zafar made some tea and we sat for a moment to recover. I tentatively spoke, while Zafar enjoyed his tea.

'Would you be offended if I came and did a little cleaning here one day? The boys are too busy with the food prep and you know boys, they don't clean as well as women, I hope I'm not being rude.'

He sighed. 'Ah, Hulya, am I going to get in deep trouble with my nephew?'

I dropped my head; I shouldn't compromise him.

He rubbed his bristly chin, as he chose his words. 'I would be delighted for some help, these kids, they ignore me, the other partners don't care, because they have money and this is nothing much to them, but I built this Topkapi business from scratch. It was a shining pride of mine back in the day, but I've been very unlucky and lost most of it. If you do help me, Hulya, it must be secret.'

I nodded, thinking of Mehmet's reaction if he found out.

'You know, Hulya, Mehmet is too proud; he will not accept his wife working, especially not in a takeaway owned by three bad Muslims.'

He roared again and I joined him.

'Ah, Zafar, Allah tells us to help our brothers and sisters, not to judge their sins unless we ourselves are without sin.'

I thought I could cover my lie with my need to observe my faith and help my brother. With a wink, I went in to the store room and started to make a list of cleaning kit.

Zafar raised his eyes to the roof and whispered, 'Insallah!'

That night when I was cooking supper for us, I felt lighter and happier than I had in a long time. Sometimes independence separates a couple, but my liberty would add to our happiness, I was sure of that. Mehmet didn't know me that well, we hadn't been together that long, I hoped he would realise eventually that I'm an educated woman and could be a very strong wife helping us reach the lifestyle that I certainly wanted. A bit of cleaning was hardly going to jeopardise the balance between us, surely he would see that?

We ate together in our tiny attic, I had bought some candles and dressed my hair the way he likes. It was a romantic supper and the scallops were delicious. That was the first lie in our marriage. I told my husband that Zafar had dropped them in to me, no mention of the trip out to the market. Zafar's words of advice had struck a cautionary chord.

We made love that night with sincere sentiment; Mehmet had three days off and promised a romantic few days exploring London.

We had exactly that; it was amazing, exhausting and exciting!

It felt so lovely to hold my husband's hand as we strolled around. He took me to Harrods department store, I was enchanted by the beauty of the intricate plasterwork ceilings in the food halls, it reminded me of the grand decoration in Istanbul. We walked through the handbag department, a stunning azure blue clutch bag took my eye and I lingered a moment.

Mehmet gushed, 'I will buy it for you my darling if you love it.' I raised the gorgeous bag in front of his eyes, holding the £2,500 price tag at eye level.

'I don't love this bag enough!' I exclaimed, with a big grin on my face.

'Mashalla!' he declared with an expression of mock horror on his face. 'Phew, I was starting to feel a bit sick,' he laughed, 'but one day, my love, I will buy you anything you desire. I'm working for us, for our future and I want the best for us.'

It was the perfect day; we ate at a fantastic Turkish café further up the road called Ozzie's, a real taste of home.

Knightsbridge has everything anyone could want. We were not simple village folk, we were raised in Istanbul suburbs, a good quality upbringing. We are used to the wealth of Istanbul but London is special. I felt like buying something as a memento, but after our simple nostalgic dinner, we wandered through the parks and on the underground tube, so we didn't pass any souvenir shops.

Arriving home tired out, we went straight to bed. As we undressed, Mehmet produced a shiny red enamel London bus, a perfect souvenir. He had sent the young waiter to Harrods to buy it. It meant so much, that shiny little bus.

I will never forget that day, it washed away all the doubts and fears I had about living here, I suddenly felt that I could fit in. I was not an unusual face in this multi-cultural city, every language filled the streets, and sitting in the café chatting with the owners and customers just like we were back home made me feel less alien; it was a joyful day.

Monday came around and off my husband went to Uni. He was coming up to his first run of exams, he had been studying shipping charts, currency conversions, import tariffs, insurance frauds, prosecutions and customs cases. The work was detailed and heavy, I couldn't really help him much as it was mostly technical disputes over cargo or breaches of contract and appeals for confiscated loads, but he was smart and diligent and I had no doubt he would become a maritime legal eagle, my Mehmet, my dear love.

The familiar beep of Zafar's car woke me from my daydream. I grabbed my purse and flew out of the attic, down the four flights.

Zafar looked sideways. 'Hmm, someone had a nice weekend,' his deep rumbling laugh filled the car. I blushed and told him he had forgotten his manners, which made him laugh more.

'Hulya, I'm a lost cause, I'm afraid. Allah gave up on me a long time ago, so you may as well. And I meant you look happy, it's good to see.'

I did have a great weekend. I told him about our exploration of London, he knew it like the back of his hand. He knew Osman, the owner of the fabulous café in Knightsbridge, and agreed it was probably the best place to eat, fresh and just like home.

I was describing some of the dishes I cooked for Mehmet and he said he was starving.

'I'll make you breakfast when we get to the shop.'

He broke in to a boyish grin. *This man needed mothering*, I thought as we drove.

Poor man was ravenous by the time I had cleaned the pans and all the surfaces, I would not cook in that mess. We shared a favourite dish, so simple and tasty, we call it *menemen*, slightly runny loose eggs with herbs. I make it with a twist: fine slices of *sucuk* sausage, olives, goats cheese, with minted yoghurt poured over the top and some warm *simit*, seeded bread.

Hard to beat and so full of flavour.

Mehmet ate like he hadn't seen a good meal in years, which wasn't true at all, his many lady friends liked to dine out, but something in this dish touched him.

He washed down his hot sweet tea, and I saw his eyes become wet and glassy.

'You OK, Zafar?'

'It's been more than thirty years since I ate that meal, Hulya. It was the last food my mama cooked for me, before I came to England. I refused to eat it here, promised myself every year I would go home for *menemen* by my mother's pan. Of course, I never went, years pass and you find yourself glued here.'

'Oh Zafar, I'm sorry if it upset you.'

'No, Hulya, it was delicious and I never had better, that is the truth. Now I've tasted yours I realise what a terrible cook my mother was!'

We roared with laughter and poured more tea. I thought to myself, *If this man is a bad Muslim, maybe Allah needs to loosen the rules and accept a few strays because he's a joy.*

The best pleasure for a smoker is the one following a hearty feed, so I got on with my cleaning while he sat at the back doors and enjoyed a smoke and a dark thick coffee. I never could take our traditional coffee, made me run to the toilet every time, but the boys were raised on it and I suppose they got used to its effect.

I cleaned and scrubbed, by the time Zafar came in to start prep for the service, he took a step back. In only forty minutes or so I had made a real difference to the grotty kitchen.

'My God, Hulya, they pay by the hour in England, you better learn to slow down, or you will never earn enough for the rent.'

I looked quizzically at him.

'You do a day's work in an hour, my girl! Don't break your back, don't wear yourself out, Mehmet may notice,' he winked roaring with mirth, so I swatted him with the tea towel for his cheek.

I felt very sisterly toward him, he was alone in many ways and he could do with a mother, a sister or better yet, a wife!

Before I knew it, the chefs were arriving and that meant it was nearly 4pm. We sped off to the house so Zafar could have his nap. Starting again at 9pm he would go on through until 4am then on to the coffee shop, not an Alan Sugar lifestyle, that's for sure.

I showered and tidied myself, just as Mehmet arrived home. I felt liberated and valid, it felt good, I kissed him heartily, he picked me up and twirled me around our tiny little home.

'I have good news, it's not official but I have a potential place at Johannsen Coeur maritime law.' This was good news indeed. 'They pick the best, they pay the best,' he talked excitedly, kissing me between sentences. 'My professor has been asked for his best two students to be suggested and I was the first choice, naturally!'

We laughed and kissed and twirled, we made love there on the sofa, which was out of character for my husband, who liked the respectability of our marital bed, but I felt uplifted. This life here in England was lifting a little of the restraints of home. His childhood was very disciplined; as the son of the Imam, he never really had the opportunity to be casual or relaxed.

Mehmet lay sleeping and I padded to the kitchenette. I had brought some delicious *sucuk* home and I started cooking my *menemen* for the second time that day. We sat lazily in our dressing gowns eating it from the pan, scooping the delicious eggs turned orange by the oil in the spicy sausage. I watched as he devoured it, hungry from lovemaking, but also, it was extremely tasty.

'Ahh, this is why I married you, Hulya, you are the

best wife a man could want, beautiful, smart, loving and a top-class chef as well.' He covered my mouth with oily kisses and we settled down to a cosy night of intimate declarations of our deep contentment and joy of being each other's love. They were sweet, simple days in our little attic.

CHAPTER SIXTEEN

Hulya

The weeks following our London weekend were fast and chaotic. Mehmet got the letter to approve his new job at Johannsen Coeur maritime law. We decided to take a trip to Ozzie's little café in Knightsbridge, to treat ourselves. Zafar joined us and soon our table became a group, everyone knew him, Osman and his wife joined us, plus another couple from a nearby table, good friends of Zafar's. We laughed and talked, it was just like being in Istanbul, the food kept coming despite us shouting 'No more, no more!' Secretly, Mehmet was panicking about the cost. As if reading his mind, Zafar shouted loudly, 'This is my chance to give you a wedding breakfast, you are my very special guests tonight.' The *raki* came out and the men drank, even Mehmet had a small tot, he would never have done so before. I was surprised but glad too to see my studious, hardworking man live a little.

Osman played Turkish music, one of the old singers, Sibel Can, everyone got up and danced to the old songs. I felt a pang of sorrow to see Zafar sitting at the table. I motioned him to join us, he made some feeble excuse about his old knees, so I didn't press him, but I started to hatch a little plot.

I had thought about my older sister, Eda. She had been widowed four years ago, a very pretty woman, warm and sweet spirited, only forty-six and too young to be alone for the rest of her days, her son was at university now, so I wondered if she may like to visit us.

'What are you thinking about, darling?' Mehmet cut into my thoughts.

'You can read me already, husband, hmm, I soon can have no secrets.'

'I hope we never have secrets, you are my best friend, Hulya, I will share everything with you, I promise.'

'And I you, my darling, I you.' A touch of a blush hit my cheeks as I thought about my secret job. I wasn't a good liar.

Zafar left to go and take over at the Topkapi. We wound up the party and made our way home. It was so romantic to walk through the streets we had seen in movies. Now accustomed to the tube system, I felt I could maybe even come shopping here, especially if Eda was with me.

Zafar was keen on busty blondes, it seemed, there had been a few leaving the house in the early hours, he never mentioned them and so neither did I. But I'm sure if he tasted Eda's cooking, ha, he would switch to brunette immediately.

Eda had the touch, there was nothing she couldn't cook. She had taught me, I learned her tricks and I had a good taste for adapting and improving recipes, so between us, we could create fantastic flavours and we loved adapting the very old Ottoman dishes. If there was any family get-together, it was Eda and I that were in charge of the food, but she was the top chef of the family for sure, I missed cooking with her.

So when we got home I mentioned to Mehmet my little plot. He surprised me again by agreeing heartily.

'Yes, Hulya, why not? It would be good for you to have her here. I'm going to be working all the hours at this new job, I must prove myself, you understand, my love.'

'Of course, darling, I know, it will be tough. Where should we put her? No room here. I will talk to Zafar tomorrow, ask him if there is any more space here coming up.' And it was agreed. I slept very well that night, happy, contented, I said my prayers and thanked God sincerely for all the blessings he had given us.

When I invited Eda, she was delighted and excited. Zafar said there was a studio coming up in three weeks and we could take it for her, only a small rent as it was very small and rather grotty. Eda had a good deal of money herself from her late husband's estate and it wouldn't be an issue, tickets were booked and visa arrangements made.

I was so busy the week before she arrived cleaning the studio from top to bottom and decorating it. One of the young lads from the takeaway, Mahmud, came to help. He fixed the leaking taps and broken shelving and laid new carpet, which Zafar paid for. He convinced his partner to spend a bit on the place, it made such a difference to the studio.

After we put the new bed together, I took a walk to the shopping centre and found a lovely lamp, candles and a vase, some gorgeous curtains and matching cushions. I found a fantastic giant throw for the sofa full of turquoise, jade and gold threads, and a lovely quality linen tablecloth for the little round table. I wanted to make this a nice place for my sister.

By the time we finished and Zafar popped his head in to take Mahmud to Topkapi, he nearly fell over himself.

'Hulya, this is amazing, so fresh and clean, looks like a flat in Mayfair, I might need to increase the rent now!'

It took me a second to realise he was kidding as I heard his familiar roaring laugh fill the studio.

'I'm glad you like it, Eda is very excited, I do need to get her some cooking things at the market tomorrow.'

'Yes, no problem, Hulya, we will get it kitted out, she cooks good you say?'

'Good is too poor a word, Zafar, you will taste for yourself, makes my food look bad.' I saw a tiny flash of interest in his cheery features.

I had seen a difference in this man since he had a touch of family around him, he had cheered up and a little support at the Topkapi lifted him up for sure. I wasn't doing much, but as they say, every little helps.

Mehmet was exhausted every night he arrived home. He showered, ate the tasty food I cooked, kissed me and fell asleep. I was feeding him the best nutritious food I could, bone-broth cassoulets, seafood, lots of leafy vegetables, pulses and protein, this was all I could do to help him manage the gruelling days at the firm. He spoke very little about his work, I didn't press him too much, my job was to make him relax and rest for those short hours he was at home before he headed off again to the city.

He had forgotten about Eda arriving and it was a shock to him when he came home to find her sitting on our sofa, but it wasn't long before they were hugging and chatting like old days.

Zafar had sent his friend and taxi cab driver to Heathrow to collect her and that afternoon she was installed in the studio, which she adored. I managed to get a few kitchen bits from the market but she would be better to choose her utensils herself from the store in our high street – the old stuff in the studio, included in the rent, was so disgusting that I couldn't expect her to boil water in those pans, let alone make her signature lamb soup, which I was looking forward to eating myself.

My little plan was formulating and conscious not to rush anything, I thought we could all have a dinner together to welcome Eda and introduce Zafar. I had asked Mehmet if he thought Saturday night was OK – he would be off Sunday, and Zafar would only be free around 7pm for an hour or so as it's his busiest night, so it wouldn't feel too awkward or set up. Yes, a casual light dinner to welcome her, and then everyone would go off to their own quarters.

I headed to the market with Zafar on Friday morning and Eda was already starting her stock for the lamb soup. Oh, the smell, it felt like I was home in Istanbul. I must have hugged my sister one hundred times already, I hadn't realised how much I had missed her. She settled in pretty quickly and she told me what she wanted from the market.

Zafar still hadn't actually met her, she had been here three days but Zafar respectfully kept his distance. I think he had forgotten the etiquette for dealing with a lone Turkish woman. He was his usual funny self at the market and we shopped with two trolleys, Eda's and Topkapi's.

A couple of the ingredients that I selected, he noticed and swapped for one of a superior quality.

'I get the feeling Eda is quite the chef, from my experience if you buy the cheap one, they will hold it against you for years.' He was right and after dealing with hundreds of chefs of all nationalities, he wasn't about to risk it for the sake of an extra few pounds.

'Looks like she's making lamb soup.'

'And sesame dumplings.'

'Ohh, my mouth is drooling already, get her some fresh parsley and chives, not that dried rubbish. And the organic halloumi, Hulya, that other one is too salty.'

I looked at Zafar and raised my brow.

'Oh, you know a few things about food, eh, Zaf?'

He roared, 'Yes, Hulya, I used to be a chef, God only knows what I am now.'

I hugged him. 'You are still a chef, you just have to sell

what they want, not what you want to cook, I get that, must be sad though.'

'It is, Hulya, I loved cooking, it was my passion. You know, I didn't lose the businesses all because of gambling.' It was the first time he had told me that he was a gambler. I didn't react, just listened.

'I actually thought that if I cooked my beautiful home food, people would flock to Topkapi, would pay the little extra money for the quality, but I made a mistake. It took me a long time to accept that takeaway food is just to fill you up as cheaply as possible or to soak up alcohol to enable you to function next day. It broke my spirit, I suppose. That's why I admire that man Bahadir, he was so determined, he never compromised on his quality, he worked and pushed to keep the standards and eventually it paid off for him. But of course he built beautiful restaurants, he matched the environment to the food, which is his magic. Nobody wants to buy a Rolls Royce from a back street car dealer, you get me?'

I didn't get his metaphor at all, my English culture not quite there, but I nodded and patted his arm.

'It's not too late, Zafar, you can start over maybe?'

'Too late for me, Hulya, I'm a wreck. Better I stop dreaming and just keep selling my doner kebab and chips to the drunks; my time has gone now. Come on, we better get going.'

That was the end of his openness, but it touched me deeply. This kind, funny man who sent his mother money every month, whether he could afford it or not, just so she didn't need to struggle or worry and so she could enjoy telling her ear-worn friends about her clever businessman son. That's a kind of love and duty bound in our culture, we are proud people.

I had just enough time to clean through at Topkapi, drop the ingredients at Eda's studio on the ground floor, shower, change and grill some whole quail, prepare a mixed salad and make some *borek* with extra *bayaz peyniri*, which is a little sharper than feta cheese, and lots of chopped parsley, just how Mehmet liked it. He arrived his usual worn-out self, ate heartily and took himself to bed early.

'I want to have some energy for dinner tomorrow, Hulya, so forgive me for sleeping.'

'Oh, sweet love, you go ahead, I'm OK. I will go and sit with Eda, she says she can get Turkish films on her computer, I don't know how.'

So I skipped down the stairs and smelled the heavenly scents of my sister's cooking before I reached the door.

We played our music on the little computer she called a tablet. Eda had always been up on the latest technology, her husband's company were the first Apple computer distributors in Turkey, they made a lot of money. He had always made Eda educate herself about the products and every new model arrived at their house before the shops got them – smart lady, my sister.

She had chatted to a young man called Roy at number 8, offered to pay half his Wi-Fi bill if she could use it. He was very happy to oblige and swapped the password for a plate of warm delicious *borek*, without a hint of concern she wouldn't pay up. He was a pretty good judge of character and this smiley, cherub-faced lady was sound.

'You are too skinny, young man, need to eat some good food,' she chided him, familiar and open like she had known him all his life. She mothered everyone, her warmth and the power of her food broke barriers, social, cultural, age, it didn't matter, two people can always share a moment with delicious food.

Roy trotted off to work stuffing the delicious layered pastry all the way into his van. He was an electrician she discovered, no family, came from foster parents and had a pretty hard life, worked all the hours and lived quietly.

'My God, Eda I've lived here nearly a year and I didn't even know we had a Roy at number 8.' It never ceased to amaze me, she could extract information better than an FBI agent, in fact people just volunteered it. It was her openness I think, she had a rounded, pretty face, always a smile for everyone and I had forgotten how safe I felt with her. She wasn't huge, but let's say of generous proportions, a hug from Eda felt like a safe place, she was a second mother to me in many ways.

I was feeling very content with my lovely sister beside me, my gorgeous husband sleeping above me and my unlikely ally and friend below me in his basement. Home can be made anywhere as long as you have loved ones close.

Saturday night arrived and we were in Eda's studio setting the small table. The smells coming from the kitchenette were likely to draw every Turk in London to our door. Mehmet was stirring the soup as we added the final side dishes; small plates of pickles, olives, yoghurt and cheeses were laid out. She had even made her own bread; it was still warm and soft with a crisp outer layer coated in sesame seed.

I heard Zafar at the door; Eda went to welcome him. As the door opened, I saw his face change from fine to fabulous, a practised art in hospitality, but his smile was for real, matched perfectly by my sister's open smile. They stood just a second longer than necessary, which I noted in my imaginary diary.

Mehmet and Zafar hugged, and he kissed Eda and me on both cheeks.

'Welcome to England, I am at your service,' he took a half bow and that smile never left his face.

We all laughed and the men were seated as we served the delicious hearty soup with dumplings. It was a pleasure to watch these men eat like they hadn't in days, a true cook's pleasure.

We all ate and chatted, Zafar entertained Eda with tales of crazy chefs and kitchen nightmares, she and he talked all night, until he shot up like a cat and realised he was going to be late for Topkapi.

He bowed to kiss her hand and said sincerely, 'This is the only night in thirty years that I have ever wished it to be slow trade at Topkapi, so I could stay longer and enjoy this wonderful company.'

I skipped and danced in my head. This was better than expected. Mehmet nudged my knee and widened his eyes.

I was grinning like a fool, I corrected myself but carried on dancing inside.

It warmed my heart. Eda became quite young and girly on receipt of the charming sentiments from Zaf, like the sister I knew when I was a little girl. I hoped for, if not a romance, then a friendship, as Zafar was one of the nicest men I had ever met. I believe the English call them rough diamonds.

It's a perfect phrase!

CHAPTER SEVENTEEN

Sherrie & Angie

Sherrie

We arrived in California. The dramatic shift in architecture from Santa Fe to Sacramento was like a leap in time, another world. We flew into Los Angeles and took the train for the rest our journey. I watched avidly as we trundled along the coastal route through to the city. The wide clear blue sea reared up at several points in our journey, I hadn't seen the ocean before, only on TV. This was like God had painted a vast canvas with the most sparkling blue-green hues; the pale golden sands stretched as far as I could see along the coast, from white shimmering gold to honey brown, and darkening to a deep nut as shore met with the waves. It was a sight I will never forget. I had an urge to stop the train and dive off the edge into the crystal blue sea.

I thought back to my closeted life in Limestone Creek. I didn't miss it, but there was still a little girl inside me who wanted to run and tell Ma about the amazing things I'd seen and experienced. A sharp stab of pain in my heart reminded me that no one back home was actually interested in my life, my world or in fact me.

Sylvia was napping across from me. She was becoming the mother I had needed, I often woke at night in a sweat from a nightmare that Sylvia had died. I didn't have anyone else in this world who cared. I did wonder about tracing my father, but I didn't really have the first clue about how to go about that, maybe Sylvia would know how.

The Sacramento Plaza Hotel was equally plush as Santa Fe, but the most obvious difference in the style was the beautiful bohemian gardens, reminiscent of art nouveaux watercolours. Slopes of flowering bushes, tiny cornflower-blue flowers mixed with poppies and mimosas, monkey flowers, desert sage and robust green bushes, dotted with tiny delicate flower heads in creamy pinks and purples, cascaded throughout the pathways, in a casual but charming abundance. It was so pretty and natural, I felt an instant connection with California.

I wandered around stretching my legs; it had been a long journey and at nearly 6ft tall, it was pretty cramped. OK for Sylvia with her little legs and 5ft 5in stature, like a small, brightly adorned Buddha she slotted in with ease pretty much anywhere, but I tended to stick out at odd angles, legs, arms and neck, all too long for comfort in a confined space. So I walked the grounds, stretching my muscles and soothing my aching back, breathing in the fragrances that were mixed with slightly salty air. I realised of course the ocean was so close, it felt like the mood of the garden reflected the Californian attitude, more natural, laid back.

I saw several gardeners working away crouched down in the huge landscape. Like all non-gardeners, I didn't really appreciate the hours of dedicated back-breaking graft it took to create something that looked like it just blew in and settled down there by chance. Such a contrast to the Santa Fe garden, which was far more formal with manicured topiary and flowering cactus plants making statements throughout the landscape.

The pavilion, stage and marquee had already been set up and it was being washed from top to bottom, the billowing VIP tents shimmering in the heat as they dried naturally in the warm air. Gardeners were finishing off the climbing plants, winding them around the painted trellis screens that gave some hidden spots on the stage. The sound guys were cabling up, and the lighting rig went through its routine, in line with the show format.

A tall dark man in a beautiful cream silk billowing shirt and sandy linen trousers was directing the work. He caught my shadow across the stage and turned to address me. I thought he was going to shout at me, but stopped himself short as he took in my appearance.

'Ah, good afternoon, miss.' He assumed I was a contestant checking the scene for the heat tomorrow. He slightly reddened, God knows what thoughts had flashed through his head to cause it. I equally blushed at that thought, then he smiled a smile so broad and friendly,

I immediately was captured by his face, a young Elvis Presley sprang to mind.

His light olive skin, deep brown eyes and dark lashes that framed them gave him a look of a loving spaniel. He had short dark hair, could have been a military cut. He was a mystery to look at, his face seeming to change dramatically with every move or new expression, a bit confusing, can a face have several faces?

Realising I had been staring at him for far longer than was polite, I pulled myself together and took his outstretched hand, up on to the stage next to him.

'Hello,' he tried again, I'm sure he thought me a dumb blonde.

I was tongue-tied, finally blurting out, 'Sorry to disturb your work, I was just...'

He cut in with that ridiculously sweet smile. 'It's no problem, we understand you need to get your bearings for tomorrow, please go ahead, just take care of the cables.' He motioned me toward the pavilion doors that led to the changing rooms and backstage waiting room.

I really shouldn't have been in there, but it was intriguing to see behind the scenes. Bays of salon chairs, with vanity tables and huge illuminated mirrors covered an entire wall of the pavilion which was the hair and make-up section, leading to the wardrobe department.

The rails were set up and raised cards with twenty girls' names were clipped to the steel. I saw Angela's section, ready and waiting for her swimwear, formal gown, ballet and daywear. I involuntarily touched the card and wished her good luck. An archway led to a lounge area with a huge TV screen, low sofas and behind them a bank of desks and a spaghetti of cables. The show producers would be editing in here, putting together the film for TV; the interviews and pre-event backstage goings-on were manipulated skilfully to build up an excitement. The TV burst into life; the cable guys had connected up and I watched as young Elvis paced the entire stage area with the rolling camera ensuring every angle was covered. It was a live feed but with no sound attached yet. I wondered what he was saying as he imitated the contestants' movements, walking from the central door and parading around the perimeter of the stage to halt in a flamingo-esque standing position. He looked funny trying to hold the pose, he was laughing with the cameraman and I couldn't look away. His beautiful face was changing with the bright lights, highlighting the tiny hint of crinkle at each corner of his dark eyes and the way his mouth curled up slightly on the left side when he laughed. He had perfect teeth and a full mouth; I wondered what it would feel like kissing it.

'Hi, miss can I help you with anything?' a female voice called a few feet behind me. I spun around and blushed furiously, and there was a tiny girl in dungarees and a massive mop of dark brown crazy, curly hair.

She had bags enough for a small army. I rushed over to help unload her, she was rather taken aback by me taking a huge holdall off her small shoulder and setting it down.

'Erm, miss, you don't need to help me, it's OK, I'm used to this, I may be a mouse but I'm strong.'

She grimaced as she eased a massive bag over her head; the wide strap had almost cut her in half.

'Hey, no problem,' I blurted out, hoping not to get into trouble for being here. 'I may be a giraffe but I'm farm-raised.'

We both laughed, an unlikely pair, she made Aunt Sylvia look tall. But then most girls looked short next to me, I was unnaturally tall and lean.

'So you are checking the place out for tomorrow then, huh?' Her curls bounced as she spoke.

'Well, erm, yes, sort of, I have tickets. My aunt has them if you want I can go get them, we paid,' I blushed.

She looked very confused, her curls smoothing as she wrangled them into a scrunchie.

'You are a contestant, surely?'

'Oh no, no I'm just watching, I'm from Santa Fe, we watched the first heat and now we are hooked, it's a fabulous event, I'm so excited for tomorrow.'

'Wow, girl, if I looked like you do, I'd be strutting my little tushy on that stage, you look like a supermodel, hun.'

I blushed and looked at my feet, it wasn't the first time I'd heard that, but it took a lot of getting used to when you had been so unloved and rejected for such a long time.

'Thanks, I'm a bit too shy I think for all that, I'd be happy doing something backstage. What do you do?'

'I'm hair and make-up. Actually, we are a team of eight, but my assistant Claire has come down with chicken pox, so no way can she come anywhere near a beauty event, hence why I resemble a camel today.'

We laughed again and I held my hand out.

'Giraffe at your service, I'll help you, if that's OK.'

'More than OK, I'm Giselle.'

'I'm Sherrie. Let's do this.'

We emptied out the packed holdalls, with all sorts of beauty paraphernalia. Hairdryers, straighteners, curling tongs, heated rollers, spritz bottles, several hairsprays, shine sprays, waxes, mousse and gels, brushes, clips, combs and trolleys. Setting out the equipment in each vanity bay, I found myself laughing and chatting with Giselle like I'd known her ages.

Then another of the team arrived, a funky, elfin-looking girl called Misty. Introductions were made and we unloaded her while she ran back for another load, bringing with her another of the team, Gigi, a tight-trousered, open-shirted mini Adonis. His shock of blond curls and a pirouette at the end of each statement gave away his sexuality. He was adorably handsome and funny and so bitchy. We finished the unpacking and setting up, everything a woman could possibly need to beautify herself was stacked up and ready.

Gigi checked the electrics for the dryers and nothing happened, so he called through to the front for the ops manager. About twenty minutes later, my young Elvis stepped into our beauty shop with a muscled electrician. Misty appeared with a bottle of Prosecco and some cakes.

'This is our treat, Sherrie, after every set-up, we relax. The rest of the team will come at 6am and we don't need to be here till about 9am tomorrow.'

'Oh, lovely.' I hadn't ever drunk alcohol before and I was underage, but I didn't want to look like a bumpkin so I said, 'Yes, sure,' and took a glass. This was the first time I had hung out with people that resembled girlfriends;

school had been a lonely place for me. We toasted and ate the best cupcakes I ever had, from a place called Coco's Patisserie. I asked if I could take one for my Aunt Sylvia; Misty insisted after all the help I'd given.

The electrical connections were made, the dryers roared, the mirrors lit up and we toasted to Elvis and his spark pal. He took a sip from Giselle's glass, they seemed to know each other well.

His eyes darted to me and stayed a fraction longer than necessary, his cheeks reddened again. What the hell was he thinking about?

'Oh, miss, is your Aunt Sylvia a brightly dressed lady, with red hair and lots of ethnic jewellery?'

'Yes, that's a perfect description, why?' Then I realised. *Oh God, what time is it?* I'd been here for two hours and not let her know, I shot up and said my goodbyes quickly.

'I'll catch you tomorrow at the show.'

They thanked me and Elvis told me she was at reception looking for me. I ran back through the gardens, nearly decapitating a gardener who was uncurling himself out of the flower border.

'Sorry, sorry,' I called as I sped back to the hotel lobby.

A very relieved Sylvia hugged me with genuine warmth and concern.

'Sherrie, sweetheart, I was worried.'

'Sorry, I fell asleep, all that travelling you know. I'm sorry Sylvia, I should have left a note.'

I produced the cupcake and we sat on the sumptuous sofas in the Hotel Centro and ordered iced tea and more cake. I told her about my afternoon and the friends I made. She sat smiling and happy to see me full of fun and excitement.

'I've never seen you look more radiant and relaxed than here, Sherrie; this Californian air suits you, darling.'

'The air and the chilled-out attitude, I love it here, Sylvia.'

I described the young Elvis man I had met. She gave me that look of an older woman who should know better.

'Ooh yes, I met him, if I was thirty years younger he would be in trouble.'

We laughed and chatted I had never felt more content than that day.

We had a stroll around the town and ate some fantastic seafood at a small funky-looking bistro on the waterfront. It was decked out with fishing nets and crab baskets, lots of nautical paraphernalia, quirky fish made from plaster of Paris adorned the rustic wooden walls, the waiting staff wore navy shorts and striped tee shirts with sailors' caps or pirate bandanas. I loved the whole easy vibe and sense of humour of the place, the food was outstanding and the little bistro was packed at 8.30pm. We finished up and wandered back for a bath and an early night, big day tomorrow.

Sylvia explained how the contest worked, I hadn't a clue. So, there were another three heats last month across America producing four finalists each and a fifth runner-up; that brings a total of twenty girls through to this semi-final in California and the four finalists from tomorrow would represent west-coast America in the final at Texas.

Further heats and semis in northern, eastern and southern states would also produce four finalists and a fifth runner-up for the Texas contest, so to gain the right to enter Miss America 1999, you had to accumulate enough points over the three events.

Angela had accumulated ten points already for her first place win.

Sylvia said, 'She can still get through with a second place tomorrow and a second or third in Texas, but don't forget, the modelling contracts they get just for top-four places pay a whole lot of money, plus the TV exposure; easy to get an agent once you have won a contest, small part on a soap and next thing you are an HBO actress. You get it now, Sherrie, why it's such a big deal?'

I really did get it, I wanted to be part of it, a world I could be part of and fit into, not sure I had the grit to be up on the stage, but fashion modelling appealed to me. I recalled the shopping trip and the white dress, which I was going to wear for dinner afterwards. We had booked a table at the hotel restaurant, it was a real treat, Sylvia had a fabulous scarlet Moroccan kaftan, heavily beaded and threaded with silver bells and coiled snakes. I couldn't imagine any other woman able to wear that creation, but Sylvia pulled if off with her flamboyant personality. I was never likely to lose her in a crowd, that's for sure.

I slept like a baby, worn out from all the travelling and walking, the excitement of the day ahead woke me up fully and I was up and dressed, all ready by the time Sylvia opened one eye, so I opened up the balcony and went downstairs to the restaurant and ordered our breakfasts to be taken up to the room. Twenty minutes later we were enjoying the freshest orange juice I ever had in my life, juicy prunes and dates, rye toast with lightly scrambled eggs and slivers of smoked salmon, washed down with good strong coffee.

We were ready for our event. I told Sylvia I'd seen some contestants in reception, but hadn't seen 'our Angela', as she had become now. I applied a little light make-up and brushed my teeth again, conscious of egg breath in case I bumped into young Elvis today. I had one of the summer day dresses on that Sylvia bought me, a very sweet, slightly Grecian-style crossover dress, in a silky muted grey, a very clever dress, not too sexy for a girl my age, it was right up to date with the latest fashion. The shoulder straps were cased in elongated brushed pewter metal, and it matched the metal-finish belt that cinched in my already tiny waist. My long tan legs were bare, and flat silver-roped sandals finished off my summer Grecian goddess look. We experimented with hair up and down and settled on down as we didn't have time to curl it, so off we went, Sylvia in a very tame turquoise shift. She said she was low key so that her scarlet kaftan would steal the night. I laughed with her, never at her, she had more confidence than a cheerleading squad, she didn't fear scrutiny at all.

As we entered the gardens of the hotel, it took my breath away. The tented VIP areas had been dressed with flowers and delightful painted wrought-iron cottage garden round tables and painted chairs, it was exquisite. There were white-shirted waiters milling with tiny glasses of fruit cocktails and champagne flutes with plump strawberries speared on the rims. I had thought the Santa Fe crowd was beautiful, but here in front of me were people with not only good looks, but a way of dressing that made it look fantastical. Hair was bouffant and glamorous, lots of gold and white silk floated around us, giving off a cool, unstructured bohemian vibe. Sylvia and I looked just right, simple lines, block colours, purity was the fashion here and self-confidence was the look.

The heat began. As before, the pavilion doors opened and twenty swan-like beauties glided out in a S-shaped pattern, terminating at the shoulders of the two hosts, Brett and Kelly. They were taking the west-coast event all the way to Texas as hosts, but it was a new set of judges for this heat and we gave a rapturous applause, especially for our Angie, standing tall and sleek with her pale pink sash. A couple of people in the audience looked at me. They had seen the striking similarity, it was ridiculous, they assumed I was her twin sister I suppose. I scoured the place for young Elvis but he was nowhere to be seen. A little disappointed, I settled down to watch the event.

CHAPTER EIGHTEEN

Sherrie & Angie

Angie

A funny thing happened when I was in hair and make-up. Before we went on stage, the little stylist girl with the mad hair asked me if I had a twin sister.

I didn't know what she was on about, in fact she pissed me off a bit. I'm trying to focus all my thoughts and energies on my performance, I didn't think she should be bothering me with nonsense chatter, but she's such a good hair stylist, that's why she keeps her job., To look at her, you would think she's here to clean the drains out, but she has magical hands, she's made my hair extra shiny, extra straight, perfect.

Today I am performing a beautiful piece from *Swan Lake*. I hope the cultured Californian judges would appreciate it, my tutu has been sewn with organza feathers and my bodice encrusted with crystals, I think it will look spectacular on this grand stage. When Brett saw the rehearsal he had gushed at me like I was Margot Fontaine; truth is he just wants to get in my pants. He was much too intense, made me feel quite sick, but I have to play along until after Texas. My mom saved me from him, but now she's in the audience and I'll have to deal with his advances alone. He was so creepy at Santa Fe, I didn't tell Momma what he whispered, she would have blown a fuse.

So here I am again poised like a circus contortionist, semi-naked, my muscles burning from walking in heels in an unnatural fashion with my weight shifting from hip to hip. God knows the damage I'm doing to my bones, hence why I need to win, to be Miss America, travel the world, hook a billionaire and retire.

I smiled like a sweetheart, my every movement precise and polished.

It became a blur, the speed between rounds; before I knew it I was being ushered into the spotlight to perform my solo.

CHAPTER NINETEEN

Sherrie & Angie

Sherrie

Sylvia nudged me as the spotlight shone on the top of Angie's feathered crown.

The whole audience hushed, the first strains of the orchestral music played and my heart beat faster. The only light on the stage was on her, it tracked her precisely as she pirouetted and danced in perfect harmony with the powerful music. I stole a glance at the judges who were in rapture with this wondrous creature before them, it dawned on me how clever Angie was, choosing ballet as her solo, it gave her a chance to show a completely new side of her. The audience experienced a completely fresh look, no sash, no long hair, no gown, it was like having a second personality. It granted an enormous respect to her as a young woman, we could easily believe she was a prima ballerina, it gave a sort of gravitas that flute playing didn't quite reach. I admired her, how much dedication this young girl had given to her craft, just keeping that perfect figure and strength for this performance was a full-time job in itself.

Sylvia had held her breath throughout the performance and gasped at the end, breaking out into applause. She actually stood up along with many others and clapped and cheered, someone actually threw roses on the stage like at the ballet, it was amazing.

I saw Brett watch her with complete love, he was smitten for sure. It looked like he was torn between running backstage to congratulate her or introduce the next contestant. He gathered himself thankfully and the next girl entered. Sadly, she had a hell of an act to follow and as I knew she would have been watching from the backstage on that giant TV, I saw her deflate somewhat as she started her tap dance routine, it was already over for her, God bless.

Sylvia and I strolled around the gorgeous terrace, nibbling miniature sandwiches and fruit. It was a hot, sunny day, the flowers emitting a heady fragrance. I had a full mouth of strawberry when young Elvis appeared at my shoulder. Sylvia almost spurted out her champagne, I stupidly smiled a fruity grin, held my hand out, whilst desperately trying to gum the strawberry into submission and swallow it. Seeing my peril, Sylvia took his attention and distracted him with a flamboyant laugh. She linked his arm and turned him to the huge burst of yellow-headed flowers.

'Darling boy, what on earth is the name of this plant, I have been driving myself crazy.'

Elvis was polite enough to give my aunt the full Latin name and that gave me the four seconds I needed to spit the strawberry into my hand. I smiled and we said our hellos.

'Sorry if I was rude yesterday, but I was stressing about the electrics, we had a few snags, I thought you were a contestant, miss…'

'Sherrie.' I extended my other hand, he took it, held it and told me his name was Benjamin.

'Very nice to meet you properly, Sherrie. My sister, Giselle, was so thankful for your help yesterday.'

A little flutter of happiness that Giselle was not his girlfriend, but his sister, rattled about my chest; Sylvia caught it.

Benjamin still had hold of my hand.

'Do you know, Sherrie, there is a contestant that looks exactly like you, Giselle was asking if you are twins.'

Sylvia interjected.

'Yes we do – Angela; we really would like to meet her if that's possible, it's just uncanny, the girls are absolute doppelgängers. Could you arrange it, Benjamin?'

'I'll see what I can do. Giselle asked me to invite you to the after-show party, please say you will come.'

'Oh that's very kind but we have reservations at the restaurant tonight after the show.' I was flustered by his closeness, dying to say yes, but would never blow off my auntie for a guy.

But Sylvia chirped in, 'What time is the party?'

'About 10.30 by the time the crew pack up and everyone is finished.'

She grinned and clapped her hands. 'That's just perfect, we will have finished dinner by 10.30 latest, Sherrie, you will be in plenty of time.'

I beamed at her, what a good friend this woman was.

Benjamin, still holding my hand, finally released me.

'Great, just come over to the pavilion when you are ready.' And he went back to work with a spring in his step.

'Sylvia, I don't know about this party, I don't know them that well.'

'Never mind that, my girl, I don't think Benjamin will leave you unguarded for a moment.'

We laughed at the smashed strawberry in my hand; I dropped it discreetly in a flowering bush.

The competition resumed. In my heart, I was sure Angela had first place, she was just special. The results came in and the judges passed the golden envelope to Kelly. The audience was silent, Brett took it and slowly opened it, I saw the twitch in his cheek, suppressing a smile. Angela had it.

She was back in her formal gown, receiving the second crown and her full ten points. Brett paraded her like his queen, and she kept her poise throughout. We stood and clapped, proud of our Angela. Still no sign of Benjamin around, so we didn't try to get backstage, it was swarming with crew and press. So we headed off to our rooms to take a rest and change for dinner, my white frilled cocktail dress hung up ready for this night. I had butterflies.

CHAPTER TWENTY
Sherrie & Angie

Angie

My emotions were bubbling up inside me, I thought I would burst. I was feeling a little wobbly and was actually glad of Brett's hand to guide me. When we went backstage, he whispered in my ear, 'Marry me.'

I just looked at him like he was a lunatic, luckily saved by the producer wanting to set up for a recorded interview. Brett was ushered out, Mrs Harris appeared to congratulate me, accompanied by my mother, she was wet-faced but beaming with pride.

'Could you come to the agency next week, when you have time? We have had a lot of interest in you, Angie, I can't guarantee it but a major brand want you, so we need to sit down and discuss it.'

Momma was beside herself. 'Of course, Pamela, we will be there day after tomorrow.' Then Momma's tone changed. 'Angie needs to rest now.'

Pamela nodded. 'Yes, of course, that's fine.' She moved on with a tight smile.

The power had ever so slightly shifted, Pamela wasn't so much in charge, she was an old wolf and she knew a rising star when she saw it, so until I was contracted fully to Harris agency I could in theory go elsewhere.

I got through the video interviews and all the stills they needed for the magazine layouts. I was shattered and also starving hungry, I needed some proper food; a sandwich tray wasn't good for me, too many carbs.

I now had a whole month off before the Texas final, I felt like living a little, which was a very alien feeling. What the hell was happening?

So Momma asked for a table for two at the hotel restaurant and we headed to our room to rest and change, it was slow progress with all the well-wishers stopping us in our tracks.

But the buzz I got from all the attention was awesome.

CHAPTER TWENTY-ONE

Sherrie & Angie

Sherrie

I entered the dining room in my white strappy heels and my white sweeping off-the-shoulder frilled cocktail dress, a few steps behind my Aunt Sylvia in her blazing scarlet kaftan. She had everyone's attention, she paraded through the tables like a sultan. I glided behind her, the exact antithesis to her wildness; I was as serene as a swan. The diners stopped eating, the waiters stopped serving and even the head chef stopped shouting, for just a few seconds.

From the other end of the dining room, my doppelgänger glided toward our table. She was resplendent in a pale pink off-the-shoulder tight satin cocktail dress, looking glorious and svelte, like a true beauty queen.

We stopped dead. Sylvia and I both shouted out, 'Angela!!'

To the surprise of her and her mom, they both stood still, open-mouthed. The waiters suddenly bounded into action. Thinking they had made a mistake on the seating plan, they dived in and put the two tables for two together, proceeded to seat us with a flourish and apologies, kissing our beautiful butts basically, so there we found ourselves, Angela's mom Rosie and my Aunt Sylvia across from each other and Angela and I face to face at last.

Sylvia and I were of course beaming. We had been desperate to meet her, we had had a month to get used to our similarity, we called her 'our Angie', for God's sake. But, I suddenly realised, they had not had that luxury.

I broke the stunned silence.

'Hello Angela, I'm Sherrie and this is my Aunt Sylvia.' They nodded and smiled weakly.

'This is so weird.' Angie stared straight at my face, taking in the incredible similarities. 'Are you a fan or something?'

I laughed and Sylvia, said, 'No honey, we are just as surprised as you, but we had some time to get used to it. We are from Santa Fe, we first saw you there at the Plaza.' The silence was awkward. 'Shall I order us some drinks? We may as well eat, I'm starving!!'

Angie looked at my bohemian aunt and said, 'I love that kaftan, it's so California.'

Rosie agreed, she said, 'I didn't know who to stare at more, Sherrie or your kaftan.'

The ice was broken and we all burst out laughing. The head waiter looked relived, there would be smooth service. He quickly attended and we told Angie and Rosie the story. Soon we were all tucking into our food and chatting like old friends. It was incredible, Rosie and Sylvia knew some of the same people, they got on like old friends, Angie was a little cooler toward me, I could feel her deciding whether she should like me or not. I remembered my initial reaction when I saw her, it was pure shock, it's not often that you find a complete stranger who is basically your physical twin sister.

I told her how we were rooting for her all the way in the heats; she softened a little with a good bout of compliments.

'Thank you. Ahhh! Now I know why the stylist was asking me if I had a twin.'

'Oh, Giselle, yes, I got to know her yesterday, have you met her brother Benjamin?' I suddenly had a little worry, I hadn't even decided if I liked Benjamin yet, but with this equal competition in front of me, I quickly discovered I did.

'Oh yes, he's a little stiff for me, all work.'

I smiled and said, 'What about Brett?'

Angie's eyes widened. 'How do you know about him?' Rosie swivelled to listen in.

'I can tell, he can't hide it, he's mad about you.'

'Err, he's mad for sure, you know he proposed tonight?' Rosie screeched, 'What!'

We both fell about giggling, our wall broke down and we proceeded to wind Rosie up about the big wedding coming up, she looked like she was going to faint, until Sylvia topped their glasses up and reassured her we were messing about.

'Anyway, sod 'em Rosie, if they do bugger off and get married we can go men hunting on a world cruise, how about it?'

Rosie relaxed and said, 'Only if I can borrow your top, Sylvia.'

The champagne was kicking in, everyone was smiling, it was a great, weird, odd night. I whispered to Angie about the party and she said, 'Yes, I feel the need to live a little, it's been pretty gruelling the last six months.'

Rosie protested, but we all reassured her that everything would be just fine. So we left our chaperones and with hugs and kisses promised Sylvia and Rosie fifteen times that we would be safe and back in the rooms by midnight, wouldn't leave each other's sight.

We walked out of that restaurant with every pair of eyes on us. Both of us in high heels, it was hard to miss us, two 6ft 3in-inch tall golden beauties linking arms and whispering about the gardeners, who had resumed watering duties. They stood open-mouthed spraying the flowers as we passed by, neither of us was fazed by the attention, we were so used to it, but it took all my self-consciousness away to have my twin friend linking my arm.

The party was in full swing. As we entered the pavilion Giselle was the first to scream, 'You came, Sherrie, Angie, oh my God! Oh my God!' Benjamin appeared and she punched him on the arm and said, 'See, I told ya, they are identical.'

We drew a small crowd, Misty joined but was barged out of the way by Gigi, who took both of our hands and led us to dance with him, the little show-off.

We both danced the same way, that freaked us out, and then we really let go and danced like we were in our bedroom, Angie laughing like a loon. I could see her relax, she was letting the stress out from competing.

I put my arm around her and said, 'I wish we were sisters, I think you are so cool.'

She hugged me for real. 'Maybe we are sisters?'

Brett suddenly appeared with a couple of girls who didn't make it to the finals. They were hoping for a leg-up in their careers, Brett was hoping for a leg over: he was creepy. He shrugged the cling-ons off and took Angie's hand, dancing with her up close and personal. Benjamin wasted no time in filling the gap in front of me and we were grooving and giggling. *He's not a stiff*, I thought to myself.

Giselle, Misty and Gigi alongside, dancing like crazy, it was a great fun party. Some people were drunk or stoned and I could see a few getting leery, a couple were arguing and one massive jock-type guy took his shirt off, I tapped Angie and said, 'Let's go get some air.'

So we grabbed a few root beers off the table and headed outside into the gardens; it was a lovely warm night and we talked under the stars about the life in California.

Brett kept trying to get Angie to go for a walk with him, but she said no several times. It was when he pulled her arm too hard and she yelped that Benjamin stood up and confronted him.

'That's enough, Brett.'

'Who the hell are you to tell me enough?' Brett was slurring his words. He screamed at Benjamin, 'Little prick, think you are a big man around here with your pathetic shiny name tag? You are nothing. I'm famous, I'm Dr Mendelsohn and you are a poxy events manager, ha, loser.'

Benjamin kicked his legs from under him and Brett landed like a small child flat on his bottom. We all fell about laughing. Benjamin said, 'Sit down and shut up or security will escort you to your room.'

Brett was humiliated and he scrambled to his feet. 'You're a bunch of kids, I'm going, last chance Angie, you coming or not?'

'Not!' she shouted

He stormed off and we carried on our fun night without the weirdo.

A few minutes later he paraded his two desperate girls past us, they were clinging on like barnacles. Urgh, it made me sick, how they lowered themselves, all because they didn't make the grade in this competition.

Angie said, 'That's the fear, they are so stressed and obsessed with winning this, they lost all perspective and self-esteem. They are both really pretty girls, they could do modelling work no problem, but beauty pageanting is like an obsession for some, personally I don't even like it.'

'What?' I said, open-mouthed. 'You are kidding, you look like you are born for it.'

'Sherrie, I started when I was a little girl, it made Momma very happy, but I have a three-step plan.' She sounded very serious.

'Go on?' I wanted to know everything about her.

'Win Miss America 1999, travel the world and marry a billionaire.'

'That is it?'

'That's it!'

We all laughed thinking she was being funny, but of course she was absolutely dead straight.

CHAPTER TWENTY-TWO

Sherrie & Angie

Angie

It was a bizarre weekend for sure. I replayed the event over and over in my mind, from the ballet movement, to the discovery of Sherrie – that freaked me out, but I already wanted to see her again. I somehow felt more secure being with her. I know how to portray absolute confidence in a performance, on any stage, but in real life, I haven't got a clue how I'm supposed to be, especially with men. It's a minefield, I feel the butterflies when Brett gets close up, but I don't like him, he doesn't meet the criteria anyway, he has a little fame from his soap, but it's hardly big league, I want a billionaire!

I called Sherrie. 'Hi, sis,' we laughed. That's what we started calling each other after we discovered we both liked crazy dancing to old 80s tracks in our bedrooms. We were so similar, we must be sisters.

'Hey sis, how you doing?' Sherrie's Kentucky accent made me smile down the phone.

'I'm cool, want to meet up before you go back to Santa Fe?'

'Yes love to, I have to go and see that agent today, you know Mrs Harris?'

'Sweet Jesus! We were destined to meet anyway, sis, she's my agent now, I'm going over at one today, shall we meet there?'

'OK great, I'm booked at twelve, so I'll wait for you, Angie.'

'Awesome, love ya, sis,' I said with a sing-song voice.

I startled myself, I never said 'love ya' to anyone, only Momma, but I got that genuine connected feeling when I spoke with Sherrie. I didn't know that, at the other end of the line, my new best friend had big fat tears rolling down her cheeks.

When I saw Sherrie come out of Pamela's office with Sylvia, I instantly hugged her, I felt so happy to see them both. Rosie and Sylvia were laughing at something, cackling like a pair of witches, I hadn't seen my mom laugh with any friend like that. She didn't have many, I suppose she dedicated her whole life to me. There was a twang of jealousy when she clearly was enjoying Sylvia's company, but it soon changed to warmth; it was healthy to have company her own age, so we went off to the mall for a little retail therapy while Sherrie had her meeting with Pamela.

When Pamela saw us both together in reception, I saw her shrewd darting eyes evaluating us; twin models were rare. Mommy and I decided to sign a full twelve-month exclusive contract with Pamela, it was a safe bet move until Texas was over and Miss America contest next year, at least we would be financially sound. The big name that had expressed an interest was Prada, you don't get much bigger than that.

If I was successful at the casting, the job was worth about $245k for a twelve-month campaign. My mom nearly collapsed, but I remained cool, I'm more practised than Mom.

We had a riotous lunch with Sherrie and Sylvia, causing quite a stir at Coco's, the chic Italian café by the wharf. The owner, Coco, was a rotund Italian man in his fifties and he flirted outrageously with Rosie, demanding proof that she was my mother and not my slightly older sister. The blatant charmer, it was hilarious, when he presented roses to us all and the staff sang 'Bella Rosa' in wavering baritones, we had such fun.

The owner wanted photos when he discovered we were supermodels, his tag not ours, so we obliged, posing together like celebs do, it was a taste of things to come, what a laugh.

Attached to the café was the gorgeous Patisserie Coco, Sherrie squealed when she remembered the cupcakes and Coco's brother Maurizio appeared with a pink box full of cupcakes on the house. Yummy. Sylvia took charge of those.

Sherrie had to return to Pamela's to sign her contract and we went together, while Sylvia and Rosie had strong cappuccinos and truffles with the very attentive Maurizio and Coco.

When we walked in together Pamela was like a cat on a hot tin roof; she beamed at us like long-lost children and she was as slick and smooth as Coco.

'Girls, please come in, I have some exciting news.'

It was that day that sealed our fate, we were meant to be together like sisters. Prada had been in touch and on discovering that we were twins, which wasn't actually true, confirmed us immediately. The fee for Sherrie was less, due to her novice modelling status, but a flat fee of $125,000 for the campaign for her was an incredible first modelling job, unheard of in this business.

It was that moment that my sis, best friend, whatever we were, broke down in tears and hugged me and Pamela. The girl was shaking, we held her up and got the pen out, she signed on the dotted line through tears and sobs.

Pamela laughed; I hadn't ever heard her emit any sound of joy previously. We both looked up.

'Girls, you two are going to be stars, mark my words, you girls are very special.'

We weren't to know her 25% cut of our fee had just made the final payment on her LA condo. She was over the moon, her joy was real.

The job was booked for October, we were going to travel to Paris and Milan for the shoot, amazing opportunity and chance to have a little freedom too, so that gave us plenty of time to get Sherrie ready. It was decided that she would come and stay with us in California for the whole of August. We could work out at the gym together and get her in tip-top condition, while I prepared for the Texas final in early September; no more cupcakes!

I wondered more and more how my father would react, knowing his little girl was getting famous. Would he know my face if he saw me in a magazine? Probably not. Would I know his face if he passed me on the street? Maybe.

Mommy had a tin of old photos from when I was a baby, she doesn't know I've looked at them several times, the top shelf in her closet stopped being a safe hiding place when I reached my teens, I was 5ft 11in at 15 years old.

I would recognise his face I'm sure, we shared the same eyes and mouth. They were pretty distinctive, I could see why my mom fell for this man, he was handsome and a little dangerous-looking. He broke her heart big time, she never even had a date since he went, fifteen years is a long time to be alone. I did worry about her, I was going to be travelling a lot, Momma had never been alone, so I hoped her new friendship with Sylvia would grow strong.

I was going to miss my new sis. They left earlier this morning, we promised to call each other every day and Sherrie promised no more cake, not that she had any fat to worry about. But she wasn't toned enough and Prada was ruthless with the models, they were notoriously small fit, and so even I would have to be on my toes for this job. But with my momma tackling her nutrition and me on her workouts, I wasn't worried, the genes were there naturally, just the fine-tuning needed.

CHAPTER TWENTY-THREE

Helena

When I woke up from my self-induced coma, I was surprised to find that I hadn't puked or shat myself. You would think I would be happy about it, but it worried me because I had read that this meant my body had got a bit too used to the filth of heroin swimming inside my bloodstream. It flashed through my mind, I knew for sure, I was addicted. I wasn't such a fool to think that I was immune to the decay of using, but I wanted to destroy myself and this was a good a way as any.

I still had that calm fog that made all this worth it.

I hadn't thought about my husband for two days and that in itself was a miracle. It usually lasted about a week, the calmness, I was able to sleep at home and get up to function, work, do my nursing act and generally live.

Without Dr Gerry, I'm sure I would have crumbled and walked in front of a train long ago.

So I cleaned my sweat-drenched body off, changed in to my street clothes and headed off to the supermarket car park. As I was leaving the folded-up duvet set for the laundry, the tall slim Jesus boy was doing the same thing. It's a bit awkward when you come out of the hit; everything seems a bit soft and sensitive.

He smiled at me, 'Didn't see you arrive.'

'Just after you, I use the locked room.'

'Ahh.'

'Feel better?'

'Yes, umm, well, you know.'

'Yes, I know,' He dropped his head.

We both left and bundled down the stairs. It was odd, he was ahead of me, but didn't rush, he turned back a few times, remarked on the stink of the place or the graffiti, we spilled out into sunshine, he smiled at me.

'Beautiful day. Want to get breakfast?'

I wasn't sure what to make of him, he looked about twenty-eight at most, maybe he wanted to bum money off me. I look like a bag of shite, I'm bloody sure he didn't fancy me. I took in his appearance, his jeans were expensive once, his demeanour wasn't like any junkie I had met before. My grumbling stomach made the decision for me.

'Yeah, why not?'

'Café next door to the supermarket is OK,' he said.

So we walked together amiably, we looked like any other pair of friends strolling along in the sun heading for brunch, hunger was a feeling I rarely felt these days, heroin did that to you, the only time you feel ready to enjoy some food is after the coma.

When you are in need of the stuff, you can't even face a bite, if you do force it down it usually comes back up; body wants the filth, nothing else and certainly nothing nutritious. So we quickened our pace involuntarily as we smelled the bacon wafting out from the little greasy spoon, Al's Café.

It wasn't long before two hot plates of steaming, greasy, full English breakfasts were placed with a flourish in front of us, the array of condiments lined up between us like a game of sauce chess. I reached out for the brown and Jesus grabbed the red ketchup.

We both laughed, 'Ahh you're a red, hmm.' I gave him a look of sarcastic distain. 'Etiquette dictates a strict sauce policy with full English brekky: ketchup or brown. It's a divide that can't be crossed and a person that has both is simply a freak of nature.'

We laughed at that. He countered that there is one mitigating circumstance that may allow for the double usage: should there be a potato element to the breakfast, a dash of red may be permitted to a purveyor of brown.

Jesus was spouting about the righteousness of being a red, as articulate as a barrister. I didn't notice the rarely heard giggle emitting from me as I chewed a very full mouth of sausage and egg, garnished with my brown sharp fruity sauce.

'Nonsense!' I shouted between forkfuls. 'Everyone knows only true condiment connoisseurs select brown. Red is for plebs!'

Jesus chuckled and semi-choked on a fat-soaked hash brown.

God it was delicious, we laughed a lot and the banter was sharp and witty, the mugs of tea arrived, and he chose sweetener, while I poured sugar from the glass dispenser.

'Sugar is best,' I declared, 'all that artificial shit in sweeteners causes cancer my friend.'

'Better than diabetes, my dear,' he countered, 'at least I'll keep my feet!'

We both laughed and the barbs started up again about who would rot faster from our food induced illnesses. It was ironic really as we regularly courted death with our lovely Dr Gerry, yet here we were debating best ways to stay healthy.

The irony was not lost on Jesus, he gave me a knowing look, and I sat back in my plastic booth, full to bursting with another hot mug of tea on its way. I looked at him squarely back, our hilarity now muted from the dulling of the senses while the digestive system tried to handle this onslaught.

'Why do you do it?'

He sat back on his side, dabbing his ketchup smears, a long sigh left him.

'It's a very sad story, sure you want to hear it? What's your name, anyway?'

I was about to say Kelly, but something made me trust Jesus.

'Helena.'

'Of Troy, I assume.' We chuckled. 'I'm Israel.'

'Israel? You're kidding me, ha.'

'Yes, it's a freak of a name; my mum was a serious Bible-basher.'

'How funny, I thought you looked like Jesus on the cross, I saw you in Gerry's lounge.'

'Was I zombied out?'

'Yes, totally, but you looked very peaceful, arms outstretched. I've been calling you Jesus in my head all morning.'

'Will you tell me your story if I tell you mine?'

I felt that prickle of anxiety rush up my neck, this had been the first time in years that I had not thought about who I was in reality and my sins.

'I don't know Israel, I...'

'Its OK, you don't have to, love, relax, enjoy your sweet, rotting, decaying, sugary brew.'

He lightened the mood so easily.

I quietly asked him, 'Go on, tell me.'

I sat and listened to this tall, slim, skinny boy with pale grey eyes and white skin tell me about his early years growing up with his mum Veronica in Dartmoor; how he had a charmed childhood, living with his grandparents, he had never known his dad. Mum was a fragile, spiritual woman, she was a deep soulful Earth child, it made her a very loving mother and he recalled how she would cook everything freshly and naturally, how her kitchen resembled an old apothecary shop. She grew most of the food they ate, sticking to a strict vegan diet.

I was amazed at this considering the amount of meat he just consumed in front of me, but I kept quiet and listened, not wanting to stop him talking, his voice was soothing, his story had me hooked.

'My grandad built us a little annex at the back of the big house, which led onto the huge garden, Mum spent all day tending it, she was at one with nature, I didn't have a clue that my mum was, how shall I put it, not well, mentally. I didn't know any different, only when I started at junior school, I started to see the difference. When I played at my friend's house, I saw that they had a mum and a dad, ate meat and watched telly, played video games and talked about all the holidays they had and the trips to theme parks, things I'd never experienced. It was more fun, if you know what I mean, I was twelve or thirteen when I rebelled against her natural ways, started staying out, hanging around with a group of lads in the village, we got in to a few scrapes, like boys do, but you know, nothing really bad.'

I just nodded and sipped my tea, he carried on talking.

'Mum started to get very upset and angry whenever I came home, she was overboard about the devil taking me into his dark side, it was heavy for me. There was nothing much to do in our little house, no television, just sitting with my mum sewing and meditating, it was not what a teenage lad wants, you know what I mean, I suppose I rejected her, she was broken-hearted. Her little baby grown up, going away from her, I get that, I didn't mean to hurt her feelings.' A flash of guilt crossed his fine features.

'We had some nice times too, it wasn't all bad,' he added gently, 'until the summer of 1984. Something changed with her, she went very low, stopped tending the garden, didn't cook, just lay on the sofa in the same clothes for days and days, unwashed, unmoving, like a catatonic state for hours, just mumbling and talking to herself. It freaked me out, I just couldn't stand being around her, my grandparents were very old, they brought in the family doctor who sedated her and got her into bed. I took her soup and sandwiches every day but she ate virtually nothing for weeks.

'I was about sixteen by then and a selfish little prick probably, but I didn't know what was going on, so I stayed away most of the time, left grandad to deal with her, I used to crash at a mate's house, he always had weed so the weekends were pretty lost in space.'

He let out a sad laugh.

When I finally went back, Mum was up and about, she was like on speed, rushing at me, babbling about the devil and how I must be cleaned from the inside. Grandad was worn out, he looked so old and tired. I stayed home with her for a few weeks, it was like hell, she spent all night raving and pacing around, waking me up and shouting passages of the Bible at my face, she threw water over me several times, trying to christen me, it made me so pissed off, I hated her, I really did. The worst was her laughing episodes, she would sit in a chair staring at me laughing uncontrollably, for hours, it made me hate her, like she and some imaginary person were taking the piss out of me. It went on for hours on end then constantly for two whole days. On the third night, she took a kitchen knife and stood over me, I was lying on the sofa, she wanted me to drink bleach to clean the bad from inside me, I was terrified and I flipped out and ran to get Grandad, he was so bad on his legs, it took ages, finally we got back there, but it was too late.

Israel dropped his head and closed his eyes.

'I'm sorry, hun,' I said very softly. 'You don't need to carry on.'

'No, I want to tell you, I think I need to.' He picked up the story.

'We got back through to the kitchen and she was there on the floor, she had sliced her own neck open, she died there bleeding like something from a slaughterhouse, we couldn't help her. Grandad had a massive heart attack that night and died in hospital. Grandma, who was already half gone with Alzheimer's, wasn't really aware of any of it, thank God for small mercies eh? She is in a care home.

'So I was there at sixteen, truly on my own in this world. I sort of lost it for a while, stayed stoned for about a year. My social worker tried to get me into a foster home, but no one had space for a sixteen-year-old stoner, so I was allowed to stay at my friend's house and meet fortnightly with her and when everything was sorted out and I received an inheritance at eighteen I really let myself go wild, travelled all over for about seven years, spent a lot of time in Australia and Thailand, until the money ran out and I made my way back here last year.

'Nothing here for me, though, I haven't been able to get myself together since I came home, can't stop thinking about what I should have or could have done to help her more, I was a crap son!'

He ordered a coffee from the waitress and looked at me.

I was speechless, I knew exactly what he felt inside, so I told him my story.

When I finished, he reached out and held both my hands. There were tears in our eyes and I felt connected to the soul of this young man in front of me, he was probably the first real friend I had ever had. I told him everything, warts and all, we shared the most personal information, exposed our deep self-hatred and yet, we both felt stronger for it.

I didn't want to ever let this man's hand go. I'm not talking about romance or sex, his hand felt like a lifeline to me. I felt frightened to actually let it go.

'Where do you live now, Israel?'

'I bum around from mate to mate, sofa surfing, it's OK. But I want to get off this drug shit and find some work. I know how to garden,' he laughed ironically. 'Maybe I'll be lucky and get a caretaker job with accommodation.'

I knew straight away what my path was, I'm not a huge believer in God or the mysteries of beyond the clouds, but I knew for sure, I needed to be near Israel and he needed me.

'Well, Israel, you are in luck, I have my own personal jungle, which is in desperate need of some work. I also have three spare rooms, so why don't you lodge with me? Nathan used to do the mowing for me, but since he moved away, it's been left to its own devices. Katie's at university, so I'm alone and need a hand with stuff.'

When you are homeless, it takes a lot less time to weigh up the options as there are none.

So Israel happily came home with me.

CHAPTER TWENTY-FOUR

Helena

When Israel and I arrived at my house, he looked shocked at the size of it... I don't suppose he's met a wealthy junkie before, but being the loving, good man Daniel was, he left me and our future child well taken care of in the event of his death or serious injury. I stayed at the house for the children, it was a daily reminder that I hated, but they felt closer to their dad here, they told me every visit. I didn't have the right to take that last vestige of father away after what I had already done.

'We better have a story how we met, Helena, I don't suppose anyone knows about Dr Gerry in this neighbourhood?'

'God yes, the nosy brigade will be asking, let's have a think about that one, do you want a drink? I've got some good red!'

It felt so easy chatting to him.

'Super,' he bellowed in an over-the-top posh voice.

'Send Jeeves to the wine cellar and fetch the Châteauneuf-du-Pape.'

'Hahah, it's his night ooorf!' I shouted up the stairs, as he bounded up to choose his room.

Only Katie's was still occupied with her stuffed toys and princess bedding, she liked to keep it as it was when her dad was alive. I thought it was time she let it go, but how could I say a word to her about it?

As I uncorked a very good Malbec – we were all out of vintage – he appeared back in the kitchen. 'Is it OK if I take the back room overlooking the garden? I love the light in there.'

'Yes, of course you can, it was Daniel's office, he often said it made paying the bills a little less painful, with that view.'

I'd put a sofa bed in there a few years back, Nathan had taken his father's oak desk to his mum's house, he wanted to study for his exams on that desk, for good luck. He'd done very well too, just like his dad, he was smart and disciplined, his mother had done everything possible to ease the grief and help the boy adjust, deal with the loss.

Katie coped less easily, despite being so young she seemed to have the stronger emotional connection with her father, perhaps because the real memories were so few. She said she often felt him around her, I hoped it gave some comfort.

I went for a long bath, and Israel was assessing the garden job. By the time I came down to the lounge, a roaring, crackling real fire was warming the hearth, sending golden flickers across the ceiling.

'A real log fire, I had almost forgotten it existed; I never used it, not since…'

Not since we moved into the house. Daniel had loved that feature, he was like an eager boy scout, we had made love in front of that fire, in fact our baby had been conceived here, feelings were flooding up inside me and I reached for the wine, Israel topped us both up and we settled on the sofa watching the hypnotic flames, both of us absorbed in our own worlds of pain.

A few glasses later, he broke the silence. 'What do you reckon then?'

'Reckon to what?'

'Our cover story! Didn't you notice the twitchy curtain over the road when I arrived?'

'Oh right, yeah, how about, you are my nephew, returned from travelling? That's not far off the truth, keep it simple.'

He nodded, 'OK, what's your sister called?'

'Umm, Sheila?'

We fell about laughing; the wine and the warmth made everything feel good.

'Asshole!'

He spoke seriously, 'Carol – that will do, Carol and Jim, your older sister and her hubby, easy enough, I don't want to cause you any aggro Helena.'

'Yes OK, Carol and Jim,' I realised what he meant, protecting me from any nasty gossip. 'Good folks, Carol and Jim, your mum and dad!'

Israel had a perfect Aussie accent from his years down under, it was natural.

'Keep the nosy buggers happy. What about the kids, will they know about your sister?'

'I don't think so, I've never really talked to them about my family, basically because I haven't got any so they won't suspect.' I felt the loss as I said it out loud, how alone I really was in this world.

We talked and laughed all night, it was strange to have company, felt like we had known each other all our lives.

The next day I woke up feeling different; the fog usually lasted a few more days. But this was only the second day and I felt bright, energy was running high and I started cleaning the house. I did clean quite often, to keep it nice for the children, but it had always been a dreaded chore, something done for appearances only, but today I felt like it, I put the radio on and got stuck in.

Israel was sleeping late, so I left him to it and by the time he appeared I was knackered and ready for a brew. He put the kettle on and insisted I take a break, he could see my work had been frantic.

'Bloody hell, Hel, you are like Robocop today.'

'I know, I don't usually get any pleasure from being a domestic goddess, what's up with me?'

He rustled up a fluffy omelette and two coffees, we ate off the same plate at the counter. It was so nice to have a friend.

I noticed his holdall was by the sink. 'Laundry room over there, Israel, you want me to put stuff through the wash? It's no bother.'

So we did his laundry. He had very little to show for his lifetime: two pairs of jeans, three tee shirts and the thick hoodie he wore yesterday, three undies and a pair of socks on his feet.

'Christ is that all, hun?'

'Yup, that's my worldly goods in total, impressive heh?'

He pulled out a small shaving bag, rooted inside and produced a small metal object; I took it and saw it was a kneeling angel.

Inscribed in the underside it said, *Israel my angel, all my love, Mum.*

'It's all I have of hers, it's really all that matters to me. The rest can go to the bin really, this has travelled all over the world with me.' There was a sadness in his voice.

I went to the kitchen drawer and retrieved a small wooden box, I hesitated a moment before opening it; eleven years is a long time to not look at something.

Inside was an intricately carved angel made from marble. Daniel bought it on our honeymoon in Italy. A small note lay in the box. *To my darling Helena, you are my angel, my love, my heart, I love you for eternity, Daniel.*

The lump in my throat lodged there and a huge sob emitted from my mouth.

Before I knew it I was shaking and crying, then the howling came, a river of tears pouring from me, no stopping them. Israel carried me over to the sofa and wrapped me up in a throw, he held me tight and rocked me while I bawled my eyes out.

I fell asleep after the outpouring. It was early evening when I came around, the fire was lit and I could smell food cooking. Padding across to the kitchen still wrapped in the throw, I hoisted my sorry self up on to the stool.

'Greetings earthling,' he said cheerily as he chopped veg and herbs, the oven was emitting an aroma I couldn't place.

'What is it'?

'Well I'm hoping it's roast lamb with herbs, your freezer looked like something out of the Ice Age, hopefully it won't kill us!'

I racked my brains to think when I had bought lamb, but my shopping was sporadic and usually on autopilot – anyone's guess. It smelled fantastic so I was quite prepared to risk it. I watched Israel sauté some potatoes and herbs with olive oil, he worked like a chef.

'Hidden talents, you dark horse.'

'I worked as a chef, barman, cleaner, gardener, you name it, I've done it, any job that paid a few quid cash and didn't require a permit, I'm your man, survived all right for years in Oz that way, but they caught up with me finally and booted me out, here I am.'

Lucky me, I thought.

We ate like medieval drunks, quaffing red wine and heartily ripping lamb from the bone, it was juicy and so tasty; we both made speeches about dying from food poisoning and laughed for the rest of the night.

Israel settled in with me very quickly, he started in the garden early morning on day three, I took him sandwiches and mugs of tea, but had to go to Daniel's bedside, it had been nearly a week I had neglected to visit, I felt like a stranger walking in, the surprised look on the nurses face shamed me.

'I'm sorry, I have been ill, couldn't come,' the lies making me redden a touch.

'Hey no problem, Helena, that's what we get paid to do, you are allowed to take a break you know, it's OK.'

Serena the staff nurse had told me this a few times before, not that I listened. I thanked her, 'How's he been?'

'No change, all running smooth, he's got a touch of chest infection again, you know the fluid build-up, can't seem to drain all of it.'

We knew this was his particular weak spot, a pneumonia risk. Despite the antibiotic mixture pumping though him, his injuries caused damage to the lung cavities and fluids often built up, infection was always being monitored.

'He's OK, though?'

'Yes, he's doing fine. Your stepson popped in yesterday, he told Daniel about his new job in America, he's getting married too, that's so good, he's moving on with his life.'

'Yes, yes, it's great news.' I mustered a normal-sounding voice but it felt like a smack in the face hearing it from the nurse. Nathan hadn't bothered to tell me his news. I tried not to be hurt; after all I'm just his brain-dead dad's wife, not really any relation to him anymore. Now he's a grown man, needs to move on with his life, it's normal, I suppose.

I stayed longer than intended, read him a few chapters of his old favourite book, *The Old Man and the Sea*, it seemed ironic that his life mirrored that story, alone and with virtually no chance of survival. I always wondered if that were some sort of omen. Against all the odds the fisherman survives and maybe deep down I hold a hope for Daniel.

When I left that afternoon I felt a bit energised, which was unusual, so I wandered around the shops, got a few things, more fresh veg and some herbs Israel liked to use. I hadn't noticed before that they had such a varied range of produce these days, from everywhere in the world, so I bought some exotic fruits and decided a fresh fruit salad would be nice. Shopping on autopilot for eleven years, this was the first time I'd even cared what went in the basket, it felt strange.

We ate well again that night and Israel was knackered from hard labour in the garden, but it was amazing the difference just cutting down the overgrowth made, it opened up the generous borders the snaked around the lawn.

I left him snoring on the sofa with the throw wrapped around him, the fire ebbing away. I had an early night and slept a solid nine hours, heading off to work early for the first time in years, but by the afternoon I was feeling like shit, my head was splitting and I had a full on fever, so I shot off home.

Israel helped me up to bed, he was worried. 'This looks like withdrawal, Helena.'

'Can't be, Izzy, I'm OK for another week normally, I never get sick so quick.'

'Well, let's see how you go, the aspirin may help but looks like withdrawal to me.' He was scrutinising my complexion like a new mother.

I bundled up under the duvet, shivers hitting me like waves, teeth chattering and I was in and out of sleep and dreams, then the nausea struck, violent retching to start with, then my body went under attack. Last thing I remember was Israel tying my hair back and holding a bucket while I evacuated every nano morsel in my entire system, loudly, violently and without any way to stop. It went on for hours, dry heaving to bile, to the point my nose was bleeding and the pain was everywhere. Israel soothingly wiped me down with hot cloths and held my stinking, shaking body while I cried out to Daniel to slow down and screamed for my baby to be put back inside me. The doctor in my dream threw a bucket of what looked like minced beef at my feet and shouted, 'Put it back in yourself, bitch.'

Horrible, devilish faces circled my bed screaming, 'Whore, bitch, murderer,' at me. Blood poured from every open mouth, every worst nightmare spinning and flashing around me, my adrenaline was so high I became short of breath. I struggled to be free of the duvet and Israel, to be able to breathe, I was uncontrollable, lurching like a mad woman for the open window.

But Israel rugby-tackled me back onto the bed and held me, soothing words and his soft voice slowly, steadily calmed me and I fell into a dreamless sleep. I was in that bed for three days. Israel washed me, fed me tiny sips of water and kept me close to him, soothing me when I woke and cleaning my foul mess when my shit and piss evacuated without warning.

I was curled in a ball on the bedroom floor vaguely aware of him changing the bedding, wafts of washing powder scent drifted around my semi-conscious brain. It reminded me of the hospital, clean and sterile, I swear I saw a light glowing around him as he crouched down to gently lift me back into the clean bed. Another deep, dream-filled sleep, nine hours later I came back.

He was there, at the foot of the bed, curled up snoring lightly, like a faithful Labrador.

I tentatively eased out of the bed to go pee. He opened a bloodshot eye. 'A basset hound,' I said out loud, 'not a Lab.'

'Huh?' he came around slowly, he looked like hell. 'So you're alive then, Helen of Troy. You are tougher than you look.'

I had lost 10lbs body weight in four days, I felt weak as a mouse, but inside of me I couldn't really describe the feeling, it was alien to know that your body wanted to live, that despite your own best efforts to kill yourself, your spirit had the final say.

'I'm bloody starving!'

He cracked a smile, and hoisted himself off the bed. 'Me too, I couldn't keep anything down the last few days, all that shit and sick, God!'

It dawned on me what hell it must have been, how this man I barely knew had saved my life. I limped over to him and threw my arms around him.

'Thank you, thank you, my own personal Jesus, you are my angel.'

I was crying, but not with sorrow, for once with gratitude and hope and love. He started to fill up too and we hugged hard.

'I'm going to cook something, before you collapse again,' he shot downstairs.

We ate and drank for two days. Every few hours, he would thrust a full fork of something tasty, and I scoffed every one. I was feeling so much better, I thanked my lucky stars that I met Israel, he saved my life.

I was thinking about heroin. I hadn't craved it yet, it was so odd, normally by now it would be my uppermost thought. How long would I make it until I had to go to Dr Gerry? I could delay it with lots of alcohol and sometimes sleep if I was lucky, but never more than two weeks, and so feeling like this was unusual.

Instead, I craved fresh fruit and herbs, lean meat and fresh fish, I started drinking copious amounts of water and even spent the afternoon weeding the borders.

We took a trip to the local garden centre and bought a boot full of bedding plants, it was while I was paying at the till I glanced back at Israel who was twitching and scratching at himself. Ah, I realised he was craving.

We drove home in silence; he had a bead of sweat on his forehead, even though the car was cool, he was getting bad.

'So Israel, when are you going to Gerry's?' I burst out with it.

'I was going to slip out tonight, while you were sleeping,' he looked at his hands as he spoke.

'It's bad, huh?'

'Yes, Troy, it's getting bad.'

'So why not let me return the favour?' I stared at him.

'You aren't strong enough yet.'

We drove a mile or so in silence.

'I could lock you in?'

'I'll break the window,' he shook his head.

'Not if we boarded it up and strapped you down,' my tone was light despite the serious subject, I really wanted to do this for him.

He looked and laughed, 'Dominatrix, eh?'

'Ha-ha, asshole! No, I'm your friend. You've done it for me; I want to repay you. You saved my life, Izzy. Let me do the same for you.'

'I'm not ready, Troy, don't push, let me go to Gerry tonight. We can get prepared for next week; you need to get your strength back.'

'Are you sure, Izzy? I can do it tonight I will be OK!'

'No, hun, next week, give me time to seal the office up, buy some locks, you won't be able to stop me otherwise, I might hurt you.'

'OK then, that's a plan, we do this thing next week. Deal?' I wanted him to commit, we shook hands.

'Deal, Troy!'

Off he went that night and I couldn't sleep a wink. I was waiting for the urge to drive over and see Gerry myself, but it didn't come. I couldn't believe my luck, it was very rare to kick the heroin habit so easily in the first attempt, not many get a second chance, I did something I hadn't done since a child, I thanked God for sending me this angel.

I prayed he would be safe tonight and return home tomorrow, so when the birds started their dawn chorus, I decided to get up and go and work in the garden, take my mind off the worry, digging over the soil, adding fertiliser horse manure to the earth was incredibly satisfying. Seeing the mounds turn jet black, ready to receive, I started planting. It was about ten thirty when I heard the front door. Rushing back in the house, I was greeted with a bouncy Israel, laden with carrier bags.

'Full English, Troy'?

'Absolutely, Izzy, got any brown sauce?'

'Of course, woman, I know your predilection for unholy condiments.'

Laughing and messing about unloading the shopping I watched him carefully, his bounce suddenly replaced by a lethargy and a peculiar grey pallor, he didn't look too good.

'You OK, mate?'

He hesitated a moment, 'Hmm, not sure to be honest, Gerry had a different mix last night, he wanted to try it out, it was a freebie so I volunteered.'

I spun around, 'Are you fucking kidding me? Why the hell would you risk it? Sit down.'

I felt his head; it was burning up.

'Christ, you need to get your temperature down,' I ran to the freezer and grabbed all the ice. Running a cold bath, I bullied him into it, the shrieks from him were embarrassing, 'Like a lobster you are!'

But even though we tried to laugh with sarcastic barbs, it was worrying, he was hot again moments after coming out of the bath.

He started to lose consciousness and it was at that point I went for the phone.

'Ambulance, please.'

'No, no, Troy, I'm OK,' his voice weak like a child.

I ignored him and told the advisor on the phone about his symptoms, she said the ambulance was on its way.

'I'm not taking any risks, Izzy, I can't lose you,' I howled.

They were fast, lucky for us, Israel died twice in that ambulance. I was there with him, holding his hand while the paramedics brought him back, a very low heart rate, but it was beating.

We arrived at the hospital and one of my husband's nurses was coming out for a quick fag break. She did a double take, and then ran over to help me.

The men unloaded Israel with practised ease and he was whisked through the emergency doors without stopping. Triage nurses followed the moving bed, getting some info, then back to me for his personal details that I was barely able to supply. I told them he'd taken drugs, unknown, his first name and rough age, but other than that I was stumped.

It was an hour before a sweating nurse appeared to tell me he was stable but in intensive care, so no visitation until tomorrow.

I got a taxi home and had another fretful night, waking at the first light of the dawn. I decided to take a chance anyway and headed for the hospital. I had two options: east wing for coma care, or west wing for intensive care.

I stood rooted to the spot for a moment.

My feet turned west and I headed off to try and see Israel.

CHAPTER TWENTY-FIVE

Helena

As I walked through the hospital corridors, I felt a maternal instinct from somewhere, God knows I hadn't had those before. They let me in, he had been moved out of intensive care just a few minutes earlier.

Laying in his hospital bed with a steady blip-blip-blip, I froze for a second, had to double check myself where I was.

But his floppy fringe swung as he turned to face me.

'Helen of Troy, come on down!'

His laughter was weaker than normal but I beamed back at him, the tears falling openly on his shoulder.

'You asshole, Izzy.'

'Well, that's a nice way to treat your best mate.'

We hugged for ages, 'You OK, though? You know you died twice?'

'I like to be special, once is for plebs.'

With that I pretended to slap him.

The nurse told us to take it easy and not get too rowdy.

We sniggered like school kids. 'She's right though, take this seriously, Izzy.'

'I'm finished with drugs, Helena. That's my big warning, only a true asshole would carry on after this.'

'I'm so glad to hear you say that, Israel. But I'm still worried because you are pretty much one hundred per cent pure asshole!'

We burst out laughing and the nurse appeared with a look that could melt the Antarctic.

We both signed up for rehab, even though I think I was clean, it's a trapdoor that can drop at any time. The centre was a small annex in the hospital grounds. Every Thursday we met with our group and talked about our experiences. Israel was on a methadone plan and his target was twelve months' reduction, with heavy counselling alongside.

We made a pledge to counsel each other daily, to be clean.

It was Israel's turn to stand up in front of the group and tell his story, I sat back ready to listen to every word even though I had heard the tale, but my mouth dropped.

'Hello, my name is Israel Jesus Worthington. I am an addict; I was born of heroin-addicted parents and was an addicted baby at birth. I've been clean for five weeks now and am on a programme. I have died more than twenty times, something or someone obviously has a plan for me, keeps me here.'

Then he looked back at me, I had tears flowing.

Jesus.

CHAPTER TWENTY-SIX

Carmella

I'm about two hours away from London, so amazingly close, I can almost feel the cool English breeze on my face as I buckle up in my super comfy, first class British Airways seat. My departure from Rome was fast and without much complication. I had left books and brochures of Shakespeare study courses for English literature students around the apartment all week, made bogus phone calls about the supposed curriculum for the eight-week residential course, not that anyone really cared. Massimo and I had stopped being in the same room after the episode with my sprained finger. I made a polite exit and told him I would be back in September.

He just raised a hand, not even eye contact, so it was an easy escape.

I had no companion in my next door seat but across the aisle I couldn't help notice the young businessman who couldn't take his eyes off me. He was a typical English-looking man, a bit like Hugh Grant, with his floppy hair and staring habit. I stifled a giggle and looked squarely back at him.

'Good afternoon,' I ventured in my best English accent, Professor Arro would be beaming.

He seemed to choke a little and splutter a greeting, in fact several greetings rolled into one. This time the giggle couldn't be held. He reddened and virtually collapsed within his seat, finally composing himself to retry his greeting in Italian. I waved him silent.

'No, no, please in English, I must polish my phrases, I'm rusty as pins.'

'Nails,' he offered.

'Ah yes, nails.'

Rusty as old nails, we both smiled. The stewardess addressed the Englishman as Lord Templeton. I was impressed. Ha, maybe prof was right to teach me to talk like an aristocrat after all. My mama would gush so hard she would burst if she saw me talking to an English lord.

We chatted throughout the flight about the Cotswolds, where I intended to stay and ease my fragile emotions; in fact the lord knew the small town of Bourton-on-the-Water very well, having dated the Earl of Brent's eldest daughter Diana, before discovering that they had absolutely zero in common other than brothers attending the same school.

'Diana was more concerned with marrying a landed gent, I knew she wasn't for me; I'm a tech nerd, can't bear the outdoor life, all those garden parties and dogs everywhere.'

Our chat was easy and flowed, it was refreshing to talk with another human, someone who knew nothing about me, it was liberating. I left the airport lifted and free, the spring in my step attracting several admiring glances as I breezed through. My lord gave me his card so if I ventured into London we could have dinner one evening. He reddened again as he blustered about the great restaurants in London, then backtracking realising his faux pas, telling an Italian about this great little Italian restaurant he goes to. We both laughed and I kissed his cheeks and said, 'See you soon.'

I was aware of his eyes following me until I was in the car arranged by my travel agent. A jolly driver talked nonstop as he whisked me from Heathrow along the dreary motorway out of the city and finally into the greenery toward the Cotswolds. He had to stop at the pub for directions to the estate cottage that was going to be my home for the next two months. We entered the grand iron gates of Medlicott Hall; it reminded me of those wonderful English period dramas, it was built in the 16th century and you could define the original from the later additions. It was a contradiction in architecture, but as a whole it gave it an honest feel, charting the success of the estate, and the tastes of the family over the centuries. The gardens were special. They hadn't been changed much and the tree-lined, long, slim drive led to a circular cobbled forecourt, with a fabulous ancient stone fountain in the centre, its cooling mist refreshing the air around us.

A young man approached and greeted us with a cheery wave and with a few quick directions, which I couldn't quite understand, a broad smile and a welcome to the hall to me, off we went around the side of the great hall, to a delectable thatched cottage, with its own gated entrance and lush gardens that gave it perfect privacy for the calm country retreat it was advertised to be. It met all my expectations and more.

The small windows nestled deep into the creamy rendered misshapen walls, which sat firm under the heavy straw thatch. It was beautifully done with rows of corn and wildflowers crafted from the straw all along the ridge line, like a fairy tale cottage.

The cottage gardens were everything you would expect to see at the Chelsea Flower Show and I immediately felt my shoulders drop and my smile widen, this was a tiny piece of chocolate box heaven.

The driver, Ron, took the bags through and we were suddenly greeted by a rosy-faced lady of about fifty.

'Welcome, my dear, I'm Jayne, I'll be looking after you for your stay, come along and let me settle you in.'

Jayne led me around the cottage explaining this and that.

'But don't be mithered with it all now.'

I nodded despite not knowing what being 'mithered' was. 'I'm on hand Monday through to Saturday for anything you need, Sunday Master Johnathon with be on call, he's the young chap who gave you directions, master of the hall he is now the late master has passed. Anyhoo, listen to me rambling on, let's get you a nice cuppa. Tea or coffee, my dear?'

I was enchanted by the lilt of her accent, just trying to follow her words to make sense was quite a challenge. Jayne opened up the French doors in the kitchen onto the amazing rambling blooming garden. I squealed with delight, there in the middle of this fiesta of scented rioting flowers was a pool, not huge, but a beautiful old ornamental swimming pool, with hand-cut stone gargoyles and angels looking over it from sandstone plinths. I rushed out to inspect it.

'Oh, you're in luck, miss. Master Johnny had that all regrouted when he knew a lady from Italy was coming,' she chuckled and mumbled a few jokes to herself as she boiled the kettle and made tea, producing a homemade lemon drizzle cake. By the time I returned, the kitchen table was set for afternoon tea.

'Now then, I don't suppose a lady with your super slim figure eats a lot of cake, but you're on holiday now, so you enjoy yourself my dear and if I may say, we have never had such a beautiful lady as you staying here, so if the gardeners cause you any bother, don't hesitate to ring me and I'll tan their hides for them.'

I laughed and said ok, still oblivious to what she was saying and I was definitely going to eat cake.

'I'll leave you alone now, Ms Matteo.'

'Carmella, please.'

'All right, Ms Carmella, the telephone is here by the cooker, press 9 for an outside line, press 4 and that goes direct to my phone, 6 for Master Johnny on Sunday, but to be honest he forgets where he puts the darn phone so you will be quicker to find him in the greenhouse, just through the gate at the back of your garden, he's always tending the plants, green-fingered like his father was, God rest his soul.' Jayne carried on chatting all the way down the path and away.

I raced back to the kitchen and took a tray out to the garden, to the lovely antique iron table and chairs with cheerful flowery cushions and a love swing for two made of wood, with a sun-bleached yellow canopy. It was all so charming and homely. I sat sipping tea and ate mouthfuls of the moist cake. Sharp lemon syrup hit my taste buds and I immediately thought of Roberto and the *torta limone* we shared in Café Giuseppe in Rome.

A little pang hit my heart. I had promised him I would let him know when I arrived, so I pulled his number from the secret compartment in my purse and called him at his office from the phone in the kitchen. It took three attempts to get a connection and then his warm, deep tones filled the earpiece.

'Cara, cara, I missed you so much, I'm looking now at our little table under the olive tree, it's filled with an old couple, I wonder, will that be us in years to come?' He let out a wistful sigh. The romance of the man made my heart swell, these words were everything that was missing from my luxurious life, wealth meant nothing really without love and care. I wished he was here in this gorgeous cottage. I told him about Jayne and her peculiar dialect. Roberto enlightened me that 'mithering' meant 'hassle'. Ahh, I understood about the gardeners now.

We laughed to think that this round, rosy lady would beat them on the bottom till it turned red for such a crime, as he explained the meaning of having one's hide tanned. England is unique and special.

'Cara, I'm in London next week for an exhibition, Vasille is showing, can you attend?'

'Of course I will, that would be wonderful.'

'Shall I reserve a room for you in my hotel?'

There was a moment's silence; the unspoken suggestion filled the line.

'Yes Roberto that's sensible, I will stay a few days in London anyway, I need to find a detective who fancies a job in Rome.'

'Yes of course, do you need any help?'

'No, Roberto, I want to handle this alone, you mustn't be any part of it; promise me, caro, you won't get involved.'

'I promise. So I await you in London my darling, we arrive Thursday, the show runs Saturday to Saturday. Your reservation will be under Carmella Carlutto, I hope you don't mind, I think it best not to use your real name at the Savoy London. I can't wait to see you.'

'Good thinking, I'm so excited, Roberto, I'm feeling like a new woman already.'

'Ciao, caro.'

'Ciao, bella.'

I went back to the sweet garden and lay down on the love swing, fell into a deep sleep and was only disturbed by a wet nuzzling at the back of my knees and a frantic calling from afar.

'Hunter, hunter where are you boy?'

Hunter was a very bouncy young golden Labrador. He couldn't decide whether to obey his master, like a good boy, or to hang around this sleeping lady who smelled of lemon cake, who was sure to give him a slice if he nuzzled her enough.

I couldn't resist his big brown oh-so-hopeful eyes. I rubbed his ears and he drooled his adoration at me, he bounded to the table and I realised my duty was to follow him, cut a slice of cake and feed this cheeky, gorgeous boy, so I did, and a chunk for me. The voice got very close and Hunter spun around with guilt and delight in equal measure.

'There you are. I'm so sorry, miss, he's a law unto himself, only a youngster, lots to learn yet, God only knows if he will though, bit too fond of sweet things to make a decent hunting dog.'

'No problem. He's adorable. Would you like some cake? It's too much for me alone.'

'Oh, it's Jayne's lemon drizzle, gosh yes, I don't mind if I do, that's terribly kind of you, are you sure I'm not imposing? You have only just arrived.'

'No, no, please, it's such a beautiful place I need someone to rave about it to.'

He laughed and settled into the garden chair with Hunter tightly packed by his right leg, staring hopefully at his master.

'How about a cup of English tea?'

'I would love one, to be honest, but I feel rather cheeky.'

'Nonsense, you are my first guest and I rather like to serve tea in the garden, it's my pleasure.'

'Well then, I wouldn't dream of denying you that pleasure, Mrs Matteo.'

'Please call me Carmella, and am I right to think you are Master Johnathon?'

'Johnny, just Johnny, I always think people are talking about my father when they call to speak to the Earl of Medlicott.'

His eyes flashed a dart of sadness and I patted his arm. 'I'm sorry for your loss Johnny.'

He brightened at my touch and held eye contact with me.

'Well,' he said, 'we can't be all maudlin about these things, it's the way of things, we are all going the same way.'

'Yes, we are indeed.' We sipped our tea and shared the cake between the three of us, Hunter getting the best of both our slices. He was in love with me from that day on.

Johnny said that if Jayne knew we gave away her best cake to this naughty boy, she'd have our guts for garters. I looked quizzically at Johnny and he explained it meant we would get a stern telling off.

I will never understand these English sayings, they are so strange.

Our afternoon tea and chats became a regular thing over the next two months. When I wasn't in London, I had dinner several times with Johnny in the great hall. He told me the family history and I explored the labyrinth of rooms that were left empty all year around, it saddened me to know that once this house had been the epitome of social life for the wealthy and titled and now stood quietly waiting to crumble. The estate had been hit hard by taxation and was struggling to make ends meet, hence the need to rent out the cottage to guests. Johnny admitted that he wasn't a great man for business. His brother Thomas had been the big hope for the estate but had sadly died in a sailing accident two years before his father.

'I was quite a disappointment to the old man; he lost most of his energies for the estate after Thomas.'

Hunter sensed his master's emotions and plopped his golden head on his lap. He comforted the sad-looking dog and Johnny revived with the contact of warm fur under his palm. He was a sensitive soul, I could see.

'Only thing I'm good at is growing flowers, I supply a couple of local florists but they need them so cheap these days to compete with the supermarkets, it's pin money really.'

I felt the loneliness emitting from this isolated, lovely young man. What a pile of responsibility he has been landed with.

I asked the question, 'Could you sell the house and make a new life somewhere else? Maybe get married have some children?'

'I have thought about it many times, Carmella. I want to be the son my father wished I was. I don't think I could handle the guilt of finishing the Medlicott line, I'm the last Earl of Medlicott, I have to find a way, must be a way.'

A flash of inspiration hit me, my new English friend, Lord Templeton, he had left Diana in limbo, that's just what Johnny needed, a good wife, someone of his own to share his love of the country, to boost the house back into life. What did Lord Templeton say about her? All garden parties and dogs everywhere, that sounds right up Johnny's road, I mean street, I think.

London was exhilarating. I'd been busy doing nothing much, pottering about the garden with Hunter and helping

Johnny in the greenhouse, I almost forgot about Thursday, the Savoy, a rendezvous with Roberto.

But by the time I was getting off the train my stomach was in knots. I knew I had feelings for Roberto, I just wasn't entirely sure what they were. He talked of love like we had known each other years. He felt like he had known me, but he didn't actually know me at all. His imagination has filled in all the gaps, watching me from his office all those years, he has built our relationship from a fantasy. I was not saying it couldn't become a reality but we were just starting out and I had changed. I was no longer scared to speak or laugh or walk around barefooted dropping crumbs from my cake on the floor, like I did at the cottage, knowing Hunter will hoover for me anyway. I have got to like the silence and meditation time, just me alone with the bees and butterflies for company, it was nothing like the depressing silence and loneliness of that apartment in Rome. I was amazed that I survived it; being here in nature was healing me.

The sound of the lazy trickle of water from the rockery waterfall that Johnny installed near the love swing sent me in to a deep, satisfying sleep. My anxiety had almost gone. In fact I was just discovering who I actually was, so how could Roberto even think he knows me? I didn't know me.

I needed to talk to him, seriously.

And while I was psychoanalysing myself, I realised that I was a little vain. I enjoyed the attention from nice-looking men and the general warmth and enthusiasm from pretty much everyone here in England. When they discovered I was Italian, they told me all about their holidays in Sorrento and the Italian men they fell in love with for a fortnight of romance. I never knew I could be so chatty and unguarded with perfect strangers. A lifetime of social exclusion, living a life following routines, instructions and codes of conduct that forbade me to really interact with my peers, had left me unaware of how it was to live free and unshackled, to develop my own personality.

But a deep burning desire was brewing. I was so inexperienced in all matters of love and romance, even talking to a man in a loving situation, I didn't know how to do it. I thought Roberto could be the one to lead me into the light, so that's why I was checking in at the Savoy as Mrs Carlutto, with my suitcase full of my best lingerie. I was here to explore, the city and myself.

The suite he booked was full of flowers. The concierge had smiled warmly at my delight. The elaborate ironwork balcony opened out giving a view of the bustling vibrant city. I felt tingles all over. There was a letter in a creamy embossed envelope propped up on the dresser. In beautiful calligraphy he had written:

> *Cara, my sweet love, I want you to live inside my heart, please allow me to cherish you, to spoil you and show you the true love of a man. I do not ask for love in return, I can only dream of this, please allow me to love you, to give you everything you deserve, starting with the finest dinner tonight.*
>
> *Your carriage awaits at seven, my princess.*
>
> *Roberto xxx*

He had charm, he had confidence, he was cultured and mature, why was I just a touch unsure about falling in love with him?

I called for laundry service to steam my evening gown. I'd just brought the one, I'd got a bit used to the easy dressing of shorts and tee shirt at the cottage, so while that got spruced up, so did I. The wonderful Jo Malone bath bombs filled the suite with amazing jasmine and vanilla scents, it reminded me of Johnny's greenhouse. I luxuriated in the deep bath, my pedicure and manicure booked and the hairdresser arriving at six: instant beauty, just a call away. I remembered the street girls in Rome, slim, toned, tanned and coiffured, they couldn't call anyone and charge it to the account, those girls had to work at everything. I wondered if I could even survive without the luxuries of wealth. What was I even capable of? I didn't know, but I knew I wanted to find out.

Shakir came to mind as I tried not to get my hair wet. He would go crazy if I didn't use the mineral salts he had supplied, but to be honest, I forgot to pack them and had used the shampoo supplied with the cottage. It didn't make much difference to the shine, in fact my hair really liked the English climate, it behaved itself for once in its life, so I dunked down deep in the bubbles and thought, *Sod it. It may be frizzy but it will smell divine.*

There was a knock at my door at 7pm.

My hairdresser gave her last spritz and left, letting my suitor Roberto Carlutto inside. She gave me a look of, 'Oh, very nice' as she swivelled to check him out and darted off. She was right, he looked very handsome in a tuxedo, his tanned skin made his green eyes shine, very sexy. He took a moment to admire me and his smile said it all.

'My God, cara, I have never seen you look more beautiful.'

This wasn't just a charming compliment. I had blossomed in just a week in the summer gardens at the Cotswold cottage, the fresh air and organic food from the estate gardens that Jayne and Earl Johnny supplied was making a difference. But it was the stress that had left my uptight muscles that really made me look better. Even the shape of my mouth had changed; I'd lost that look of apprehension, my smile was sincere and not just a mask I wore daily to make everything seem fine.

Roberto saw the change and I saw it in the mirror. This steeled me further to free myself of this dreadful farce of a marriage and to regain some semblance of self-esteem and identity.

He extended his elbow and I placed my arm through the crook, we made quite a pair, gliding through the foyer of the Savoy, many stopped to look at me and at my gorgeous companion Roberto, a few envious glares from the ladies who were of a similar age to him. I understood that it was an unfair system for ladies over forty, often discarded for younger versions. I was a little uncomfortable about that, age didn't really matter much to me generally but I was so inexperienced in romance and relationships I did wonder if it was OK. Roberto on the other hand looked proud as punch to escort a much younger woman on his arm and the continued attention the men gave me didn't go unnoticed.

'I see I will have to guard you day and night, my darling, there are many suitors who would like to swap places with me.'

I laughed and brushed it off as nonsense.

'It is the last thing I'm looking for, Roberto, I am not ready for another marriage.' And there, I said it, as we travelled to our rooftop destination, a beautiful al fresco dining room at the top of the most beautiful mansion house in Kensington, a very private, exclusive place where only the wealthiest guests were permitted. We were seated in a semi-covered private booth, overlooking the skyline of London. The décor was serene, calm and immaculate, manicured trees dissected the booths giving intimate space and a feeling of being the only people in the whole of the roof garden, yet a few feet away were sheiks, film stars and billionaire business tycoons all enjoying the same feeling of private luxury.

Our head waiter was perfect; he recommended we sample the chef's special taster menu, a series of tiny but ingenious delicacies sure to please our discerning palates.

We agreed. The Cristal champagne was poured and we toasted to many things: freedom, new beginnings, serendipity and fate.

Roberto hadn't reacted to my declaration of independence, but I felt it had to be discussed; it was as if he was on page 100 of our relationship and I was just reading the front cover. This disparity was bound to rear its ugly head at some point, but not tonight. I intended to enjoy this lovely evening, with this lovely man. The food was exquisite as promised and we ate heartily, unlike the cold, austere dinners with Massimo and his dreadful mother. I didn't feel self-conscious about enjoying the meal, there were no disapproving glances from Robert, in fact, he enjoyed feeding me the best morsels of each dish, it was a culinary experience I hadn't even experienced in Rome.

We were discussing the English fayre with its terrible reputation when our head waiter advised us that the executive chef was of Middle Eastern descent and therefore expert at creating amazing food for kings and heads of state, sourcing the finest ingredients from around the entire world.

We passed our compliments to him.

The sun was setting and the tiny twinkling lights started to illuminate randomly along the trees. We bet each other which tree would be next, I was winning, he raised the stakes.

'Cara, if I guess the next tree, will you kiss me as my prize?'

'Pick well, Roberto.' I winked and smiled.

He really studied those trees and finally chose the ornamental maple. Holding my hand, we waited, I felt his hand squeeze mine and it lit up, his smile brighter than the tree.

'A deal is a deal, caro.' I turned to him and drew closer to his lovely face, he cupped my chin in his hand and drew me in, our lips touched fleetingly, then his full mouth closed around mine, he kissed me like I had never imagined a kiss could be. My heart was beating fast and my instinct was to pull away just from the sheer intensity of being so wrapped up in another person's space. I was unable to maintain any coherent thinking as his passion lit the flame burning inside of me. I kissed him back urgently, with feelings of lust and desire. We were lost in each other, like the last two people on earth, oblivious to the world around us.

The absolute discretion of our waiter ensured we were undisturbed until we finally broke our flaming embrace. My vision was blurry as I focussed on Roberto's face, the look in his eyes gave him an almost pained expression and I read him perfectly. I whispered the words he so wanted to hear.

'Roberto, take me to bed.'

He emitted a tight sound from the back of his throat and waved for the waiter, who had already alerted our driver to be ready at the front. Our waiter earned around £100,000 a year for this kind of intuitive action, and he rarely saw a wealthy man and a beautiful young woman order dessert and coffees.

Roberto whisked me to our car, the urgency was palpable. I felt the desire burn through my shimmering dress all the way back to the Savoy as Roberto kissed my neck and mouth, whispering words of *amore*, his strong hands running along my back and legs, stopping short of my breasts. I was aching for him to rip my dress off and take my hard nipples into his mouth. I gasped and called his name as quietly as I could but inside I was singing and wailing. The driver had raised the black screen. Roberto could have taken me right here in the back of the Bentley if he wanted, I would have gladly received him, but he had more control than me. His maturity and experience were there to guide me into this world of passion and pleasure, I was his willing student.

It was a blur arriving in my suite. The lighting had been set low and the bed turned down, the Savoy was the best. My silk negligee was arranged at the end of the bed but I never got to put it on, I was as eager and frenzied as he was to take off my dress and give my body over to the pleasure of lovemaking. He didn't disappoint me, from the moment the door clicked shut, he was master and I his willing concubine.

My dress dropped without fuss, his expert fingers removed my thong as he lay me down on the bed. Parting my legs he went straight into my sweet spot and kissed, licked, sucked and caressed me until I was crying out to climax, but moments before I reached the top he stopped and kissed a trail down my inner thighs, cooling me off. I've seen animals in the wild displaying their desire to mate, I felt that animal want inside of me. I stood up and took charge of his tuxedo, I stripped him naked, kissing and caressing every naked inch as it became free. He groaned and called me his witch, his queen, his love, but I was not acting from love, I was burning up with the pent-up frustration of years without sexual attention. I had one goal, to feel what it is for a man and woman to connect intensely.

We fell naked onto the bed and I wriggled out from under him. My turn to explore. He lay back on the pillows and watched me with such lust and pleasure it spurred me on to be more daring. I stood above him and widened my legs so he could see my most private, intimate part. He wet his fingers and circled my bud gently with his thumb and driving his forefingers inside me, he drew me to his mouth. Fiercely he licked and sucked until I felt the tsunami of heat rage through my entire body, trembling and crying out I climaxed over and over into his eager mouth. Without letting me recover, he flipped me onto my back and then I felt him; his generous penis, swollen with want, entered me. Slowly at first, he was being sure I was ready to receive and I was, almost delirious from multiple orgasms I was open and wanting more. He dove in, deep and powerful, his focus seemed to take him away somewhere else, I watched his cheekbones catch the light as he thrust forward and back, his muscular arms rippling with each exertion. I arched and widened my legs encouraging him on, next thing I knew my legs were over his shoulders and the depth of his thrust doubled, I was moaning his name over and over. I had never felt anything like this, pinned and immobile, I never wanted this pleasure to stop, the burning came fast and furious as he pumped hard and steady into me. He opened his eyes and we locked contact, both of us powering ahead in exquisite lust-fuelled harmony, his breathing laboured and fast. I felt the shuddering in my groin, I was coming to climax again, he was with me in every heartbeat, every panting breath, we rode and rode together, groaning and crying out, the sweat beading on his forehead, droplets of salty liquid skimming my mouth as they rolled down my chin, I jerked forward unable to control my shaking body, he took my cue and he halted, deep inside, I felt every inch of his body tense and slowly relax and he let go and released his seed deep inside of me, burying his neck in my hair, he called out, '*Amore.*'

We stayed locked together, spent and weak as kittens, for a long while. Finally releasing me, I tentatively left the bed and went to the shower. I could barely stand up, my jelly legs giving way as I washed myself. I felt the soreness of my labia as I washed, but the sharp pain was attached to a sharp pleasure as the sponge washed away his seed and sweat.

I nearly came again as I washed, I was so turned on and incredulous that I had been so open and burned up with lust. I remembered my wedding night and cried a little as the warm water drenched my aching muscles.

Roberto appeared in the shower and we kissed passionately under the waterfall. I washed him gently and he was getting hard again, so I dropped to my knees and for the first time in my life, took a man's penis into my mouth, having no idea what to do, I was glad he was not fully raring to go, it was a gentle and intimate moment, he ran his fingers through my wet hair as I kissed and loved him. He filled my mouth with warm salty juices and it was a shock at first, I didn't know what to do with it, so I opened my mouth and let the shower water wash it out. He lifted me up and we kissed softly.

Roberto wrapped me up in a huge fluffy white towel and carried me back to bed, drying my body like I was just a child. His love was total, I felt it through his silence and his gentle handling of my body. We had shared a moment that connected us. I understood for the first time in my life why women can fight like dogs for the love of her man. This feeling was like seeing and knowing the core of yourself, the id, the self, whatever name you give it, I discovered my essence that night, I was a woman.

CHAPTER TWENTY-SEVEN

Carmella

My appointment with Mr Havilland, private detective, was a light and humorous first meeting. He didn't look like any PD I had seen in the movies, in fact he looked more like a writer from a romantic novel: crumpled linen suit, tanned and slim, with a laid-back attitude and a quick wit. He had been recommended by the concierge at the Savoy who knew Mr Havilland was 'just the ticket', as he put it.

So here we were. I told him about my unfortunate marital status and he shook his head and assured me it was a travesty that I had wasted my years with this idiot. I liked the way he didn't mince his words and I decided he was the right agent for this job, so we continued our briefing at the Rope and Anchor pub on the corner. We ate hot roast beef and horseradish sandwiches and I had a very good Pinot Noir and he a pint of flat brown liquid that smelled like yeast. He made notes as I regaled him with names of private clubs and restaurants that Massimo frequented. I told him that Shakir was gathering more intelligence as we spoke and I would call him to find out anything new to report.

Mr Havilland insisted I call him Tim. I very much enjoyed our lunch and after, we agreed the fees and that I would be paying him in cash because of the secrecy required. We concluded that he would head off for Rome in three days' time. He gave me a mobile phone so he could text me with updates or questions. It was a bit of an odd thing to carry around, took me ages to find out how to turn it on, but it was so handy to have when he called me five days later asking if we had a lodger living in the apartment in Rome.

'No, never.'

'Ahh, I see, well it seems you have a house guest who has his own key. A good-looking male house guest. According to the maid, this guest is called Eric, so I'm following up what has happened to Giorgio these days.'

But it was only the next day that Tim called me to advise that Giorgio and Eric were now in fact both house guests at the apartment.

Massimo's mother was in Switzerland and so the place had become a bit of a *ménage à trois* love nest, so to speak.

I felt repulsed as I digested the fact that Massimo was blatantly living his real life, no regard for my reputation or even his mother's. I wondered if she knew her little golden boy was a bitch.

Tim laughed and said, 'There will be time for revenge later, Carmella, for now keep calm, enjoy your holiday and leave these bastards to me.'

So I did.

Earl Johnny took me into the village several times for dinner at the Ring-a-Roses pub, every head in the pub swivelled to get a good long look at us. He waved and smiled to most and Harry the landlord served us with his wife's homemade steak and ale pie, and fresh beetroots from his allotment. Crusty country bread was the absolute best for mopping up the thick rich gravy. I have eaten in the best restaurants in London and Rome, this food may not look fancy or have a whole page dedicated to the description, but when you have been gardening all day and starving hungry, it's the tops and better still you can wear shorts and flip flops to dinner and no one cares.

I was very happy in the cottage messing about with Hunter and Johnny. The gardeners had been a little nosy and I overheard Jayne giving them a hell of a roasting. She was shouting the words so fast that I couldn't catch many, but they got the message loud and clear, that guests came here for privacy and retreat, not to be perved on by nosy buggers like them.

I chuckled to myself as I took a dip in the cool garden pool. It was heaven, just the sounds of distant tractors going up and down, the birds and crickets and the occasion call to Hunter from Johnny in the greenhouses.

I had absolutely no inclination to return to Rome.

I was going back into London next week. Roberto would be back again to curate the next artist. He had been so annoyed to be called back to the office halfway through the exhibition, a major meltdown of one of his artists and only Roberto could possibly sort things out.

It was a woman artist called Jocasta Wilde, not her real name I'm sure, probably something very ordinary like Sally Smith, but she had certainly built up quite a reputation and following in the art world for her daring explicit female nudes. She was hot property in the USA and China, but not so hot in Italy. We have nudes on every corner. Beauty and the female form holds up half of my country, so it's no surprise to me that her harsh, vulgar exposés of womanhood didn't sell much in Mediterranean countries.

Her work had been ripped to shreds by the Italian critics after her show at la Scala, she refused to exhibit again, threatening to cancel her New York show and this was the crisis that only Roberto, with his gentle persuasion and abundant charm, could possibly resolve.

As one woman to another, it was quite obvious to me; she was in love with him, she hated him being out of the country, out of her grasp. I wasn't sure if it was a pang of jealously that had struck me, but it spurred me to call him that night and I found myself getting rather horny as he chatted and told me how much he missed me, how he couldn't get any sleep thinking about making love to me, so we agreed another date in the Savoy was called for on both sides.

I had four days to get myself ready and I noticed that, despite the gardening and walking, my waistband was a little snug, so I donned my trainers and went for a run. The thought of where to run to made me remember Earl Brent's daughter Diana. I decided I may as well run across the top side of the village which would bring me about the Earl's estate, according to the tourist map at the pub. It couldn't harm to see if she was around; who knows, maybe she already knew Johnny. I needed to dig a bit before I acted as matchmaker. I set off and the heat made me realise I was pretty unfit, no more steak pies for me, it's the carbs that get you. Mama would have a fit if she saw what I was eating here.

It took an hour to cross the village and I was intending to feign exhaustion at the Brent manor house and beg a glass of water, but no acting was required. I was absolutely knackered when I reached the gates. By sheer good luck, a muddy Range Rover halted at my side as I nursed my stitch that had me bent double.

'Good grief, girl, you look near dead, hop in and I'll get you some water.' I couldn't speak but gruffly heaved myself in the seat, while Diana used one arm to fend off the three springer spaniels that were desperate to rid me of my sweat and the other to handle the huge car at speed toward the grand manor house.

'Diana Brent, and you are?'

Her accent was sharp and clipped like the old BBC newsreaders. She was dressed like the Queen in a tweedy skirt and frilly blouse, and her blonde hair was tied back in a neat schoolgirl ponytail. When we got out I noticed her flowery wellies and imagined her feet must be sweatier than me, but she bounded over and helped me to the house, straight through to the massive stone-flagged kitchen. It was like time had left this vast space alone, a huge Aga and thick pine table were the dominant features and I sat gratefully in an old walnut grandfather chair that didn't match but looked so right.

She busied herself sorting out the dogs' water bowls first and then us, a teapot and a lovely crystal jug of water was placed before me and yes, a huge slab of cake. I laughed and explained, 'That's the bloody reason I'm nearly dead, trying to lose the cake off my tummy!'

'Oh, life's too short, sweetie, if a man doesn't want me to eat cake I'd rather not have the man.' Her faithful springers landed around her feet as she settled into a chair and poured the tea. She broke chunks of cake and fed her furry babies first and then us. She was just perfect for Johnny.

She quizzed me with several questions in quick succession about who I was and where I came from and what on earth an Italian heiress was doing running through the fields of Bourton-on-the-Water, so I obliged her with the answers and dropped Earl Johnny's name in frequently. I saw a hint of a blush when I declared what a sweet man he was.

She agreed. 'Yes, I went to a dance with him when we were about seventeen, I thought he was a handsome boy, but his brother was the big mouth and he used to spoil everything for Johnny when he was a lad. Any girl that liked him was seduced by Thomas or ridiculed and put off by his bully-boy ways.'

'Oh, I didn't know.'

'No, well, you don't speak ill of the dead do you, but Thomas bullied Johnny all his life. His dad encouraged it, trying to make a man of him apparently, not very nice situation. I remember my dad and his dad had words once at a charity gala, he made some unpleasant reference to his weak son and my dad defended him, they had a spat and that was that. Our families sort of avoided each other for years, silly really as we are practically neighbours, I kept meaning to go and see Johnny after his dad died, but I got wrapped up in a relationship with a chap from London and you know how it is.'

I thought about Lord Templeton on the plane; she must mean him.

'Are you still seeing the London guy?'

'Oh no, God, what a mismatch we were, he was constantly glued to some screen or other, a real computer fanatic, every time we went outdoors he got ill, allergic to dogs too, so we called it a day.'

I danced happily inside, my matchmaking spoon stirring a huge imaginary pot.

'What about you, have you run away?' She winked and smiled.

I decided to tell her the sorry tale, God knows why. I never had a woman friend before and something about Diana was so damn decent and down to earth, I felt I could tell her anything. She listened avidly as I described my sorry life, wedding night and then my night of passion with Roberto. I skimmed over the details but she understood the vast polarity.

'Wow, he's a keeper then.'

'That's just it, Diana, I don't know. I feel like I want to have him for myself but not lose this sense of liberation I have waited so long for. He's very serious; I think I could easily get swept along.'

'You are in control, Carmella; remember, a woman always dictates the pace, don't do anything you don't truly want to do. Now listen, my friend, I'm due to collect my pops in town about six, shall I run you back to Johnny's? You might die if you try and run it back.'

'Thank God, Diana, I was dreading that, yes please.'

And that is how I got Diana and Johnny to meet up, he and Hunter had started tracking me as they were worried sick when I hadn't returned, sure I was stuck in a ditch with a broken leg. Hunter greeted me like a god when we pulled alongside them in the hedgerow path.

'Diana, how are you, dear? he exclaimed with genuine good heart. 'You rescued our guest I see, thank you so very much.'

'Good to see you, Johnny, you're looking very well, jump in I'll run you back.' Hunter didn't need asking twice and bounded onto my lap then spent the rest of the drive trying to lick Diana's mouth. Unlike most women, she didn't complain, she kissed him back giving him a tantalising hint of the madeira cake she'd eaten. I caught a glance at Johnny who was watching Hunter and Diana with a look of happiness I hadn't seen before.

CHAPTER TWENTY-EIGHT

Hulya

My darling husband Mehmet had started his new position as junior lawyer at Johansson Coeur maritime law. We had skyped the family back home and everyone sent their heartiest best wishes. I felt a little sad for a few days after that, I missed my mother and Istanbul, I would have liked to go and visit but this was the time Mehmet needed me most. He was getting very stressed and tired, coming home every night, his head like a cauldron of information to be processed, understood and mentally filed away.

I did my best to sooth his headaches and rub his aching back from too many hours hunched over a desk, thank goodness for the hot strong shower in this old building, being at the top had one advantage.

Mehmet fell to his bed exhausted, I fed him and left him to rest. I spent most nights with Eda watching Turkish movies, which she downloaded from our country's movie share site. I had no idea we could do that, clever girl.

She paid Roy his monthly half and dropped him some homemade soup and grilled halloumi, he was in love with her cooking. When I popped into see Eda, there he was installing an extension socket so she could watch her movies while working in the kitchenette. I was a little taken aback, they were chatting like old friends, her English better than mine.

Hearing a familiar 'rat tat tat' on the door I went to get it. Finding Zafar there with a pot plant, he looked a little bashful when he realised Roy and I were there too, but we pulled him in and he was soon helping Roy clip the cable to the skirting board. I grinned like a lunatic at Eda, who was suddenly adjusting her hair and changing to a clean apron. *Ahh!* I clucked inside. *She likes him.* I gave her the look and she glared back, irritated at my ability to read her mind. We laughed, made some tea and the men sat at the table.

Roy was complimenting eda on her English and I saw Zafar bristle a little, jealousy perhaps?

He left shortly after and Roy went on his way, Eda handing him a Tupperware full of goodies.

'*Teşekkürler abi.*' Young Roy looked rather happy. '*Teşekkürler annecim.*' He was calling her sweet mother, it was touching.

'What! You are learning Turkish now, Roy? We better find you a wife from home, a girl who can cook.'

He lifted his head. 'I would love that, Hulya, if you know anyone who would want a scruff like me.'

'Hmm, leave it with me, son,' said Eda.

Once we were alone, we sat at the little table shelling pistachios.

'So Eda?'

'So Hulya, what?'

'Zafar?'

We both burst out laughing.

'Well, he's funny, he makes me laugh and he appreciates my cooking, maybe Hulya, maybe! It's nice to have someone to cook for and be appreciated.'

Next day we both went shopping and we popped in to the Topkapi. Zafar and the young lads were starting to prep the sauces and so I busied myself with some cleaning in the fridges. Next thing I hear raucous laughter coming from the prep room, Zafar had started the mixer for the tomato pizza sauce but forgot to secure the lid, the chopped tomatoes had flung everywhere, covering the ceiling, floors and every inch of his white chef jacket, the thick red mix dripped from his chin.

I tried not to laugh, but catching a glimpse of Mesut the young chef, doubled up shaking with hilarity set us all off, we laughed like loons and I sent all the boys out, while we sorted the mess.

When we finally got it clean, the boys were so far behind in the prep so Eda and I rolled up our sleeves and got stuck in. It was like being back home, something we would do if there was a family party or Eid, it felt so nice to be part of this, just the little niggle in the back of my mind that I was lying to Mehmet spoiled my mood sometimes.

When everything was ready, we cleared our section and cling-filmed our dishes, I got our coats and Eda moved everything to the cooler room.

We had made a big pan of a home food we call mousakka. Layers of courgette, potato, aubergine, onions, layered like lasagne with tomato sauce and béchamel, covered in a cheese that becomes a crust, baked in the oven until the vegetables are soft and juicy, everyone loves it.

'Bring it home with you tonight,' she called to Zafar as we were leaving, 'we can have it tomorrow. Mehmet will love this; Hulya has been promising her husband a big plate of mousakka for weeks now.'

Off we went home, discussing recipes all the way back.

Next day I saw Zafar. He looked a little sheepish. He said, 'I've got a confession.'

'What?' I screwed up my eyes waiting.

'You know the tray of mousakka? It's gone!'

'You ate it?'

'No, the customers did,' he was starting to laugh.

'How?'

'Well, we brought it out about 11pm to have a quick bite before the last big rush and the regulars saw it and wanted it, so we sold it. Hulya, I could have sold ten trays if we'd had it.'

'No way,' but I was impressed.

'I'm telling you, it was selling like hot cakes.'

'What cakes?'

'Never mind, can you apologise to Eda? I have sixty pounds here for her. I sold all fourteen portions and a cheeky request, could she make us another tray? Because we didn't get to have any'

He grinned like a naughty boy.

I laughed at his cheek, but another little plot started hatching and I said, 'Walk with me, Zafar, I think you should confess this face to face with my sister.'

His grin turned to concern but she was delighted to hear it was a sell-out. 'I can make as many as you like, the one you had last night was Hulya's recipe actually. Shall we come over later and cook?' Eda asked him.

Zafar's big smile answered her.

So that's what we did.

Every morning after Mehmet left for work, we would pile in Zafar's car and head to Topkapi spending the day cooking in bulk for the week. We introduced Zafar's favourite original dishes he had tried back in the early days; he was pretty negative about the chances of success.

I popped next door to the newsagent and bought stiff card and marker pens. We had our new specials menu propped up on the counter and in the window. Five of our most delicious homemade traditional dishes.

Zafar rubbed his chin as he inspected the menu.

'I tried these twenty years ago, Eda, but people didn't want anything new or unpronounceable.'

'Nonsense,' said Eda, 'I don't know anyone who can resist our Tas Kebab.'

And she was correct. We made a great big pan of slow roasted lamb, steeped in parsley and oregano, with a light garlic tomato and onion jus. It went like those hot cakes he was telling me about, I still had no idea what he meant, cakes are usually cold.

The customers were not just our Turkish neighbours, every nationality loved the dishes, it was the right time and the right place, customers' taste buds were far more advanced these days. It was a great success, we attracted people from other areas, word had spread that the best home-cooked food was at Topkapi, so we carried on cooking, Zafar carried on selling.

I was doing all the buying and accounts for the takeaway and Topkapi was starting to show a healthy profit. Zafar's business partners Hakan and Aycot appeared one day interested to know why the takings had drastically improved and he caught us up to our elbows in flour. The smell coming from the kitchen drew them in.

'Sit please,' I instructed and Eda served them a small bowl of *hun kar begendi*, which means the king's favourite, a rich lamb dish with béchamel and goat's cheese and some fresh sesame bread. Aycot stopped eating after two mouthfuls and asked,

'You girls made this?'

'Yes of course,' I rolled my eyes.

'From scratch?'

'No other way, *abi*, we don't buy in processed sauces.'

'It's amazing, it tastes like… just like home.'

'Yes!' Zafar agreed. 'It is the best I ever had. It's on our specials menu,' Zafar chuckled.

Hakan spoke with a full mouth, 'So that's why profits are up, delicious!'

The partners spoke quietly then called to Zafar.

'*Abi*, brother, we made a decision, we both are so busy with the haulage company, really we don't think we have the right to share in this success, this was always your business, we would like to hand it back to you, you obviously have found your passion again, it is the right thing that you enjoy the fruit.'

A speechless Zafar is a very rare thing, like hen's teeth, I believe the saying is here? The three men hugged and Zafar cried a few generous tears.

Everything changed that day, my funny uncle and friend was back to life.

That night Roy popped round, he said, 'Hey, you know the sign at Topkapi, it's not lit up, do you want me to have a look?'

'Would it be expensive to fix?' I asked.

'How about in exchange for a dinner, I fix the light?'

'That's a deal, Roy!' I shouted.

'I'm addicted, Hulya, I love your food, you and Eda are incredibly talented.'

It was a good deal, next day Roy fixed the illuminated sign and Topkapi's light shone bright. I was so proud of my sister and Zafar and a little bit of myself, only tarnished by the fact I couldn't share any of this positive energy with Mehmet. He was very distant these days, extremely tired. I was wrapped up in my world and I suppose I was almost glad that he fell asleep by eight at night, so I could spend more time talking food and business with Eda.

It wasn't the way I had imagined my married life in England to be, but I still thanked God every night for the good fortune and friends that surrounded me, for the food in our bellies and the roof over our heads.

I said a silent special prayer for my husband.

Topkapi was still pretty tatty, twenty years of neglect couldn't be fixed with a new light and a deep clean, but

Zafar was motivated. He was full of energy as we shopped and chatted, I noticed him call out cheery words to fellow caterers, they remembered the old Zafar when he first arrived in England, full of passion and fire in his belly, and a couple of the guys patted him and kissed his cheeks, gave him blessings, it was sweet to see. He was buying everything fresh and he was excited to find some herbs that he didn't normally bother with.

I listened to him chatting as he squeezed and sniffed the produce, 'Eda will love this, Eda will love that,' I noticed he was talking about my sister an awful lot.

Bahadir was in the market, he stopped to say hello to Zafar.

'*Salem Alikum, Nasillsin abi.*' (How are you brother? I hear you are making the home food again.)

'Yes, with my wonderful niece Hulya and her sister Eda.' He smiled a warm smile at me. We made our introductions, Bahadir looked directly into my eyes, it was like he saw deep into my soul, he had an intensity about him, slightly unnerving, but then his wide grin cancelled that out almost immediately and put me at ease again.

'Good to see that, never give up, Zafar, Aycot was raving about your new menu like he was sitting at his mother's table, I swear he cried a little.' They both roared with laughter and said something a little derogatory about Aycot – he wasn't a nice man – but then Zafar remembered the very generous thing that his partners had done for him and uttered a warm compliment about the men, which made Bahadir's thick brows rise up.

After his encounter with Bahadir, Zafar appeared a few inches taller walking around that market, or maybe he just straightened up, I don't know, but we drove back to Topkapi with a different Zafar. In the food industry and the local Turkish community, having the respect of Bahadir really meant something.

CHAPTER TWENTY-NINE

Hulya

When Zafar and I arrived back at Topkapi, Eda was already in the kitchen prep room making *pide* again. She was using one of my recipes that we used to cook at home together, minced seasoned beef and feta cheese, olives and herbs then drizzled with whipped egg yolks. Her dough had been resting and she rolled out the softest thin base for her foot-long slim pizza-like dish.

Zafar was always hungry after market.

'Can I?' he ventured.

'Go on then, you look like Oliver Twist, standing there.' Roy had given her the book to learn. 'And those boys are like Fagin's gang, watching me, waiting to steal it.' She pretended to guard her dough from the prep chefs hanging around waiting for it to rise.

I giggled thinking I wouldn't mind a big slice of that!

Zafar quickly loaded his flat steel paddle and expertly lay the *pide* in the oven, it took only four minutes to cook and rise, that was the quality of the dough, and the finest grade double zero flour with a handful of semolina flour made it so light.

The prep boys landed by his side and it took less than four minutes to disappear. The compliments rained in. Since this dish had gone on the menu, sales of heavy pizza had dropped dramatically and the locals had actually made it the bestselling item in Topkapi!

We finished another batch and left them to get on with cooking and selling. The boys were learning how to handle this lighter thin dough but they had only made heavy pizza bases before and it left them in a mess sometimes. We were patient teachers and to be honest we didn't really want to hand over all the cooking to them, it was our daily routine and it was a lot of fun in that kitchen.

Two months had flown by and I had given Zafar the figures and he sat and whistled.

'I felt how busy we have been, Hulya, but I didn't realise it would make such a difference to the profits.'

'We are used to cooking from base ingredients, it's much cheaper in the long run and we waste nothing, there is no reason it can't continue to grow.' I was very pleased to be reporting this success.

Zafar even took a long overdue wage rise, but he spent most of it on decorating the front of the shop. He bought a new shiny sign and Roy's brighter lighting track made it visible from the end of the high street, the vibe at Topkapi was lively and happy.

I noticed Zafar wasn't going out to the coffee shop after closing up, he stayed in the takeaway, doing the odd jobs that had been neglected for years, and was home and sleeping a good seven hours a night. I could see him looking less lined and the dark bags under his eyes were fading. *He's a handsome man under all that exhaustion*, I mused to myself.

Roy was a regular visitor to Topkapi, he was learning to cook with Eda one afternoon a week in return for English lessons, they had become big buddies and it felt like family, he did many odd jobs around Topkapi for a delicious feast in return and he was coming out of his shy shell.

I was teaching the young chefs how to make the special menu from scratch and they weren't quite ready to take it all on, but they could manage the prep for us, so it allowed us to do more quantity in the time we had spare, so, in addition to the brisk trade at the takeaway, I had some flyers made from the printer along the road, offering outside catering and business buffet lunch service. It proved a hit with the local offices and with the help of Mesut and his little van we delivered all over our town. We used our halal option a lot, no one else was offering this guarantee in catering in our region, which was common sense to me, it was a huge Muslim area, that money was like a bonus every week. We made efficient use of the staff and it cost us virtually nothing to run, the orders came in on the answer machine and off we went daily, servicing our local business community.

CHAPTER THIRTY

Hulya

It was Thursday and Eda was at Topkapi, I was at the market with Zafar. We had a lot to buy as the bank holiday was coming up and a big football match locally meant Topkapi was going to be hammered along with our biggest order so far, a hot and cold buffet for thirty people at the town hall, it was our full range of specials and if we got it right, they suggested it would be a monthly booking. We were 'over the moon', according to Zafar. What funny phrases he has!

So when we got to the takeaway, I naturally rolled up my sleeves and assisted Eda, barked my instructions at our young chefs and completely forgot about time.

I dispatched the lunch buffet with Mesut, Zafar and I followed in his car, off to the town hall. It was a huge hit, we got the thumbs up for the contract, we were so elated on our return from the positive feedback and compliments, telling Eda all about the event as we rolled more dough, that it was only when Roy popped his head in, on his way home to pick up a *pide* to go, that my heart sank.

'What time is it, Roy?'

'Nearly 6.30, Hulya, do you girls want a lift home?'

I flew to his van, Eda stayed to finish off, her face full of concern as she watched me run.

We drove back and I caught a glimpse of my husband's back as he climbed the steps of our mansion house.

'Oh no, Roy, I'm in trouble'!

I was covered in stains and flour from cooking, so I hung back under cover of the shrubbery until he was inside. I left my apron outside our door and crept inside. Mehmet saw me enter, so I flung myself through the studio at full speed pretending I was desperate to use the loo, once hidden in the bathroom, I quickly wiped away the flour and evidence from myself as thoroughly as possible, flushed the loo and headed back out.

When I came out, my heavily stained apron was on the kitchen table and my husband was sitting next to it.

'So Hulya, is there anything you want to tell me?'

I'm an honest person and I'm not an easy liar, I knew this wouldn't go down well and having expressly gone against his wishes and in fact his insistence that I don't work or go anywhere with Zafar, I was now a bit scared. Not knowing what else to do in this situation, I spilled the beans, as they say in the American movies.

Mehmet listened to me trying to justify my actions, but it was futile as there was no justification for lying that sounded reasonable to a son of an Imam who valued honesty above most things.

Mehmet is not a rough man or highly aggressive in any situation, he's an educated scholar, so I didn't expect him to stand up, throw the table to the floor and shout at me like I was five years old, this wasn't my Mehmet.

'What other lies do I not know about, Hulya?'

His eyes were like black daggers.

'Maybe you are seeing other men? Gambling? Drinking with Zafar? Who knows?'

His voice was getting louder, his accusations, just crazy.

'Maybe you are a prostitute in the daytime while I work, I wondered where you found the money for your home decorating, I wondered why you never answer the phone when I call you at lunchtime to hear your voice, in the ten minutes I get for a break! I wonder so many things about you, Hulya.'

My mouth opened and shut like a fish hauled to the deck. I felt the anxiety rising in my chest, this was ridiculous.

I'm a decent girl! A virgin up to our wedding night, I'm not this bitch he was portraying me to be, but every time I tried to answer him and reassure him, he just got more mad and I heard the hurt, the distrust in his voice, he was staring at me like I was a stranger.

I had never seen him so angry, it scared me to see this other personality of the man I loved, the tears burst through my lashes and I felt my control slipping away, so I ran from our tiny attic to Eda's studio, thankfully she was at home, Zafar had driven her straight away after I left with Roy and I stayed there with my sister, crying and in shock.

I didn't know the man upstairs in the attic, I knew I had betrayed his trust, of that I was guilty, but I was so lonely and my motivation was good hearted, never did I intend to hurt my husband or our marriage. It was the first time ever I had been separated and wary of my husband, I didn't know what to say or do, I knew I was guilty but he was guilty too, it was all unfair and stupid, I was conflicted and truthfully didn't want to accept the possibility that I would have to give up this new life I had carved out, I finally cried myself to sleep on my sister's bed.

Zafar went to talk with Mehmet next morning but he had gone very early to work. I was very upset, I couldn't settle anywhere knowing he was angry and our relationship in a mess. I told Zafar I wouldn't be coming again and he understood, he said he would try and take the blame off me.

This was a kind offer, but I knew Mehmet wouldn't be that easy.

I had to face this situation, this was my mess and I must try and apologise for going against him. A little voice inside me hoped I may even convince him that it was such a good thing that we were doing, but I didn't fancy the odds, because Mehmet didn't really know his uncle like I did. He hardly saw the man and to Mehmet, Zafar was a bad Muslim, a gambler, a philanderer, it would be hard to convince him that his uncle was one of the most creative, warm, funny, sweet-natured men walking on the planet, who had changed his ways and was a son any mother would be proud of.

I waited in the attic for him to come home, pacing and unsettled. I had a lovely CD playing, our traditional folk music which Mehmet used to play on his acoustic guitar when we were courting back in Istanbul.

I had a nice dinner ready and the flat was spotless, I have to admit that I had neglected things a bit. It had been a whirlwind few months with Eda and the Topkapi doing so well with our food, we got a bit carried away. I hadn't even thought about what I would do with the rolls of twenty pound notes stuffed in the tin box in my dressing table. Finally the door opened and he walked slowly inside, I went to take his jacket but he blocked me with a hand.

I stung inside, the rejection hurt me.

'Please darling, don't let's ruin our marriage, I made a mistake, I'm sorry, I got so lonely and bored.'

He fired straight back at me, clearly still boiling with anger.

'So that is what you will do every time you are lonely and bored, Hulya? Disobey me and my wishes, run around with men, working in a takeaway? What else will you do while I am killing my soul working eighty hours a week in the city for us, for our future?'

'Killing your soul? I thought you loved your job?'

'Yes Hulya, killing my soul! I had to discard everything that made me enjoy my life before, everything that nourished my spirit; I have nothing left inside me.'

He sat heavily at our little scrubbed table.

I spoke gently, 'Let me get you some chai at least.'

He nodded, a surge of relief hit me, at least he didn't tell me no.

My husband, my lovely studious, serious husband, who used to make me laugh and pick flowers on the way home to put behind my ear while he kissed my neck, had changed and I had been too busy to notice. I looked at him properly for the first time in a month.

'Tell me, my love,' my tone full of care.

He did, in detail, how every minute of every day, he hated it. How he had been shocked to the core at the blatant illegal goings on that he was supposed to be party to and sign his name to, his respected family name!

Lying daily and manipulating regulations to defraud people of money and trade, smashing the lives of decent men, he felt his soul was being wrung out, with every lie, every devious clause used to crucify hard-working people, for the benefit of insurers or corrupt agents.

It made him sick to the stomach, the bribes, the backhanders, the blind eye that he was supposed to turn in order to keep the wheel of this conglomerate spinning.

He said he would rather go home to Turkey as a failure and go and herd goats up in the mountain, than spend his life doing this work that he had trained so hard for but had disillusioned him so quickly.

'I am raised as a religious man, Hulya; I can't live my life hurting people for profit.'

He spoke to me with a kind of sorrow I had never heard before.

He told me about a case he had been working on where a group of employed crew had been severely injured due to the neglect and penny-pinching of the shipper, all seven men had lost their health and would never work again. His task, his objective, was to find ways to mitigate the liability of the shipping company, who had declared profits of more than $180 million that year. He was knowingly causing the men such stress and treating them with such disrespect and callous disregard for the hardships they and their families were going through, it was making him physically sick to do this.

But the final straw was when he was called into the head of the insurance company and given a congratulation speech on his excellent work, basically a giant pat on the back for being such a royal bastard.

'That's the moment I knew I have to stop, I'm so sorry, Hulya I can't carry on.'

I listened with deep sorrow, I had been oblivious to the pain and discontent my lovely man was enduring alone. While I enjoyed a carefree existence cooking with my sister and laughing with Zafar, he was alone with this burden, I felt like I had not been a good wife to him.

Once the gates had opened he was talking rapidly, emptying out the hurt and shame he felt.

'Darling, you saw my parents' faces on Skype when they knew I had landed the amazing job, the relief, the pride, the faces of two people who sacrificed everything for themselves to get me to this position, how can I turn around and tell them, hey, I don't want it anymore? How can I let everybody down, Hulya?'

I watched him walk slowly to the bedroom; his shoulders were lower than I remember them being on our wedding day.

He was crying, curled up in our small bed, his words thick with self-hatred, it was unbearable to watch.

'You married a young man with a good financial future, I feel I have let you down the most, I'm not the strong man I pretended to be, just leave me alone with my disgrace.'

He shouted at me to leave him alone, so I reluctantly went to Eda's studio. Zafar was there too. I told them both what had happened and Zafar shook his head.

'Damn! He has the weight of the family on him; it's a gilded cage, nothing is free in this life, he's trapped by his own sense of duty, I know how he feels, you know how my mother feeds off the imaginary success she believes I have?'

We both nodded.

'How can you break the illusion? It gets worse the longer it goes on, trust me, my mother thinks I own half of London, she would die of heart failure if she saw how I live, I should have admitted to my mum years ago that I was a loser, too late now, it would kill her.'

We were all silent in our thoughts.

Eda spoke first.

'Zafar, you are not a loser! Why don't we open our own restaurant, extend Topkapi, if we can get next door to sell us the lease. When we make a big success it will be easier for him to tell his family that he switched to restaurateur?'

Zafar laughed at the idea.

'They will think he has lost his mind, all that study all those exams, he won't go for it, it's not that easy, Eda, thanks for the confidence, but it's a massive leap from a few specials on a takeaway menu to a restaurant that could pay Mehmet the sort of salary he can earn as a lawyer.'

Eda didn't agree, but kept her mouth shut, until I spoke up.

'He's so down, so lost, full of self-hatred, Zafar, he just might have to, because I'm sure he is never going back, and we don't have too many options.'

Zafar rubbed his bristles, 'You do know I've tried and failed, more than once?'

We nodded, held our breath, I could feel the energy in the room, we all wanted to try.

'We will need some investors.' Zafar reddened. 'I'm embarrassed to say I don't have much, I had some debts to pay, what I made the last few months has gone.'

Eda said, 'I do, I have an inheritance that is doing nothing at all. My son's money is in trust and the rest is mine to do with as I please.'

'I can't take your money, Eda, it's not right.'

She sat back and looked him in the eye.

'You aren't taking it Zafar, I'm going to be your new business partner, along with Hulya and Mehmet, I can get my business visa straightaway, it's a logical solution. I love London, I want to stay, I realise how lonely I was back home and I want to be near Hulya.'

So the night was spent discussing food menus and ideas, and I felt a little guilty for being happy and excited when I knew my husband was feeling so desolate above.

'We have to make this work though, if this fails and we have to tell the family we lost everything, I don't know if Mehmet could take that.' I felt a burn of fear as I spoke. 'He's already so beaten down, he's talking about herding goats in the mountain for God's sake!'

Eda hugged me. 'Don't worry, Hulya, it will work, with our food, Zafar's experience and connections and a bit of good luck, I'm sure we can make this a success, we must try!'

So it began.

The next day Zafar called around his cronies. No one wanted to invest, he had a long-standing reputation as a heavy gambler and that mud sticks for an awfully long time. It felt uncomfortable for Zafar to use Eda's money even if she was a partner. He had actually wanted to ask her if she would go out with him on a date to the pictures one evening. Now he decided it must go on the back burner; it's not good idea to mix love and business, and it was definitely feeling like love was creeping into his old heart. He hadn't felt that in a long time.

CHAPTER THIRTY-ONE

Hulya

Zafar had everything to lose now. This was the last shot at making Topkapi a success, if this failed, there wouldn't be any more heart left to crush.

His mobile rang; an unknown number and he tentatively answered it, an old habit in case it was a debt collector.

But to his shock it was Bahadir's deep voice on the line.

'*Merhaba abi*, I heard you were looking for investors.'

'Yes I am.' Zafar's heart was in his mouth.

'Are you planning to do our traditional food? Give me some competition, eh?'

Zafar coughed to ease the lump lodged in his throat, a wave of bravery coursed through him.

'Yes, that's the plan, no more shit takeaway, we want to do everything authentic, home-cooked recipes the old way!'

'I'm interested, Zafar, but I won't be involved if Hakan and Aycot are involved, you know we have bad blood.'

'Didn't you hear, they passed it back to me, the whole takeaway? Unbelievable.'

There was a silence, 'That's surprised me, Zafar, they must have found their conscience at last. You have two excellent chefs with you, two home girls, will they stay?'

'Yes, Eda and Hulya are sisters, they will be partners, they are magnificent, everything done the old way, properly.' There was a pride in his words.

Bahadir was a straight talker. 'Your new menu, everyone is talking about it, I even had customers in my restaurant telling me about your *burek*, I had to agree with them. I remember your food from the early days, well done, Zafar. Let's have coffee and a bite to eat, let's see what these girls can do and what we can do.'

The surge of adrenaline hit Zafar, this was going to happen! With the backing of Bahadir he wouldn't rely so heavily on Eda.

'Thank you, Bahadir, you won't regret this.'

'*Mashalla*.' He hung up.

When the phone went dead, Zafar sat in his car and cried for five minutes. He shed the tears he hadn't dared let out for many years. Someone believed in him again, more than that, he believed in himself again.

He had a shot to create his beautiful food in a beautiful place with friends that were as passionate and skilled as he ever was, maybe finally he could invite his mother to sit at a table in his restaurant and let her see he was a success.

He pulled himself together and ran up the steps to tell Eda all about the phone call. She went to hug him and they awkwardly missed and ended up cheek to cheek, which turned into a gentle kiss, which became a deeply sensual introduction to each other's beating hearts. Both had been alone for a long time and this feeling was special. They were flustered when the knock at the door broke the spell and I frantically scrabbled into the studio.

'Please come and talk to Mehmet, he won't get out of bed, he says his legs won't move, please come, hurry.' I was frantic.

We all dashed upstairs and crowded around Mehmet in the bed, who was curled in a foetal position.

Zafar spoke first, 'Brother, what is it?'

'I can't move my legs, Zafar, my head has been splitting with pain all night and this morning I woke with no feeling from my waist.'

I called 999 and we carried him to the sofa, he was in severe pain. Thankfully it was only minutes until the flashing lights were outside, they helped me get him down the four flights of stairs and I jumped into the back holding my husband's hands, with Zafar and Eda following behind in the car.

It was two hours later, when he reappeared in a wheelchair and to everyone's relief, slowly but firmly stepped out of the chair and walked gently out of the hospital.

'Severe stress reaction, they have given me some sedatives to get proper rest, they said if I hadn't had that seizure I may not have noticed the stroke that was on its way.'

He let me help him in to the car; he kissed my hands and talked to the floor.

'The decision is made, Hulya, will you forgive me? I'm not going back to that job, you married a loser, I will understand if you can't love me.'

I wrapped my arms around him and kissed his sad face.

'You fool, Mehmet, I love you with every inch of my being, I could never leave you and never love anyone else, I don't care one bit about maritime law, I only about you and me. And anyway, we need you at the restaurant!'

I gave him a massive cheeky grin and a wink.

'What restaurant? What are you up to now, wife?'

'I'll tell you all about it when we get home. But bed rest for you, nothing but rest and being served by your loving wife.'

'Ah, Hulya, how did I get so lucky, to have a love like you?'

I smiled at him, touched his chin and whispered in his ear. 'Remember that thought when we are knee-deep in customers and screaming chefs, it's going to be amazing darling, something we can be proud of together.'

Eda held Zafar's hand as he drove us home. I was so busy looking at my husband I didn't even notice. But inside, I felt the seed of a new chapter in our lives and it felt scary but so exciting. Our own restaurant, what could go wrong?

CHAPTER THIRTY-TWO

Sherrie & Angie

Angie

Here we were mid-August, it was hot, the weight always fell off naturally in this month, so it made things easier. Sherrie was living with us for now and she had followed every regime to the letter. My God, the girl had a stamina that most boys would envy, she said it was down to the farm labouring, she had worked from eight years old. Mommy didn't need to put her on a hard diet because the weight fell off her too quickly, her metabolism was fierce, she actually had to have some sugar and carbs, no one would believe a Prada model could eat cake, sweet Jesus.

I was ready as I could be, I never really averted from my regime, I found it a lot easier to stay on it, no yo-yoing or bingeing for me, which just aged you.

We were arranging the stylists and Tina, the event coordinator for Texas, advised me that a different stylist team were booked for Texas, meaning my tiny curly Giselle wouldn't be with me.

This was a blow, it's so stressful getting every look perfect in a short time, I didn't want to trust anyone else. I asked if I could employ my own, she said yes, there would be a small amount of paperwork needed but no problem.

So Sherrie called her and asked if she and Misty could come to Texas, after a few calls to and fro, it was a yes, and even Benjamin had arranged a week off work. He would drive the girls over and act as security and assistant. I saw Sherrie blush at this news. Hmm she liked him more than she was letting on.

So it was all arranged, Benjamin would hire a motorhome, pick us all up from New Mexico, and drive us over to Texas, this way we could keep our costumes and kit with us. It was a great idea, and we could stay with Sylvia a few days before we set off.

Mommy booked us flights to Santa Fe for the last day of August and Sylvia was so excited to have us, she had missed her Sherrie a lot. The last few days were frantic, getting outfits packed up and ready, all my ballet gear was wrapped in clear paper and folded like origami.

We were ready and so we had a day at the mall. Sherrie bought several dresses and shoes, she hadn't got used to the fact she was about to be paid a huge sum of money from Pamela, she still shopped like a bargain hunter but we were identical sizes so we could swap and mix our clothing. I loved having a sis, I saw Mommy a little pushed out at times and I did try to include her, but at the mall we were hounded by guys and it was awkward with Mom in tow. I wished Sylvia was here, we made a fantastic four.

Arriving at Santa Fe was quite an experience, I am totally used to being stared at and complimented, but now it was the two of us, even I felt a little cringey at the awestruck, love-struck and plain gobsmacked men that flocked and grovelled at our feet. Ridiculous is the word I'm searching for. Rosie ushered us along as best she could, but men just brazenly handed us cards, asked us out, invited us everywhere basically, private villas in Italy, superyachts in Cannes, penthouses in New York, we had invites everywhere.

Rosie had no chance of keeping them at bay.

So the arrival at Sylvia's Moorish mansion was a total relief. It was wonderful to see her again, she and Rosie picked up where they left off and Sylvia presented her with a gorgeous aqua and gold kaftan. They squealed like girls and we had a fun girly night.

The next day Benjamin, Misty and Giselle arrived. They stayed a night to rest, Benjamin's back was like a rod after that massive drive. Next day we had a good lunch, packed up and set off, Texas here we come. We sang and played cards, Giselle shared the driving with Ben so he could join in as well. We were like a travelling family unit. About eight hours later after a few pit stops, we arrived at the Chateau Lulu-Mar in Austin. It was an amazing venue, built like a French chateau, with enormous sandstone turrets flanking the main stately building, giving it a fairy-tale feel.

Giselle whistled like a cowboy. 'Geeeez Louise, what a place!'

Stewards directed us and we were soon ensconced in our suites. I couldn't wait to go and look around this enchanting place, so we dumped our bags and Misty kindly offered to stay with Sylvia and Rosie to unpack and hang it all up.

The elevated staging for the competition had been built in front of the stunning lake, the backstage cleverly located at the rear. A level down from the stage a hydraulic platform elevated the contestants up to the staging as if floating, while illuminated fountains sprayed undulating flumes high in the air behind them. It was a spectacular backdrop.

Such a grand event attracted the great and the good, the venue alone ensured the wealthiest and the most influential guests would happily attend. Many of the movers and shakers of the modelling world, TV celebrities, pop stars and paparazzi would be here tomorrow, along with the business elite of Texas, which I hoped included some billionaires.

Even Pamela was flying in for the event. Now I was her minion, if I won the final, she could charge even more for me. Ruthless industry this, but once you were in it, very hard to come out. Where else can you earn thousands of dollars for wearing someone's dress in a magazine?

We had iced tea at the pool bar and I would have loved to go for a dip. Giselle read my mind.

'Don't you dare get that hair in the pool.'

I was way too professional to risk it, any chemical in that water could wreak havoc with my hair, eyes and skin and it was not worth it.

I had to go backstage to register my arrival and they would send for my costumes around 8am when we would do a full dress rehearsal. We all gathered in the terrace café and ate a light easy supper and made reservations for the seven of us in the formal restaurant for the following night.

So an early night for me, I wouldn't alter my pre-competition routine for anything, the stakes were too high at this stage. Mommy came up with me, she liked to give me a pep talk before events, it was our own ritual, it sent me off in an easy slumber. I suppose she had been practising that technique since I was a tiny baby, she had it to a fine art.

CHAPTER THIRTY-THREE

Sherrie & Angie

Sherrie

I quickly took my seat next to Sylvia and Rosie, having been backstage helping Giselle and Misty with Angie's gown and hair, just as Brett appeared on stage to introduce the twenty finalists from throughout the United States. 'Representing west-coast America,' he called his girls, leaving Angela to the last, a flicker in his cheek gave away his feelings for the beauty in cream satin. She shone as always.

Next, a very handsome man called Arron introduced his ladies from north America. There was the most beautiful caramel-skinned, auburn-haired, princess-like girl called Cara. She hardly looked real, nature had given her a full deck of aces; her green eyes glittering in the lights with high cheekbones and a full Cupid's bow slick with a hint of lip gloss made her an absolute goddess. I worried a bit.

Two more hosts introduced their lovelies and again another girl stood out, from the southern states, Christie. The audience applauded, it was home ground of course, she had that mix of blonde and brunette, like elves had found every shade of gold, blonde and rich hazelnut and painted each strand of hair in a medley of hues that culminated in a moving artwork. Goddamn, it was natural. She was brown-eyed and sultry, fuller in the figure than Angie and Cara, but it just made her look like a woman next to girls.

I wasn't sure if this would go against her or for her, but clearly they loved her, she was a finalist. Sylvia shot me a look, I understood it. We didn't say anything as Rosie was staring at the line-up like a hunter. There was a distraction in the elevated VIP section and I turned back to take a look. A very elderly man in a cream linen suit and a matching Stetson was being assisted to his booth. His assistants, despite being well dressed, looked like nurses, the way they anticipated his movements gave it away.

I didn't want to stare, the gentleman was clearly frail and not well. I wondered if maybe he had a daughter in the event, perhaps the sultry gorgeous Christie was his daughter or granddaughter, it was hard to put an age on him from a distance.

Sylvia went to the ladies' room and she was gone a while. It was the first break for the girls to change into bikinis, so Rosie and I went backstage. Still no sign of Sylvia, I thought I caught a glimpse of her up in the VIP booth, but couldn't hang around to see her and she was back in her seat when we plonked back down with just twenty seconds to spare. The gliding bikini-clad sirens cheerily waved and smiled as they walked in a snake-like pattern around the stage. The gorgeous Arron had the job of calling out their stats, home towns and their unique skills, which we would see next.

I could see why Angie didn't really feel the love for this event, it was a touch cheesy and sexist actually. Knowing Angie and how smart and talented she actually was, it did seem a bit fake that external beauty was so all-important. Granted, modelling may be vain, blunt and capitalistic, but it didn't patronise anyone.

The moment had come for Angie's solo. We were all holding our breaths. The spotlight touched Angie's ballet pumps, the light shaft opened up and illuminated her in a perfect oval, she was *en pointe*, her head at a right angle to her body, her arms arched high above, she was regal, every inch a prima ballerina.

As the fountains in the backdrop sprayed the golden soft twinkle lights flumes high in the air, she pirouetted and began her magnificent dance. The audio quality here made California's sound system feel like a junior school disco, this was truly heraldic. I couldn't take my eyes off her and she spun and leapt in time with the rhythm of the music and light show.

Gasps and muted cheers were emitting from the audience. It was as if she might just fly away into the twinkling fountains, I had never seen anything like this in my life.

As she finished her performance with a dramatic high spinning pirouette, she crouched into the smallest ball with her long slender arms stretched out in a low prayer pose, as the light cut to black.

The whole audience was up on their feet. 'Bravo, bravo!' The calls were loud and sincere.

I hugged Rosie and Sylvia and discreetly excused myself and made my way backstage. I had to go the long way around the seating to not disturb anyone. I was acutely aware of the elderly man in the VIP section watching me, he never took his eyes from me.

The beautiful, luscious Christie did an amazing job of singing Whitney Houston's 'I Will Always Love You', it brought tears, the girl was super talented, but I still didn't feel anyone had come close to Angie's performance.

Cara, too, had bewitched the audience with her exquisite mandolin playing, she was at one with the instrument, the most endearing plucking of those strings in her tiny hands moved us to tears again. She should have been the clear winner with that talent, it was an eye-opener to see the level rise so high. I thought back to the cheerleading girls at Santa Fe, they were worlds apart.

Back in my seat for the interviews, I turned back to see if that man was looking but he had gone. I didn't give it much more thought, but Sylvia turned to look in that direction just after me.

I'd bumped into Brett in the backstage lounge, he was watching the screen and sulking a bit, he wasn't the main host and Arron had rather stolen his shine.

Angie had a beautiful tailored suit and matching pumps, she reminded me of Lady Diana from England, elegant, feminine and fashionable. I crossed my fingers because honestly I didn't know if she would get first place. She would qualify for sure, even third place gave her enough points and automatic entrance into the Miss America contest.

I spotted Benjamin sneaking his way to the rear of the audience. He looked a bit of a lost soul, his duty had been watching Angie's costumes for any sabotage attempts, now she was in her last outfit he was relieved of his duty. So I joined him and we found a discreet spot at the back to watch the interview round.

I felt the butterflies flutter when he brushed against me to let a lady pass. He blushed. It was a seriously awkward moment but when he smiled at me with that sweet mouth, it wasn't butterflies I felt, it was something entirely different, almost a physical pain, starting in my tummy but ending up further south.

I stared back to the stage, scared he could read my mind, I lost myself for a moment, the heat and tingles getting the better of me. I needed to talk to Aunt Sylvia about this, it was freaky.

We watched Angie be interviewed by Arron. Of course he wasn't secretly madly in love with her like Brett, so she didn't get such an easy time but she held up well. I noticed a lot of warm smiles in the audience so we headed backstage to prepare her back in her gown and sash for the results. Off the girls went to the platform, we stayed in the green room to watch it on the big screen. I'm sure

I was pissing everyone off getting up and down out of my seat.

Arron led the ladies through to the front of the stage, criss-crossing and ending up in their regional groups. Brett was ready to receive his five lovelies.

The judges passed the golden envelope and Arron read the results. I noticed Brett flash a glance at Angie, she ignored him completely.

'Fifth runner-up, Marianne Mountford from Nebraska.' Huge applause from her crowd. 'Fourth place, from Illinois, Chicago: Deirdre Callahan.' A large round of applause for Deirdre, she had done a fabulous acrobatics display, fit for Cirque du Soleil if she ever binned beauty pageants.

'Third place, Miss Cara Del Vigne from New Jersey, this entitles Cara automatic entrance into Miss America 1999, let's hear it for Cara!' The audience obliged, there was a change in light setting and the audience stilled once more. Arron proceeded.

'In second place, with automatic entrance to Miss America 1999, Miss Christie Salverson for our home ground, Austin, Texas.' There was a massive applause and Christie was beaming. She didn't show any remorse for being second, she had done enough to get through.

Arron had to quiet the crowd, who were calling out their favourites, many shouting, 'Angela, Angela.' They finally settled and a small drum roll ensued.

'Ladies and gentlemen, I would like to present to you, the winner of the Miss American Beauty contest 1998, is...'

I felt a lump stick in my throat. Benjamin grabbed my hand.

'… Miss Angela Devereaux from Sausalito, California!'

We cheered and Benjamin grabbed me, hugging me tight. The next thing I knew, I was kissing his Elvis lips, the tingles and heat that hit me were overwhelming and I pulled away, rushing off to find Sylvia and Rosie in their seats. Rosie looked like she might expire, she was feeling faint, so I rushed off to the bar to get a drink of water for her. There were no bar staff attending, it took me ages to get a porter, by the time I got back the speeches had finished and the stage had cleared, so I headed to the backstage where I found Rosie was already in a heap by her daughter crying silently.

I rushed to Angie. 'What happened?' She was tight-lipped and quiet.

Rosie blurted out, 'She's not going to compete in Miss America.'

'Oh.' I was a bit taken aback, but I could understand why. We had a fantastic trip lined up, six months' travelling and modelling in Europe, we had a huge fee that we never dreamed of. I was selfishly a little bit glad that she would be allowed to live her life not Rosie's dream but of course I kept my mouth shut, just squeezed Angie's hand.

'Rosie, how about we go get a stiff drink?' Sylvia appeared behind her new friend. 'I got a few things to talk to you about, leave the girls to relax.'

Rosie was compliant, glad of Sylvia's take-charge attitude. They went to the lobby and ordered dirty martinis with extra olives. Despite her upset there was a tiny hint of a smile on Rosie's face. As two craggy Texan gents tipped their hats to them as they passed by, Sylvia blushed a little; she never could resist a cowboy.

'I don't fancy yours,' she said chuckling, they burst out laughing like the two young girls they still were, on the inside.

Benjamin busied himself helping Giselle and Misty, packing up all the costumes and beauty kit, still trying to decide whether he just dreamed he had kissed me.

Finally alone, I hugged my sis.

'It's your life, Angie, you got to live it your way and if it means anything to you, I can see you are doing all this for Rosie and that three-step plan, I don't buy it. Always sounded like rodeo bravado to me!'

'Where do you get these wise proverbs, Sherrie?' Angie managed a small smile.

'It's Prada's fault, that's what really changed everything. I always wanted to be a ballerina or a fashion model, I'm too tall for professional ballet and modelling is a life that couldn't really include Mom, you know. I felt like I owed her, she gave her whole life to me, after Daddy left, I was her world, she was a beauty queen and it was her dream.'

'Yes I know, it shows big time, I was actually a little jealous of how close you guys are, my Ma just basically forgot I existed when her new boyfriend arrived and the twins, I was a bad memory for her.'

'I didn't know that, Sherrie, sorry, I didn't want to pry, but I wondered who Sylvia was.'

'You know, Angie, I don't even know myself.' And I told her about being taken from hospital to the bus stop by my granddaddy and basically shipped off like a parcel to this lady I was told to call 'Aunty'.

'Don't get me wrong, Sylvia has been more of a mother to me in this six months than I had in eighteen years. I love her like a mom, she saved my life in every way. Since I got off the bus in Santa Fe it has felt like a huge jigsaw just falling together. I can't yet see the full picture, but it's a hell of a lot better than the lonely existence I had in Limestone Creek.'

'Do you know who your daddy is, Sherrie?'

'Nope, not even a photo, Granddaddy says he was a very tall, good-lookin' fella, with a strong back and an easy smile, that is all I have.'

'I don't know much more, I have a photo in my purse, I stole it from Mommy's tin, I always think it brings me luck, stupid really, hankering after a father that didn't stick around, but you know...'

'Yep, I do know.'

'Hey, maybe we are related, ha ha, he could be both our daddies, this mysterious tall cowboy.'

'My daddy is very tall too! I'll go get the picture, hang on...'

But Benjamin had already packed up the purse and it was loaded in the motorhome, so I never got a chance to look at it. After a long session of interviews and photo shoots, Angie was finally released, so we all went for a swim in the massive lake. It was glorious. Ben, Giselle, Misty and some other contestants joined us, all of us relieved to let some steam out, it was a high-pressured event.

A figure appeared in red trunks. It was Brett and he tentatively joined us.

'Where's your harem?' called out Giselle.

He just ignored her and swam across to Angie, so we swam nearer, none of us sure of this jerk.

He got the message and said, 'Look I'm sorry about what happened at California. I was stressed out and drunk, my show got cancelled and they called me to tell me just before the heat, I wasn't thinking straight. Sorry guys, sorry Angie.'

'It's OK,' we all murmured forgiveness and a few commiserations about the soap. Soon the splashing and fooling about started up, this time I pulled Angie's arm to get her in the water.

'You can get the hair wet now, sis.' She shrieked and dived down into the clear waters, emerging slick as a seal with her blonde goddess hair flat to her head.

'Oh that feels so freakin gooood!!'

Suddenly we heard a familiar voice.

'Careful of your hair, Angela, Golden Goddess are paying good money for that shine!'

It was Pamela yelling from the bank.

Giselle yelled, 'No problem, ma'am, I'll have that shining like they never saw before.'

Angie dived down again, blocking out Pamela's squawking.

Dinner reservations were at 8pm and so we retreated for a little rest. We all agreed to dress up tonight, just to compete with Sylvia and Rosie in their kaftans!

We arrived in the beautiful formal restaurant, our table was on the terrace, with a view of the gorgeous twinkling lush gardens, we had even invited Brett along, we had a spare seat, so the eight of us discussed the world of pageanting, the good and the bad. Everyone was fun and sparkling in this company of new friends, only one person was subdued: Rosie. She joined in sporadically but was in her own world of thoughts for most of the night, I assumed she was upset about Angie's decision.

So I didn't push, just complimented her on the beautiful kaftan and praised all her efforts and support with my fitness regime, she was gracious but looked so lost, I was concerned.

After we toasted Angie for her win, Ben, Brett, Giselle and Misty got up to leave.

'Oh, where are you guys off to?'

After a quick flash glance at Sylvia, which I didn't understand at all, he made some waffled excuse about signing off some papers for release from the event.

'Shall we meet in the lobby later then?'

They agreed but it seemed a bit wishy washy.

Sylvia caught my hand. It was just the four of us now, and Angie looked cautious.

'What's going on?'

Rosie sat forward, she joined the living world again.

'Girls, Sylvia has something to tell you, I know, she told me this afternoon, please hear her out.'

I was feeling very scared now. I hadn't seen Sylvia in this solemn mood ever and I held Angie's hand.

'Girls, I want to talk to you about your daddy.'

We looked at each other and Angie said, 'Told ya.'

'Our daddy? You mean we have the same daddy?'

'Yes, Sherrie, you do indeed. Teddy Rae Boutine.'

Tears stung my eyes but I fought them back, I wanted to hear every word, Angie slid close up to me and we held on tight.

'Sherrie sweetheart, please forgive me, I haven't been entirely honest with you. I'm your stepmom,' said Sylvia.

I was dumbstruck.

'Go on,' urged Angie.

'Your daddy is my husband, I'd like to tell you about him if that's OK?'

We nodded like kittens.

Sylvia took a large sip of wine, and Rosie smiled a gentle smile at Angela. 'It's OK,' she mouthed, 'don't be upset.'

'Your daddy, Teddy Rae, was a rancher. He travelled around the States in a nomadic fashion in his youth. Sherrie, when he met your mother, they were not much more than kids themselves. He had been dating Rosie back in California for a few months prior and panicked when he heard about the pregnancy. He ran, he's not proud of that, he's very sorry for that.'

Rosie spoke, 'Try and forgive him, honey, we were crazy kids, no money, no real jobs, he went off working but came home a few months later. By that time, Sherrie, you had been conceived, I didn't even know that until this afternoon, but in my heart, when I saw you in California, a little voice told me you were his child. I mean, look at the two of you, how could you not be!'

Sylvia continued. 'Sherrie, your daddy didn't even know you existed until years later, your granddaddy tracked him down when you were about thirteen years old. He was here in Texas, he's an oil man. We married in 1975 and in the oil strike of 1977, your daddy was supervising a massive drilling operation. There was a terrible accident and Teddy nearly died, his injuries were so severe that he spent a full year in hospital, one operation after another, to save his charred lungs and burned body. I tried to nurse him and be there for him, it was horrendous, he needed around the clock specialist nursing. When he regained some health and was not critical, he had a special nursing wing added to our home. We tried so hard to carry on our marriage. I love Teddy still, but he made a decision to be alone with his condition. We bought that lovely home in Santa Fe and I moved there in 1981. I'm his wife, we are best friends and I love him, he has given me a wonderful life, he asked me one thing, to find a way to bring you girls together. Your daddy won't have much longer left, his lungs have perished now and this was his only wish.'

Rosie had tears in her eyes.

'Angela, I loved your father, I forgave him a long time ago, he tried so hard to be a family man and stay with us, but he was from a long line of ranchers and oil men, it's in his blood to chase danger and travel. I couldn't hold him and we were both unhappy trying to make it work. When he had his first oil strike in the seventies, I received the deeds to our rented home and a handsome cheque, I never had to go out and work to make ends meet, your daddy made sure that I could be mommy and daddy to you, which is why I was never bitter toward him.'

Sylvia spoke, 'I believe he sent your granddaddy a generous sum when he discovered you, Sherrie, but your granddaddy sent the money back, he asked one thing, that if he needed to send you to him, he would make that happen, this was agreed and Sherrie, I've been waiting four years to meet you, darling.'

Everyone sat back, the waiter could decide whether to approach or keep back, trying to read the mood on this table needed an FBI profiler on staff.

I turned to Angie and hugged her.

'I'm so happy we are truly sisters,' the tears couldn't be held back now, 'I don't feel like an orphan any more.'

That was it, all four of us were crying now and Rosie rushed around to hug the both of us, I felt accepted and loved.

Sylvia summoned the waiter and ordered more martinis.

Rosie posed the question gently, 'Would you like to meet him?'

I looked at my sister, I desperately wanted her to say yes, to feel the same need as me.

'Of course I do,' she said through streaming tears.

Teddy Rae sat in a reclining chair in the best suite in the chateau Lulu-mar, he had an oxygen tank just behind him, ready should he need it, he had waited nervously all evening for the call.

Finally he was going to meet his girls. He had seen his little Angie a little over fifteen years ago but had never met me, now he would.

There had been bouts of tears and emotion during the last few hours, the nurses were concerned about this meeting and a light sedative had been administered, they had insisted he rest after his visit to the pageant, it had exhausted him.

Rosie had visited him earlier that evening and they had made their peace, in fact they had nothing but admiration for each other, Teddy thanked her twenty times or more for the wonderful mother she had been to his child, and she thanked him for all his help, she told him this had been the most wonderful gift she could have ever wanted, a darling child from the man she had loved. There was no bitter feelings at all.

The knock on the door quickened his heart rate. As he blinked back the tears, there in front of him were his two perfect girls. We were crying and holding hands, this unity was what he had wanted to see, we were sisters, we had found each other.

He beckoned us to the ottoman next to him. And Sylvia made him as comfortable as she could, bolstering his pillow so he could see us better.

'Hello Sherrie, hello Angela.'

We both shyly said 'Hi.' I held his hand, I couldn't not. I wanted to feel the touch of my father, and Angie followed and held his other.

'Thank you so much for seeing me. I want to tell you both how proud I am of you. I want to apologise for not being there for you growing up. Sherrie, I'm so sorry I didn't know, I heard you had a hard time, I'm so sorry, if I can make it up to you in any way, I will.'

'Daddy, you have already, it's OK.'

He looked humbled by her kindness, she was more than entitled to give him a roasting, but she was so sweet-natured.

'You gave me Angie, my sister, Sylvia, a mother, she's more loving than my own, Rosie is a second mother, I have a family, I am so happy and now I have you as well. It's all good, I'm so very happy.'

Teddy shed large, even tears, Sylvia wiped them away and she kissed his head.

'Angela, it was the hardest thing to walk away from you. Can you forgive me?'

Angela was crying openly, it took a few moments, not because she didn't want to say yes, just her throat was so constricted with emotion, so she knelt down and hugged his torso, like a child would do, like she did when she was his tiny little girl, eventually through the sobs she said, 'Yes, Daddy, of course, I never forgot you.'

Rosie came with some tea and we all sat together, Sylvia held the china cup to her husband's mouth, they shared a loving look and a little in-joke.

'I told ya, Teddy, one day we all be sitting around taking tea together.'

He laughed a weak but warm rumbling laugh and let out a weary long-held sigh.

'My Sylvia, my best friend in the world. I love you with all my heart. You have been such a good wife to me!'

CHAPTER THIRTY-FOUR

Helena

Israel sat with me in our garden, it was mid-June and a lovely warm night, I felt so protective toward this young man, like the son I never had, maybe I was the mother he never had. Whatever had drawn us together, it was a blessing for both of us, he hadn't told me about his terrible start in life, his revelation at the group meeting left me speechless.

'Israel, can I ask you about your parents?'

'Yes of course.'

'Was your mum on heroin when you were growing up?'

'No, Helena, she was still taking it when she was pregnant, my dad was a serious smack head apparently and he led her into that life, he died of an overdose before I was born and my mother was taken into hospital until I was born. Unfortunately it was too late, her usage had affected me and I was born craving, addicted!

'I stayed in the hospital for my first three months under court order and mum was sent to rehab, she had to be clean to be allowed to have me back. Granddad acted as guardian for the court and did everything for her, he was such a sweet man, the stress affected him badly.

'My mother wanted me back, she quit all drugs and found God, she found natural remedies to clean the system, using herbs and old methods of cooking, she was convinced that feeding me in this natural way would keep me clean from cravings and addiction. It was only as an older man that I realised this was what drove her mad, the guilt of what she and Dad had inflicted on me as an innocent, it drove her to obsession about keeping me clean and healthy, but of course I couldn't understand that, I didn't even know about my dad.

'I didn't think much about the diet I was raised on, or how I changed after she died. Once I was alone I started to be drawn to the negative, attracted to the dangerous clubs, dodgy people and inevitably, drugs.

'It wasn't until I began cooking in Australia, talking to chefs with real knowledge about food, that I understood there is a direct correlation to what you eat and how in control of yourself you are. If you have this chat with the man on the street you will be called a loony, but in Thailand I spent time in monasteries, tending the land and living amongst very spiritual, clean people. They are vegan in the main, but more than that, they grow special herbs, they use them in everything from prayer to cooking, they make tea with them and even sprinkle them on the land for good luck, it's no coincidence that my mother grew many of these obscure herbs in Granddad's garden. She was a true spiritual healer, she loved me so much she wanted to take no risk that I would succumb to the drug addiction I was born with.'

I listened intently, and cast my mind back to the lamb, with all those herbs.

'Did you use them with the lamb, Israel?'

'Yes, Helena, I did. I couldn't get all of the ones she used, you can't buy them here, just seeds to grow for yourself, but we didn't have time for that. When I saw you at Gerry's, I knew you were almost crossing the point of no return, I had to try, you were my guinea pig, I'm sorry. That's why you were so sick, the missing herbs would have countered the voracity of the vomiting. I couldn't find any substitute, but Helena forgive me because you are rid of your addiction.'

'This is incredible, Israel. Do you realise what you are sitting on, what your mother knew?'

'I do now. She was a great healer, she was out of her mind with worry, when I turned my back on her and started living like my friends, I suppose she saw my dad in me, it was too much for her and poor Granddad. I have evidence now that this natural medicine can work for addiction. Yes, it's crude and risky but we know heroin kills you fairly quickly and so it's got to be worth a try for many people. We are lucky we got rehab, but many won't go or don't get a chance.'

He was right, there isn't a long life for an addict and anything is worth a try. Earlier that week, I had a letter from my boss, regretfully letting me go as my work had been unsatisfactory for a long time. I had to agree with him wholeheartedly, to be honest I was amazed he had waited so long, so I accepted a month's salary and a dismissal.

'Israel, we could start our own rehab centre. I can't think of anything better to do with the inheritance from Daniel.'

'Helena, the government won't let us, not without years of trials and testing.'

'But Izzy, we are not prescribing any medicine. Just natural herbs, the residents can work in the gardens growing them and live in with us as guests, a private rehab clinic, no fees, just donations from the wealthier clients and free for those who can't afford it. Sell this place and buy a remote farm somewhere.'

Israel smiled. 'I know they grow well in the Dartmoor earth, my mother's crops were abundant.'

Yes, yes, then a cloud formed in my head. That would mean I couldn't visit Daniel as often.

'I don't know if I can leave him.'

It was hard for Israel not to state the obvious, that Daniel wouldn't even notice, but it was never about Daniel, it was me that had to be ready to let go.

'Of course, hun, I understand, we could find some land around here I'm sure, doesn't have to be Dartmoor.'

But it kind of did, it was a legacy to Veronica Worthington and a great part of the healing process for Israel, there were practical reasons too, the abundant farmland in that region, we needed lots of private space for addicts to recover.

We knew those herbs grow well in that particular region, in all honesty what was there left in this Lancashire town for me anyway? No job, no family, few friends, whom I didn't even know well anymore, and Daniel.'

I mused out loud, with a sidelong look at Izzy, 'The Veronica Worthington Healing Centre, Dartmoor.'

Israel leapt over to my side of the sofa and hugged me so hard.

'I know it's the right thing to do, Izzy, like going for breakfast with you that morning, it feels just right.'

The house sold very quickly, with the lovely abundant garden that we created it was a wonderful family home, these generous rooms should be filled with happy children roaring around, pet dogs and hamsters, PE kits scattering the hallway. This house needed a new start too.

We found a huge rambling farm with twelve hectares, outbuildings, barns and the most handsome farmhouse, with eleven large bedrooms. It was perfect, with unspoiled views for miles, the ideal retreat.

As we packed up our final bits and pieces, we drove to the hospital. Katie and Nathan met us there and we went in to say goodbye to Daniel. The blip-blip-blip greeted me as I approached his still body, but it somehow didn't feel so oppressive. To my surprise there was a lovely bouquet of flowers for me and the children hugged me warmly. I kissed Daniel on the cheek, brushed his hair with my hand and said, 'See you soon.'

However long 'soon' was, I didn't really know. Katie held my hand and spoke with gentle kindness.

'Helena, thank you for being by his side all these years, you have done everything possible for Daddy, it's way past time that you had your life too, you can't wait any longer to start living again, you will do wonderful things with your centre, helping many people, Daddy would be very proud of you, we will come more often and we can email you with any updates, don't worry.'

It was the approval I needed to hear.

These were his flesh and blood; I was his wife, a long time ago. If I wasn't a good wife in the beginning I hope I have been through the last eleven years, enabling the children to live freer lives instead of sitting here wishing for a recovery that can't come. If nothing else, I took that role so others didn't have to, I hope that made up for some of the disservice I did to Daniel.

It wasn't more than a month later that I got the call from Nathan, that Daniel had died from pneumonia. The lungs were perished and even the machines couldn't keep him going, it was as if he had finally let go, perhaps he had been hanging on all those years for my sake, maybe he knew in his soul that it was me who needed that routine, he stayed until I could finally let go.

I cried buckets and my closest friend in the world, Israel Jesus, held me tight and rocked me back and forth, soothing words to ease my pain.

We started our centre in the June of the following year. After the renovations were done, the builders raised a few eyebrows fitting locked grilles to the inside windows, triple reinforced doors and heavy-duty bolts.

We took a trip to Thailand and sourced our seeds, which were now sprouting well and looking to give a great stock to start us off. Our brochure had been sent to all of the private hospitals and doctors around the country, all the drug addiction charities and in the back of high-end celebrity magazines. We knew that the majority of our clients would be privileged, but we hoped that these would fund our referrals from charities working with underprivileged young men and women, to give them a chance to come here. It was a start, it was a hope.

Israel had become a vegan again and was off all drugs, finished his programme and was now a qualified nutritionist and addiction counsellor; he was a son that any mother would have been proud to have.

Me, well I have a handsome builder called Mike who takes me out to the pictures and the village pub for brunch, with his two golden Labradors.

Israel has a love affair with a beautiful Thai girl, Mishai, she is the daughter of our main farmer, he goes every two months to see her and order seeds. I think there will be a wedding soon, he's a handsome young man, Mishai loves his pale skin and grey soulful eyes, she called him an angel, that's when I knew she was the girl for him.

We have had some success with our herbs, it hasn't been smooth sailing, escapees tearing around the Dartmoor countryside, one got shot in the leg by a short-sighted farmer thinking it was the legendary great panther, silly sod had dressed from head to toe in black to escape. We retrieved him and he is back in his city bank earning his millions and sipping his herb tea daily, his contribution alone to our charitable fund enabled us to heal seventeen young men and eleven girls from the inner cities, who were sure to die. Four stayed on to work as volunteers and our farm is growing rapidly.

Katie came to visit me, bringing a handsome shy young man with her, Barnaby, he's all set to be something big in the city, from a super wealthy family, and I realised that's what Katie was waiting for, she needs to be someone's princess, he was devoted to her throughout the visit and she will want for nothing.

Nathan called off his wedding and his move to America, he decided to stay in the UK so he could stay near his mum and sister. I felt that he had been running away from the pain of seeing his father dying slowly in that hospital bed, now Daniel had passed, he didn't need to run, he embraced family again and his career flourished. He became a pharmaceutical head for the largest lab in Europe. We have been skyping regularly about our evidence of herbal properties in treating drug addiction, I have a feeling the Veronica Worthington Healing Centre may just make a difference in this world.

My Israel, my Jesus, my angel, my best friend, he walks tall these days.

When we can, we take the quad bikes across the fields and loon about like the two assholes we really are and we laugh like kids.

At the gated entrance we had two angels made, one in a kneeling pose and one with wings outstretched.

In loving memory of Veronica and Daniel.

CHAPTER THIRTY-FIVE

Carmella

I went to London a day earlier than my rendezvous with Roberto, for two reasons. The first, to have a face-to-face meeting with Tim, my funny, laid-back private eye, who had spent a week in Rome checking on my errant husband's activities. He had a dossier of photos he wanted me to see. I wasn't looking forward to it, but it had to be done. My second, more pleasant, meeting was a dinner invitation to the famous Ivy restaurant, with Lord Templeton. He said he had a regular table with some interesting guests I might enjoy. This made me accept without hesitation, I was not looking for a romantic dinner for two, so I packed my fabulous rose pink silk 40s-inspired cocktail dress. It was fitted, corset-style, with a full swing skirt, matching pumps and bag, it was my most chic semi-formal dress and I always felt great in it, hadn't had a chance to wear it much, as Massimo and I generally attended formal balls or galas and evening gowns were required for that.

I spun around my hotel room at the Savoy and decided an Audrey up-do was in order. The concierge arranged a stylist and it was Holly again from last week, she cooed and sighed at the lovely dress and set to work on my hair.

Holly added the three-diamond rose hair clips that matched the dress at the back of my sophisticated chignon, and helped me put the dress back on. The final touch was a gold flower pendant that my grandmother had given me on my wedding day, it was very old and treasured, I felt a slight pang of homesickness, but that soon evaporated as I stepped through the lift doors in to the Savoy and came face to face with Roberto.

He was taken aback but recovered almost immediately.

'Cara, my darling, I didn't know you were here already, where are you going looking so beautiful and dressed up?' There was just a hint of annoyance in his tone.

'Roberto, hi, yes, I arrived this morning, I'm off to the Ivy with some friends, I wanted to see a little bit of London before my holiday is over, Lord Templeton has asked me to join his dinner party tonight.'

'A lord? My goodness, Carmella, I didn't realise you had such important friends here, I will not hold you up any longer and perhaps we could share a nightcap when you return?'

'That would be lovely, Roberto.' I kissed him formally on both cheeks and strode confidently through the lobby to the waiting Rolls Royce. I arrived directly outside the restaurant and Lord Templeton had the good manners to be waiting in the entrance to escort me to his table. Englishmen had such a reputation for manners and etiquette, it was all part of an aristocrat's training to be a perfect gentleman when the occasion demanded. As I had been drilled and groomed to be the good wife and social escort to an important husband, I understood Lord Templeton completely.

As we approached the large round dining table, I couldn't help staring at the blond-haired man sitting down in deep conversation with a skinny young man who was drawing something on a napkin. As Lord Templeton pulled back my chair to seat me, the blond man raised his eyes upward and we made our first eye contact. I don't know what the feeling was, how you know deep inside at your very core that this person is the man of your dreams. He hadn't uttered a single word yet but I had fast-forwarded a whole lifetime with him in my mind, a wedding, children, holidays, retirement and growing old, all in a fraction of a second.

I must have appeared a dumb mute, as I snapped back to reality when a bosomy woman in green sequins sitting next to me was calling my name with her hand outstretched.

Flustered, I took it and managed to get through all the introductions, very sure I couldn't remember any of the names.

'Forgive me,' I said, 'I am a little overwhelmed, this place is so iconic and so beautiful, I don't know where to look first.'

The group laughed and agreed, then started telling tales of famous rock stars and movie stars that ate here, the exquisite décor and stunning floral displays really were worth a visit in their own right. I thought of Johnny and his flowers and I wondered who supplied the Ivy. I took a good look at the golden-haired man while menus were being handed out. He had been introduced as Sir Alan Hamilton the fourth, I wondered if the earlier three were as handsome.

He caught me looking and I had an electric current run through me, I turned to Miss Green Sequins for a distraction and recommendation for the starters, she suggested a few things but the head waiter suggested quails' eggs in Burgundy. I thought, *Why not?* Golden boy chose the same and flashed me a look.

My breath caught in my throat every time he looked at me, I was scared I would pass out, the corset dress was tight but it had never made me breathless before.

The chatter and banter around the table was fun and although the friends were obviously close, they included me all night and didn't let me feel left out. We had a mix of aristocrats, city bankers, actresses and even a High Court judge amongst us, bright, smart, intelligent conversation with eleven young London A-listers, I felt rather proud of my social gravitas after such a short time here. Only thing missing was Johnny, he would fit right in and it would have done him good to have a night away from the responsibilities of Medlicott Hall.

I suddenly heard myself announce a garden party at Medlicott Hall on the last Sunday of August, I promised a fabulous party with a great jazz band and amazing food, I invited everyone at the table. Filofaxes flopped out all around me and seven of my dining companions confirmed there and then, including my golden-headed boy, who made a direct hit with his pale, icy-blue eyes. 'I wouldn't miss it for the world, Carmella.'

I felt that bolt of lightning hit my sweet spot and he ever so lightly licked his lips. My knees were literally knocking, I felt like I might actually pass out. Lord Templeton bawled dramatically and said he couldn't make it as he was in New York that weekend. I forgave him and promised him a dinner in Rome next time he was free. They all asked if they could come too, it was a great feeling of being accepted and liked, I hadn't had too much experience of that. I was not even sure if I wanted to go back to Rome, I seemed to have fitted in here like the Proverbial glove.

Dinner was divine and it was with genuine regret that we broke up the party and went our separate ways. Lord Templeton and Alan were heading to Annabelle's nightclub and they convinced me to go for just the one cocktail, another must-see place in London. So I did, it was everything I had imagined it to be, the art deco designs, heavy gold metal walls and sumptuous velvet seating with heavy marble statues and gilt mirrors. It reminded me of Venice in lots of ways. We took a booth and sat back to people-watch. Alan sat to my left and Lord Templeton to my right. Soon we were joined by three beautiful supermodels and two ageing but still amazing rock legends. It was heady and wild, the people in London knew how to be themselves, they looked weird and wacky at times but somehow blended and fitted in, it was a freedom we didn't enjoy in Italy, the most minor fashion error in Milan made headlines, pathetic really.

With my heart in my mouth, I watched Shika the

Amazonian beauty trying to engage Alan. She was like a queen, her smooth dark skin was glossy, her cheekbones like blades, I was sure he couldn't resist her, but he did and turned to me, handed me my elaborate cocktail and said, 'Shall we just get married, Carmella?'

It took all my control to not spray the peach concoction at his face. Instead I dropped my gaze to my lap, where he picked my hand and placed it squarely in his.

'I better get divorced first, Alan.'

'Do that, Carmella, I've been looking for you for a very long time.'

Our faces drew closer and the next thing I knew I was in his arms, being kissed in a way that felt like home, not like Roberto's strong, demanding passion, but like two pieces of a jigsaw that fitted perfectly and didn't need anything else at all to complete it.

Lord Templeton raised an eyebrow but zoomed in on the stunning Shika, not wanting to miss a chance with this beauty, he was used to never getting a chance with the most beautiful woman at the table, Alan always got there first, and he had again. He was fine with it, he could see the spark from the moment his good friend and I had set eyes on each other. His matchmaking spoon had been busy, he later told me he knew I was perfect for Alan when he met me on the flight, he and I were made from the same cloth.

We danced, drank, kissed and laughed into the early hours, I confess I didn't remember Roberto at all until around 3am, when I suddenly became stone-cold sober. Alan reluctantly let me go after I promised to meet him for dinner tomorrow night after my meeting. I agreed and we kissed each other like young lovers, my driver a London cabbie was cheeky and was singing 'Love is in the air' as we drove. I couldn't laugh along because I now knew that I had to break Roberto's heart. The little niggly voice that had stopped me falling in love with him had done so for good reason, my heart was waiting for this golden boy, Alan.

It was simply a twist of fate that led me to him via a last-minute flight to London with the floppy-fringed Lord Templeton befriending me, it was all meant to be, call it destiny.

Arriving at the foyer, the night porter gave me a note that had been left for me three hours earlier, it was from Roberto. I waited until I got to the room before opening the familiar creamy embossed card.

> *My Dearest Carmella*
>
> *I had a dream of love but I think I may be just an old fool.*
>
> *I hope my instinct is wrong; my confused mind cannot reconcile the two encounters we have shared, one so hot yet, one so cold.*
>
> *Am I mistaken?*
>
> *Please put me out of my misery, my dearest love.*
>
> *Roberto*

The guilt tore through me, it was horrible and unfair to

him, I hadn't intended to fall in love with any man, I was confused myself, up until I felt Alan's lips on mine and his arms around me. Actually, I knew it the second I walked to the table in the Ivy, but that was love, you didn't choose it. Like my farcical marriage, it's a sham to think that love can come if two people haven't felt the hammer blow that hits you when you find the one. I suddenly forgave Massimo.

He was as much a victim as I was, his love was never going to be with a woman, perhaps he had the hammer blow the day he met Giorgio, so his bitterness was so much stronger than mine. I resolved to start divorce proceedings immediately and free both myself and my desperately unhappy husband and further to that, I was prepared to shoulder the blame, I had no intention of living in Italy again for a very long time.

England seemed to suit me so much more. Let Massimo save his family name, I no longer cared about mine.

But first I had to speak with Roberto. I walked to his suite, the floor above mine and tapped gently on the door. He immediately opened it like he sensed I would come. I entered the suite and took a seat at the writing desk. Roberto understood the tone and he stood by the tall windows looking out.

'I'm so sorry, Roberto.'

His chin dropped to his chest. The words he never wanted to hear tumbled out of my mouth, I excluded the detail of Alan, he didn't need humiliation. I blamed my mixed-up life and need to be free to build a new one here in London. He shot me a curious look at that remark.

'You seem to have made a lot of friends very quickly. Young friends more your age, I understand Carmella; I'm too old for you. I knew it all along, I just hoped.' He stifled a small sob in his throat and I went to him at the window.

At first he stiffened, but I held him in silence, he regained his composure and held me away from him by my shoulders.

'Carmella, when a man truly loves a woman, he wants to own her, consume her, but with that love comes an overriding desire for her to be happy. Even if this means you lose her. My heart will be forever yours, my darling, but most of all I want you to be wondrously happy, so I must accept this decision and let you fly. I will always be your friend and if you ever need me for anything, please remember it is my desire to help you for the rest of your life.'

I was crying openly and the tears flooded his chest, we kissed and held each other close.

'I will never be able to repay you, Roberto, for everything you have done to free me from my miserable prison, can I tell you that without you giving me the confidence to hope for a better life, I may not even have stayed alive, there were many nights I cried and planned to end my life. I owe you everything, Roberto, and I will never forget this, I am also at your service and if you ever need me, I will not let you down.'

CHAPTER THIRTY-SIX

Carmella

The emotion of that last night with Roberto, meeting Alan and the breaking of Roberto's heart left me wiped out. I slept late until near my appointment with Tim, which was here in the Savoy.

We drank good coffee and ate the splendid three-tiered afternoon tea, like civilised friends, whilst scrutinising the lurid photographs of my husband with various good-looking young gay men.

The last photograph, the 'money shot', as he put it, was a long-distance image into our master suite, through the billowing curtain, you could just make out the king-size carved bed. The image had been enlarged enough to make out two naked men wrapped in each other's arms, Massimo and Giorgio.

The grainy image wouldn't allow me to make out the features of my husband's face, but something told me that there was a relaxed happiness about his expression, something I rarely saw when I was around.

It spurred me on to forgive him, to understand his nasty hatred and bitter attitude was because of his abject misery being forced to go against his true nature, denied the right to choose his mate. Even Massimo deserved to love and be loved.

I knew my next step.

'Tim, can you arrange a divorce lawyer for me, please?'

'Certainly, Carmella, in fact it's usually the next call I make for most clients, I can ring my good friend Bernard Havers, ask him to pop along and join us, and he's the best.'

Our meeting lasted all afternoon and I sat with Bernard Havers until Alan arrived to take me for dinner. We concluded our business and he assured me that it would be a straightforward case, with evidence like this, it need never come to court, in his experience.

I was painfully conscious that Alan and Roberto were in the same building and wanted to avoid them meeting, so I was glad that Alan was dressed in jeans and a shirt. My turquoise Capri pants, white silk shirt and high heels were fancy enough for the intimate Italian restaurant he took me to.

I got an even greater surprise when he spoke to the owner in fluent Italian. I was amazed to learn he spoke several European languages fluently, so he wasn't just a pretty face.

The conversation flowed all night, it was like we had known each other all our lives and we told our stories eagerly and at times warily, hoping never to put the other off. Nothing could, this was the love I had read about, I couldn't take my eyes off him, everything felt perfect, his voice, his laugh, looking at his hands as they held mine in the candlelight, the way his thumbs gently rubbed my skin, told me this was him.

I told Alan about Roberto and we decided that I should stay at his home so we rushed back and I packed up my bag and checked out. His home was beautiful, a Georgian townhouse in Chelsea, it oozed character, full of English and French antiques, wonderful artwork adorned the walls and we made love in his grand mahogany four-poster bed. It was so similar to our Rome apartment, but such a contrast in emotional warmth, this home was put together with love, by a collector who admired beauty and rarity, his taste was impeccable. The connection we felt as he tasted every part of my body gave me no doubt that my heart had passed its key directly to him, I trusted this virtual stranger with my entire being, love is indeed a form of madness.

I reached heights I never imagined existed, just his gaze made me hot and ready for sex, we seemed to know how to please each other, or maybe we were already just so pleased to have found each other. The feelings ran very deep.

We were snuggling close and I let out a giggle, he asked what it was about, I described my Nona's advice on sex, he roared with laughter and off we went again, this time like crazy people laughing and Alan shouting in Italian, 'Brace yourself, Carmella.' He was my joy.

I reluctantly left London and Alan's bed three days later, starving hungry, we ate a massive brunch at a lovely café near Hyde Park. We held hands and walked off our food admiring the parkland and the young families corralling small children and dogs. I could see us in the future like those parents. I imagined having lots of golden-haired children, I was mentally toying with names while we sat for a while on a bench eating a 99 ice cream with strawberry syrup dripping off my chin. Sir Alan got down on one knee and proposed with his late grandmother's antique wedding ring that he'd tucked in his jeans pocket.

Claps and cheers from the passers-by filled the air as I said 'Yes!'

Our kisses lasted all the way back home, he couldn't stop picking me up and swinging me around, announcing to people in the street, 'We're getting married!' It was as if all my years with Massimo, my wedding, my life, my family, were just erased in one second. This was the beginning of my life. And I owed it all to Roberto Carlutto.

Alan was an antique dealer and he travelled Europe to find his treasures. His next trip was only a few days away, so we made the most of every minute together until he jetted off to somewhere near Prague on the promise of some medieval trunks and I bundled myself on the train back to the Cotswolds.

Johnny was meeting me at the station and was desperate to hear my news, we had lunch in the Ring-a-Roses and I ate like a farmer.

He said, 'You lost weight, Carmella.'

I didn't feel it appropriate to tell him that marathon sex with Alan left me a dress size smaller, but he worked it out I think as I gushed about him and our love.

'I have a little news myself, Diana and I have been out several times since you went, in fact,' he blushed and grinned, 'we are an item.'

That was such good news, I called over to Harry and ordered champagne. Harry looked thrilled, lunch had been slow today and that topped his till up nicely, he served us like royalty, and we toasted to love, friendship and new beginnings.

It was then I remembered I had commandeered Medlicott Hall for the grand garden party at the end of August. I confessed all.

'I'll pay for everything, Johnny. I was thinking we could use it as a bit of a networking thing as well, have you seen the floral displays in the Ivy?' To my surprise, he had. 'And all the hotels in London are full of the most glorious flowers, you grow them, Johnny, I'll arrange them and let's get busy getting the contracts, I'm sure we can pull a few strings, just got to be cheeky and ask.'

'Carmella, are you here to stay then?'

'Johnny, I have no home, no family and no friends in Italy, since I will be the disgraced daughter who ran off to England and ditched my husband. They will prefer I fade away into an uncomfortable memory and that suits me just fine, I'll be living with Alan in London.'

We discussed the party we planned to throw and Johnny asked Harry to secure a good jazz band for the date. Invites were given to all the regulars in the pub, except old Sam, who tended to pass wind while napping after two pints.

Arriving back at the cottage made me grin, it was so pretty, my special retreat. Here in the peaceful garden, I could think clearly about my new love and my new life, it had been such a whirlwind, I needed a few days to ground myself again.

After taking a dip in the pretty stone pool and a nap on the love swing, a great idea suddenly dawned on me. I rang Johnny who for once had the phone near him in the kitchen. Diana was cooking a roast dinner so I joined them and thrashed out my idea to use Medlicott Hall as a wedding venue.

Starting with mine and Alan's wedding!

Diana squealed, 'What a bloody brilliant idea! Super glamourous pics of you and Sir Alan will be in every magazine, guaranteed publicity for the venue, and darling, with your flowers, mine and Jayne's cooking and this darling house, we will rake it in, do you know how much a wedding cost these days? I blooming do!! My wedding has been planned for years now; Daddy says he could pay off the national debt with what he's put aside for my big day.'

Johnny looked to the ceiling with a peculiar expression.

Diana and I looked at each other.

He stood up and went across to the heavy oak mantelpiece. From inside a brass snuff box, he produced his mother's antique wedding ring. Silently he dropped to one knee at the foot of Diana's armchair, shoving Hunter, who hoped it was cake, out of the way.

'My darling Diana, my beautiful rose, will you do me the great honour of becoming my wife?'

She reddened like a poppy and without a moment's hesitation gushed, 'I jolly well would love to Johnny, yes.'

They kissed and I wrapped my arms around them both, Hunter danced around not sure what he had missed, I sobbed a little and explained it was joy not sadness, how Diana and Johnny were a perfect match made in heaven.

He produced a bottle of champagne from the fridge and Diana said, 'I wondered what that was for,' and the three of us drank and toasted to good fortunes, new adventures and love.

I crept off early to give the fiancés some privacy and I rang Alan to tell him the news, but the hotel where he was staying couldn't connect me. So I went to bed, dreaming of white lace gowns and golden-haired children.

What a trip this had been, if I hadn't set much faith in God before, I certainly did now, there was no way this chain of events could have been started by my own efforts, it was Roberto who had been my guardian angel, I called him at the Savoy and embarrassingly had to cut the call short when I heard the Canadian female voice in the background, calling his name. Jocasta Wilde, my intuition had been correct, and although I had absolutely no right to feel jealous, I did a little.

Roberto had been Jocasta's lover for many years, but always on a casual basis, refusing to commit to any woman until he had known for sure that our love could not be.

CHAPTER THIRTY-SEVEN

Carmella

Lying under my comfy quilt in the antique iron bed, I reflected on this turning circle of life, how fleeting happiness could be. Roberto had said something very poignant, that if you find a love that makes you feel like home, you must follow it, grab it and hold onto it, because it may never come again.

I intended to do exactly that with my golden boy Alan, wishing he was here with me now I drifted into a steamy dream which woke me up a few hours later sweaty and a little embarrassed, still discovering what my body could feel, how my emotions were upside down and inside out. I took an early shower and walked about in the garden, where I saw Johnny sitting quietly with a cup of tea outside his greenhouse.

'Hey, Carmella, come and join me.'

This friendship of ours was growing into a brother-sister bond, he felt the same, he called me his Italian angel, bringing Diana back into his life and now all these amazing plans for the hall, it was a future he hadn't dared imagine he would have. Small tears filled his eyes up and he rubbed them away.

'My mother would be the happiest woman in the world if she knew I was marrying Diana, she loved me the most. Dad and Thomas thought she made me soft, but she didn't, she just loved me, we shared a love of nature and creative things. Dad and Thomas said I should have been born a girl, horrible bullies they were. Wish mum could be here.'

Hunter climbed up onto Johnny's lap like he had as a puppy and licked his tears away. It was a sweet moment as we sat admiring the full to bursting greenhouses and the rows of topiary, rhododendrons and hydrangeas ready to go to market.

'If you will have me as your business partner, Johnny, I know we can make a magnificent wedding business here, it will secure the estate financially, I'm a lost soul looking for roots and I feel like I've found them here in England. Shall we give it a go?'

'One hundred per cent, Carmella, let's go for it.'

So we used the garden party as a marketing event for weddings at Medlicott Hall.

We had brochures made and a website, which none of us could work out how to use, so Lord Templeton found us a nice nerdy tech guy to show us how to respond to emails and send the e-brochure.

It wasn't long before we got our first enquiries and they turned into confirmed bookings. Diana took the role of event coordinator, to be honest she was as good as any army major leading the troops. She and Jayne worked furiously on wedding menus, they hired Harry's wife and some young girls from the village, everyone was impressed with the quality of the food served and word spread that this was the perfect exclusive private wedding venue for London's rich and famous.

Diana and Johnny tied the knot in the late September, the first Medlicott Hall bride and groom, which was perfectly right. I cried more than a few tears that day watching how Johnny was treated like a loved son by Diana's family, her parents had watched him grow up in the village, seen how rotten his dad had treated him. They would envelop him into their own family, he wouldn't feel loneliness again.

My divorce was going through without much stress. Bernard had suggested to the repulsive family lawyer Marco Ginetti that there was some rather unpleasant evidence that would serve neither party to be made public, and so the notoriously slow wheels of the Italian legal system turned rather quicker than normal for the Matteo family. Clearly his mother was well aware of her son's predilections and made no fuss at all, which made me despise her even more. How could a mother force her son to endure a life of misery, just to preserve some facade of an image that to be frank died out in the fifties?

I actually felt sorry for Massimo and told Bernard to agree to any reasonable settlement that finalised the divorce as fast as possible.

It looked like it would be February time when things were complete, Bernard had negotiated a very handsome financial pay off for me, as I was not wishing to stake any claim on the Matteo properties or investments, I never wanted to step foot in that apartment again or hear that name.

I would be financially wealthy in my own right, which gave me great satisfaction; no one could accuse me marrying Sir Alan for money. Alan's family welcomed me in with warmth and acceptance, his mother Marion had confessed she was afraid her Travelling Wilbury son would never find his true love and settle down, but she said she could see we were so very happy together. She reflected on my patient attitude with her rather energetic, spontaneous son. I didn't tell her the battle of my marriage was the reason I learned inner calm and control, being goaded day and night for years can do two things to a person: drive you mental or make you strong, luckily for me it gave me steel. Alan's enthusiastic approach to life was a pleasure for me.

Marion turned out to become one of our greatest allies with the flower business, she was in the heart of London's society and well connected. She arranged several meetings with hotels in London and Diana and I secured the contracts. We landed a particularly lucrative deal with the famous Royal Mandarin hotel, thanks to Marion. We decided to celebrate at the trendy champagne bar opposite the hotel, we strode in full of excitement about our deal. As I scanned the room for a table I saw Roberto and Jocasta, snug together in a booth drinking champagne. He didn't see me, so I watched for a few moments and realised something: Jocasta looked at him like he was a god, he was saying something probably incredibly romantic knowing Roberto, she was entranced and I felt any old feelings of guilt just evaporate. Roberto was loved, truly loved, it was the right order of things, a man needs his love reciprocated, if he doesn't get it, it will break his spirit. They are all little boys at the end of the day, looking for something akin to the idolisation of their mother, I was very sure Roberto would be just fine.

I didn't want to disturb them, so I pulled Diana discreetly away and out of the bar, filled her in with the full story in the nearby pub.

The invitations to our wedding, set for the middle of July the following year, went out to the great and the good of London and the Cotswolds and RSVPs were flying in through our letterbox daily. I had flown back to see my mother and sign some documents for the final divorce to go through and to secure the huge settlement that I was awarded.

My father walked with me around the gardens of our old villa and surprised me by telling me how proud he was of me that I found my own path to happiness, he had never liked Massimo, but it was the tradition. He apologised to me, I forgave him of course, I knew he wanted the best for me.

Mama had been frosty and the air of disappointment filled our salon until Papa mentioned Alan's title. The 360 turnaround of my mama's disposition was hilarious, I wasn't sure whether to laugh at her or slap her.

But my father gave me the look and I played along, invites were sent and unfortunately they accepted, which I really didn't want, but family is family and Marion assured me that she would manage their stay, I wouldn't have anything to worry about. I loved Marion, she had been more like a mother to me this last eight months than my own had ever been.

It was Marion who tried to get me to forgive my mama, she pleaded her case. 'Try and understand, Carmella, she is a woman of a different generation with the weight of responsibility to hold up the family image and reputation that has gone generations before her, it isn't easy to find the right balance.'

'Maybe one day,' I said.

I couldn't wait to get back on the plane to London, I had no feeling of loss leaving Italy behind me.

Diana was the head of events for Medlicott Hall, I had absolute faith in her abilities, she had done so much in the short time I was away. The hall had been smartened up, it looked amazing, no more crumbling stonework, the gargoyles and angels that butted out of front elevations of the main building had been beautifully restored by a French stonemason that Alan had worked with for years, he gave it as a wedding gift to Johnny.

The splendid gardens were blooming and bursting out with colour all through the estate, the cottage was converted to the working base for the caterers and mobile bar, they could service the grand marquee easily via the gate at the back of the garden. I checked out the table settings with Diana, we were using antique gilt-edged fine china crockery, fabulous cut crystal tall flutes from Geneva, they were the best I'd seen anywhere, along with the intricately carved silver cutlery all supplied by a speciality hire company that Diana found on the internet. She was enthralled by having the whole world at a push of a button at her disposal and the tech boy Graham had stayed on with us to get the business working smoothly.

Our gardeners had done us proud, they were growing lilies, roses, sweet peas, lavender, hollyhocks, lupins, gardenias and a gorgeous wildflower mix to recreate the quintessential English country garden, and they were proving a huge hit in the outside terraces of hotels and restaurants all over the city.

Alan had old marble urns on tall plinths shipped in from Tuscany, planted with clipped topiary to give a hint of Italy. He thought I would like that touch, but when I saw them in situ I had a prima donna moment and asked that they be replanted with double-headed tea roses, much to the dismay of the head gardener. But Jayne stepped in and gave him a look. They just reminded me too much of my wedding to Massimo, I had fallen in love with England and it welcomed me in so I wanted my flowers to be English.

Alan realised his error and agreed heartily with my choice, he was a lovely, caring man.

We had produced a flower brochure for weddings and hospitality events, corporate contracts, and this paid for a team of gardeners all year round. The hall was running like an estate should, maximising the assets and employing local labour, Johnny had a pride about him these days and he credited Diana wherever possible. 'She's a very good wife indeed,' he said.

Even our risky project growing tropical flowers in a separate hot house further along from the cottage was proving very profitable. The head gardener virtually lived with the young specimens, so proud to see the young earl bringing life back to the hall, the future of the estate looked healthier than it had for years.

Diana and I had invested money and we were already seeing a return. The days were counting down and we were watching the weather forecast like sea captains. I hadn't quite realised how changeable the English summers can be, I listened with amusement as my new family sat around sharing tips on how to predict the weather from sky colours to animal behaviour. Country folk were pretty accurate as the day came and the skies stayed blue, the warm air shifting the sweet scents of sweet peas around the illuminated marquee.

The tables were set and the music tested, the waiters and caterers had taken every inch of the cottage. It was ready, all that remained was for me to go and get dressed, the hair stylists and make-up artist were ready in the master suite in the east wing of the hall. This had been specifically redesigned for the bride and her maids to spend the evening in prior to the wedding in the hall. It proved very popular. The men were confined to the west wing, which housed a grand lounge with leather armchairs, large TVs with all the sports channels showing, top-notch brandies and cigars for those pre-wedding man-to-man talks.

It had everything a wedding party needed and made for a hassle-free day as everything and everyone was ready on site for the event. It wasn't uncommon for bride and groom to sneak out and have a romantic tryst in the gardens but it made it even more sweet for the couples to regale that tale years on.

The heavenly smells coming from Jayne's kitchen made my mouth water and despite eating a good breakfast with Diana, my mother and Marion, I felt starving, so I sneaked in and cuddled Jayne, who was double checking everything for the twentieth time.

'Time for a cuppa tea, Jayne?' I asked.

She looked fit to drop and I put the kettle on.

'Shouldn't you be getting dressed, Carmella? It kicks off in three hours.'

'Always time for a cuppa and a slice of lemon cake,' I winked and grinned, she took out her old tin and brought out a juicy slab. Hunter appeared from nowhere, then Johnnie.

We sat around that huge table and sipped our tea and broke chunks of cake for Hunter. Jayne was about to protest, but she was too exhausted to muster much drama, and Hunter wagged at her, plopped his head on her lap and licked his lips.

'Well, a compliment is a compliment, even if it is from a dog.' Jayne looked at me and placed her hand on my cheek. 'I never had a chance to say thanks to you, Carmella. Thank you for bringing the energy back to Medlicott Hall, you made a lot of good things happen and I'll always be grateful for that, my dear. I feel Edith, Johnny's mum, here in the kitchen some days and I know she's smiling at us, she would be so proud to see what you are doing here.'

Johnny gulped. Jayne patted his knee. 'You were the apple of her eye master Johnathon, and mine too.' With that she planted a big kiss on the top of his head, and picked up where she left off counting canapés.

'Well then, Carmella. Time isn't it? Can't get married in shorts and flip flops. I've seen your mama and Marion flapping looking for you and Alan is suited and booted waiting like a nervous cat. If he asks Lord Templeton to check he's got the ring one more time, I think he'll throw it at him.'

I thought of my handsome golden boy in his wedding suit, I suddenly felt the need to rush and get ready.

'Thank God for that,' I heard Jayne mutter as I flew out of the kitchen.

The reason you get ready a bit early for your wedding is so that when your mama makes you cry, you have chance to re-do your eye make-up. Marion had cried all morning with Diana as my bridesmaid trying her best to keep her together, which had somehow thawed my mama's heart and now she was sobbing in true Italian style at the sight of me in my dress. In stark contrast to my wedding with Massimo, she was cold as ice that day, only concerned with the deed being done. But this time, she showed her motherly love and that brought a wave of tears and choking emotion to my throat. My stylist handed around the tissues. Very used to this situation, she had not applied my mascara.

'That goes on five minutes before lift-off, after everyone has made you cry.' We were laughing and crying at the same time. When my papa walked in, he hugged me and Mama, and the tears came again, I seemed to be getting good at this forgiveness thing, so I let them pour out their feelings and we had something like a family moment.

Time was running out, Papa had come to walk me down, so we made our repairs to our faces and final touches to the dress, we were ready. The photographer stalled us at the top of the grand sweeping staircase, it was a stunning backdrop, ornate plasterwork covered the walls behind the polished wood and ironwork staircase, which swept in a half circle to the grand foyer, where our guests were waiting to receive us. There was a hearty cheer and we glided down the staircase, the guests went ahead to get seated and we had a few moments to wait before we got the cue to enter the old ballroom, which we had converted to the ceremony room.

The floor-to-ceiling French doors looked out onto the terrace and beyond to the gardens and marquee. It was picture perfect.

The vicar from our village church was marrying us today and he beamed heartily as my father walked proudly down the aisle to the beat of the English wedding march. As Alan heard the entrance doors open, he turned back to see me, the smile as wide and warm as ever. He never took his eyes from mine as I neared the altar.

Lord Templeton gave me a big grin and it took the nerves away. My father handed me over to Alan. We faced each other and took a long deep drink of each other in silent communication, I felt his love, he felt mine. It was a magical moment, the audience were silent, the vicar patient, and as if we had both said yes already we turned at the same time and smiled at the vicar.

'Ladies and gentlemen, we are gathered here today to witness the coming together of Alan Hamilton and Carmella di Rosa.'

The rest of the words I didn't hear, I repeated the phrases like a parrot, to the point he asked the question, 'Do you take this man Alan Hamilton to be your lawful wedded husband?' and I said, 'I do.'

'I pronounce you man and wife, Mr & Mrs Hamilton.'

Next thing I knew I was kissing my beautiful golden boy and the cheers and whoops from our families and friends filled my ears. I felt elated and speechless actually, it felt a little unreal, but we were happy, deliriously happy.

The party lasted until the early hours, more and more friends arrived for the evening party and when the older guests retired for the night the DJ changed the tempo and we danced until my feet couldn't take another step, so my husband picked me up and carried me to our wedding suite.

I'd like to say that we made glorious love that night, but truthfully we fell to sleep in each other's arms and stayed that way until the morning. When my husband's energies were revived, we made love like we hadn't before, I'd thought it couldn't get any better than it had been, but this golden boy told me a thousand ways how much he loved and adored me, I never felt more complete and fulfilled as a woman in my life!

CHAPTER THIRTY-EIGHT

Hulya

The Jewel of Istanbul, our Turkish restaurant, was set to open on the first of September; we had nine weeks to get ready.

It was the most crazy, exhausting, exhilarating time of my life.

I had no idea that we needed so many things in order to create this little slice of home. Thank God for Zafar, he knew exactly what we needed and led us like a small army. At times it was hard to take his barking orders and we had to bite our tongues, but we all understood the pressure, he couldn't fail again, this was the last shot for my funny uncle, we felt the fear of failure inside him and so did everything he asked of us.

Bahadir was a serious restaurateur and without him we wouldn't have met the deadline. He had contacts everywhere, builders, plumbers, electricians, they fitted our place out swiftly and, more importantly, with no bill, everything was sent to his office.

The neighbour at Topkapi wouldn't let us have the next door building. A seedy, jealous man, he felt we would not be able to pay the rent, a nasty insult to Zafar. So we signed the lease on the old Town Hall, just across from the park in the busy town centre. It was a lovely Victorian stone building, with a large terrace at the front that we could use in summer. The huge central arched entrance gave it a charming, church-like feel. The building had been used as a public library for years and then a community centre. The inside had absolutely no charm whatsoever, just old lino flooring and partition walls hiding all the traditional features that thankfully hadn't been ripped out, so it needed total refurbishing inside, this was my challenge, with a limited budget and a vast space, I had to get it right!

I got stuck in with the builders pulling down the plasterboard, the gods smiled on us again as we revealed elaborate carved wood panelling that hadn't seen the light of day for more than forty years.

I ran to get Zafar and we inspected the beautiful oak together, deciding a good clean and polish was all it needed, so as the skips filled up we scrubbed and waxed the exposed wood. It shone like amber, a real bit of luck, using this as my base for the design, I ordered the furnishings to work with the glorious old oak.

Roy bought a second-hand compressor and staple gun and we made our own seating, upholstered with rich kilim fabrics sent over from Zafar's brother in Antalya. Vibrant reds, golds, turquoise and silver geometric traditional patterns ran along the fixed seating, it looked fabulous against the old oak panels.

Using silk and muslin drapes, we created bedouin-style tented circular booths and strung flickering lanterns inside, to give a warm intimate feel. I was imagining them full with friends and families experiencing eastern-style dining, it was starting to feel real, our goal was to capture the essence of home with every aspect of our food, atmosphere and friendly warm hospitality.

Bahadir arrived with boxes of fabulous multicoloured glass lantern light fittings and his team of men fitted them in less than a day. They cascaded down in three, four and five drops, emitting hues of blues, reds, pinks and golds throughout the dining room, each glass bulb bouncing light off the wooden panels, giving a glowing amber effect all along the walls. I clapped my hands in appreciation, it was beautiful. I thought of the grand souk in Istanbul, and the magic of that place was coming alive here.

It was like Aladdin's palace; I wondered if it was too opulent, a bit over-the-top for suburban London, but when I saw Roy arrive and watched him spin around open-mouthed at the décor, I knew we had got something right.

'Oh Hulya, this is magnificent, what a transformation in just a few days, I guarantee you will be a success; I can't wait to bring my friend.'

It was authentic, it was bursting with flavours of home, it was wonderful and I was rapidly falling in love with it like a newborn baby. Everything came together on that final week, all the planning paid off, and when Roy rigged up the sound system and the dining room filled with the strains of our favourite Turkish folk music, the tears came.

In my mind's eye, I saw the future, I envisioned Mehmet's family and mine seated on the grand banquette feasting and celebrating together, I prayed to God to be able to reach that goal one day.

My husband had stayed at home like a good patient for nearly two weeks. But he was restless and so got busy setting up the till system, the office and the accounts with Bahadir. They discovered they had a few relatives in common and that made them good as family, they could be heard all day bantering and laughing together, I saw his spirits revive and it made me feel guilty again that I hadn't really noticed him having a nervous breakdown working for that legal firm, I vowed to be a better wife to my husband.

Two nights before we opened, we all sat in our restaurant and sampled everything on the menu, we ate a hearty feast. I looked at my companions: Zafar, Eda, Mehmet, Bahadir and his wife Hazel, plus our newly recruited waiters, bar staff and chefs. We dissected everything so that the waiters understood the food. I would be in charge of the front of house, I knew the ingredients of every dish, so I was sure we would be just fine, it wouldn't take long for them to catch on and serve the customers perfectly.

Osman and his wife joined us after they closed up the café and Roy arrived with his friend, his very pretty lady friend Aisha, a local girl and his patisserie tutor at the night school he attended, the dark horse, he had told Eda that he was studying the language!

Aisha and Roy laid out several desserts in front of us, we dived in and sampled exquisite sticky baklava, just like at home, layered pastry slices full of pistachios, honey and vanilla cream, juicy fruit baba that oozed fresh raspberries as you cut into them with drizzles of kirsch that moistened with the sweet soft sponge, tiny layer cakes stacked high with honey, almonds and Chantilly crème fillings, they were just out of this world, they were the perfect finishing touch to our menu.

Aisha told us she was in her final year training as a patisserie chef and taught beginners at the college. She and Roy just hit it off when he came to the open night to enrol, so instead of the language course he joined Aisha's patisserie course. 'He's my best student,' she giggled, 'he helped make all these, I have a little business on the side making cakes and desserts, could I supply you perhaps?'

Roy was beaming, he was so in love with this little lady, it was obvious to see, they were a perfect match.

Zafar's mouth was too full of confection to speak, so I spoke for everyone.

'Absolutely, yes! People will come here for the dessert alone; these are excellent.'

You couldn't find this style of home-made authentic Turkish sweets in the markets; we were blessed again by the people around us and the love in the air.

Eda hugged Roy like a mother, shed taken quite a shine to him, she was so pleased he wasn't alone anymore. We sat around eating and raising our glasses to the god of good fortune, asking him to look kindly upon us. It was a great night.

Only one thing marred the night, Mehmet's mum had called to ask how we were getting on; she hadn't heard from her boy in two weeks, he had to tell a lie to his family and that was alien to him. I saw the pain in my husband's eyes and tried to reassure him it was just a white lie.

'She will forgive it when she knows the whole truth and sees us happy and successful.'

He didn't buy it really; a son of an Imam doesn't lie easily and especially not to his parents. I saw his mood drop, it did so very easily these days, his old resilience and good humour was diminished, it didn't take much to upset him. It was Bahadir that snapped him out of it, I don't know what he said to him, but he bounced back with a positive air by the next day.

Our gorgeous restaurant was open. Our first night party was a riot of personalities and ethnicities from around our town, shopkeepers, bar owners, fellow restauranteurs, all the tradesmen and their wives, the accountant, solicitor, our suppliers and all the old regulars from the Topkapi and everyone who had worked on this building, even Zafar's old partners Aycot and Hasan came, they slapped him heartily on the back and wished him well but gave Bahadir a wide berth.

The music was loud, the food was devoured with rave reviews, the laughter and dancing went on until the early hours, when guests said they couldn't take another mouthful they soon found space when we brought out Aisha's dessert buffet with a champagne toast. Everyone cheered with cake-filled mouths and genuine warm wishes for the Jewel of Istanbul.

If we had felt hard-pressed and busy during the run-up to opening, it was nothing compared to the relentless pace of running the Jewel. It was a great success from the first week, the phone rang constantly for parties, couples, families and businesses, all keen to try this new and authentic Turkish eatery, but it was the building as well that had attracted a lot of interest.

Many local people loved the old Town Hall, people had been married there, met loved ones at the dances in the old days, it was a kind of nostalgia. Photos of our interior design had been featured in the local newspaper. They had given a great review with some super shots of the flaming grill with Bahadir and Eda either side of Zafar: head chef.

It captured the excitement of the place, many wanted to see the beauty of this important building brought back to life, we had done that, we had the faith in it, we invested every penny we had in it and the community loved us for it.

Bahadir was telling us that there were many ways a business can be blessed; sometimes it's a gift you get and hadn't planned for, like this Who knew this building was so loved?

We were a full house every weekend and a nice steady trade in the week. Aisha and Roy were at full pelt keeping up with the desserts as it became the place to enjoy the last bit of summer warmth on the terrace having coffee and cakes.

Before we knew it, winter was approaching and the Christmas bookings were flooding in. It seemed like every business in our locality had decided to celebrate the company party with us at the Jewel. Mehmet was working the plans and sending the menus when he got a call from a customer called Mr Smith, a booking for a party of twelve people for the start of December. That was fine, he booked them in and thought nothing of it, his day was full of bookings, confirmations and sending out menus. I was out with Zafar at the cash and carry, Eda was leading the team of prep chefs, this was our routine, we hardly stopped to take a breath, landing at home exhausted after sixteen-hour days, we slept like the dead. Mehmet and I managed one romantic evening and I felt some of the old closeness come back between us. I was sure he had forgiven me now, the success of the Jewel was paying us well, with both of us earning it was better than his salary at Johannsen Coeur maritime and we had a future, one that wouldn't compromise our integrity.

The weeks flew by and the weather turned, the icy winds reminded us that it was December and we better had get ourselves ready for the onslaught that is Christmas. Roy gave up his electrical job and came to work with us full time and Aisha had been virtually full time here since autumn, so it was becoming a very tight-knit team.

Our first Christmas party bookings were starting tonight and I had decorated the restaurant with extra twinkling coloured lights and natural pine cones and holly decorations, subtle but festive. With a good busy night ahead, we started our service as normal. Several tables were reserved and we seated people arriving without a booking in the available tables until it was only the tented booth for twelve left reserved for the Smith party. They were late, we had a policy that if they didn't arrive within forty-five minutes of the reservation, we let the table go.

Mehmet checked his plan and called the phone number Mr Smith had left with his booking, it just rang out. By the time he got back to the restaurant floor, the party arrived and his mouth fell open, he turned visibly white and ran out through the kitchen to the car park to grab a mouthful of fresh air and steel himself.

I walked to the party with butterflies bouncing in my gut.

There stood Mehmet's parents and three younger brothers, my parents and my brother, his wife and their two daughters and Eda's son, who was searching with his eyes for his mother.

With a room full of happy diners, I had to be a calm and serene as possible. I gave my biggest welcoming smile, and I saw nothing back but stony-faced family; my heart beat fast I tried to think of something to say.

But nothing came; I stood beaming like a lunatic, with my arms outstretched.

A horrible cold silence, which seemed to last an hour but truthfully was a nano second, then suddenly a roar of noise from the Smith party.

'Surprise!!!!!'

Their faces broke into enormous grinning smiles, the kissing and hugging began and I felt Mehmet return by my side, then Zafar and Eda, all rushed together. We became a scrum of giddy, happy family. Aisha took my place as host and the waiters jumped to action taking the many coats that our families had wrapped up in. 'England is so cold!' they all called out in unison. I realised I had got quite used to the climate and hadn't worn the heavy layers that they had on, like I used to when I arrived.

Our night was chaotic between looking after our customers and keeping our big family happy it was a bit of a circus, but eventually we sat down and I poured out the explanations of how we ended up owning a restaurant. It was quite a story and some of it was news to Mehmet who hadn't known quite the extent of my involvement from way back, shortly after we arrived in England. I felt my stomach knot, the truth was out and the extent of my deception: while he went out working every day I was with Zafar at the market or at Topkapi. He looked at me with a side glance, an expression I couldn't quite decide the meaning of.

The families had booked a hotel just further into town and so they took the young ones back, which left just our parents and Eda's son, Denis.

The restaurant was finally empty and we sat having some of Aisha's delicious cakes, when Mehmet's father, Kubilay, said, 'Son, please explain what made you leave your profession.' The atmosphere changed, I saw Mehmet's shoulders drop, Eda quickly disappeared taking Denis for a tour of the kitchens.

With no place to run, he faced his father.

'Father, please forgive me, I appreciate and thank you and mother for all the sacrifices you made for me to study and gain my place as a lawyer. I know I have let you both down...' His father tried to interrupt him, but he stood up and walked quickly away, I followed him, not sure what to do. He was gone again through the kitchen doors into the back and into the night.

I called to him but he didn't turn back, I ran for Zafar who was chatting to Eda's son, they grabbed their coats and ran out in the direction in which Mehmet had gone.

I marched back to the table with the adrenaline rising. I was about to give them a mouthful, when my father took hold of me and stopped me.

'Hulya, please listen, Kubilay isn't upset or disappointed with Mehmet, he knows all about his son's breakdown and hatred of the corrupt business he found himself part of.' I stopped and sat down to hear this.

Kubilay took over. 'Dearest Hulya, please talk to him, I am so very proud of him, I raised him to be a scholar, to succeed in business and build a quality life for you both and your futures, but I could never ask him to go against our faith and harm people for the sake of financial profit, he should know me better than to think I would ever value money over integrity.'

Senem took my hand in hers, her lovely smile reassured me that her husband was sincere.

'Hulya, we are one hundred per cent behind you and Mehmet in whatever choices you make in your lives, no parents could be more impressed with a daughter and son like you two.' My mum and dad agreed heartily.

Senem kissed my cheeks and my mum wiped my tears away and hugged me as Senem talked.

'It is us that feel we let you down, by not realising or taking the time to hear the emptiness in Mehmet's voice when he told us everything was great, we were guilty of being impressed by the corporate world, not realising we were killing the sweet soul of our boy, you must convince him of that, I know how deeply he takes his responsibilities. We will go back to the hotel and please arrange for us to meet up as soon as possible. Maybe this was a bad idea surprising him like this, we didn't mean to upset him, tell him we love him, we need to talk so we can assure him of our approval.'

I was totally relieved to hear this from Mehmet's parents, they left and my mother and father hugged me a thousand times, my mum said she had never been so proud of me in my life, how I had adapted to this new country, she kissed me many times until finally they sped away in the taxi.

Zafar, Eda and Denis came back without Mehmet and they looked very worried.

'Where is he?' I felt lost without him next to me and worry was setting in, his face had been ashen when he walked out and it was very cold outside.

The phone rang, it was Bahadir.

'Hulya, Mehmet is here with me at the Istanbul Grill, he's pretty upset, leave him here with me for now, it's my fault the family turned up.'

'What?' I was pretty confused.

'I'll get him home, couple of hours, don't worry he's safe.'

A little bit of me stung. Mehmet turns to Bahadir at times like this? I thought I was his best friend? Was the gap widening between us? I thought the Jewel had brought us close again. We locked up and went home but I couldn't sleep, so I waited on the sofa for Mehmet. Finally, around 4am, he appeared. He immediately joined me on the sofa and held me tight. I repeated what his parents had said and he cried, the relief and anxiety leaving him.

It had shocked him too much to see them all without warning, I realised how much damage had been done to my sweet husband, it would take a long time to get his confidence back.

I asked him what Bahadir had meant when he said it was his fault, he had told one of the shared cousins about the fantastic restaurant that we had opened, and not realising this titbit would travel around to his parents in Istanbul.

Mehmet called the hotel and left a message with reception for our parents to come for early dinner tomorrow and so we slept in each other's arms until our alarm roused us at 10am. Our families arrived at five after we had set up the restaurant ready for the night service. Everyone left us alone after serving a nice traditional mezze of dishes, my parents very impressed with all the food the compliments raining in.

Kubilay finished his meal and patted my hand.

'My dear, you do our country proud, this is delicious and just like home. Have you seen the breakfast they serve in the hotel? It's not food at all.'

We all laughed, it was true, the standard was poor in this area, Bahadir was no fool, he picked this spot exactly because of that, not one good place to eat in this town and again the bad luck of not being granted the next door unit at the old Topkapi takeaway had in fact been a gift.

Kubilay turned to Mehmet. 'Son, please listen to me now, I want to tell you how proud both your mother and I are of you and Hulya. You can forget any kind of guilt about changing your career, son. I am so sorry that you had to hide your feelings and continue with the soul-destroying situation, I admire the bravery of you both to start out on a new unknown path and look at the success you made of it all, who wouldn't be proud of a son and daughter-in-law like you both? Sorry if we shocked you by just turning up here, it was a conversation not suited to Skype.'

The belly dancers were warming up and the Friday early crowd were heading in so we sent our parents off to the hotel. They needed a rest after all the travelling and emotion. We made a promise to all sit together on Sunday and eat like a family, so Mehmet blocked off the reservations for the daytime, it was our special day, we wouldn't have another chance until the following year, there was a new lightness about Mehmet, as he organised the party.

Zafar called Bahadir, Roy and Osman to join us with their partners for a celebration on Sunday, the chefs were given a list of dishes to prepare and the tables and seating were rearranged so that all twenty-two of us could be seated together, the last time we all sat down together like this was at our wedding, so we were a loud and boisterous lot. We had much to celebrate, and lots to catch up on with all the gossip and goings-on back home.

There was a chair added to the top of the table, I asked Mehmet who it was for, he didn't know, I asked Zafar who it was for, he didn't know.

'I thought you put it there for one of your guests, Hulya?'

So it remained empty, but I noticed Eda disappeared a few times to make a phone call. Denis excused himself and went outside, just as zafar was about to bring the desserts, he swivelled around like he'd seen a ghost, as his tiny wrinkled elderly mum Amina was slowly escorted in.

'*Anne-cim, anne-cim*,' he caught a sob in his throat, and left the desserts and ran to her, she squinted her brown wrinkled eyes and found her favourite son's handsome face with her bird-like hands. She called out, 'Zafar, *bebe-cim*,' her smile so warm like only a mother to her son can express. He picked her up in his arms, crying and kissing her leathery cheek, her brown button eyes shining with love and pride, being with her most cherished adored son after nearly thirty-two years apart. It made everyone's heart swell.

I caught Eda's eye and she winked, she had arranged this, she loved Zafar by the looks of things. I'd been too busy to notice they had been arriving together and leaving together for nearly a month now.

Zafar's mum was seated like the queen at the top of the table, a plate of dessert was placed in front of her and she gave her hearty approval to Aisha. Zafar told Aisha, 'That was quite an accolade coming from this queen of the kitchen.' We all laughed. Truth was, Zafar's mum couldn't boil water really.

Seizing the moment, he tapped his glass with a spoon and asked for silence so he could say a few words. We settled and watched as he took Eda's hand in his, led her to his side and asked her if she would be his wife.

The whole table erupted in applause and cheers as Eda without hesitation said 'Yes.' Amina kissed and hugged

Eda like the daughter she never had and we did what we always do as a family, danced around the restaurant clapping and laughing, kissing and hugging.

And my Mehmet kissed my hands and told me I was a very good wife!

CHAPTER THIRTY-NINE

Three years later

Hulya

We now have six Jewel of Istanbul restaurants, our lives are busy and we have our own sweet house, near the park. We had to find a place pretty quickly after I discovered I was pregnant with twin girls. How it happened in the middle of such a crazy year I just don't know, but as always things in life never run to plan, you just have to roll with them and pray to God that it all works out for the best. We moved into our home with me as huge as a hippo and useless, but it was fine because our great friends all pitched in and got us set up in a matter of days. The nursery was fit for princesses and they are just that.

It wasn't long before Roy proposed to Aisha and she got pregnant almost straight away so her little boy Jack plays with our girls, they baby him like a little brother. Denis finished his studies and joined his mum and Zafar, he's now a manager at the third Jewel in Piccadilly, he's doing a great job and has met a real London girl, Sally, and fallen head over heels, so our family is growing rapidly. Eda and Zafar bought an old Georgian town house and I redesigned and refurbished it, of course they only really cared about the kitchen part, which is the heart of the whole house.

After designing and building six restaurants I have my own contact book of builders and suppliers and quite a reputation. I set up a small consultancy for hospitality interior design. I'm working on interiors for a chain of coffee shops. It's a lucrative contract and Mehmet has no qualms about having a working wife, it allows him to spend lots of time with our girls, he is a wonderful daddy.

We converted the conservatory to be my studio, so I could work from home and be at home with our family. Our life has turned out better than we could have expected. Mehmet and I often think back to the tiny attic flat and remember how it all began, how little we knew about each other really and how we grew up together to make this life happen.

I would never have dreamed that we could make such a good life in such a short time. I often think back to our first month here, hardly understanding a word of English, frightened to get lost, we hardly knew anyone here, in fact we hardly knew each other but I thank God daily for the good fortune we have received, the kindness of friends and colleagues and the blessing of having our beautiful daughters.

But privately, I thank my funny, raucous Uncle Zafar.

We laugh like we always did, he calls himself a bad Muslim and I call myself a bad wife, but that's just our little joke.